Isis Unbound

Allyson Bird

Dark Regions Press
-2011-

FIRST TRADE PAPERBACK EDITION

Text © 2011 By Allyson Bird

Cover Art © 2011 By Daniele Serra

Editor, Norman L. Rubenstein

Editor and Publisher, Joe Morey

ISBN: 978-1-937128-005

Cover and Interior Design By
Stephen James Price
www.GenerationNextPublications.com

Dark Regions Press
PO Box 1264
Colusa, CA 95932
www.darkregions.com

Dedication

To my husband, Alan.
For his devotion and kindness.

'To live is to war with trolls
In the holds of the heart and mind:
To write is to hold
Judgement Day over the self.'

Henrik Ibsen.

Acknowledgements

Writing a debut novel isn't an easy business. An author needs inspiration, guidance, advice and support. I'd like to thank all who helped me in that regard. Joel Lane, Joe. R. Lansdale, Lisa Tuttle and Ramsey Campbell. To all who helped me keep my sanity. Well. They tried. Norm Partridge, Jonathan Maberry, Laird Barron and numerous others, who have read my work in the past, and commented. To my wonderful editors, Norman L. Rubenstein, and Bobbi Morey. Joe and Chris Morey.

Prologue

Who telleth a tale of unspeaking death?
Who lifteth the veil of what is to come?
Who painteth the shadows that are beneath
The wide-winding caves of the peopled tomb?
Or untieth the hopes of what shall be
With the fears and the love for that which we see?

Percy Bysshe Shelley (1792-1822), from 'On Death.'

In 41BC a terrified young woman, her skin a deep olive colour, and her black hair flying wildly about her, ran for her life up the steep steps, making for the temple in Ephesus. They dare not take me from there, she thought. She stumbled once, cutting her knee on the sharp stone, blood oozing down the inside of her leg, and staining her white gown. Before she reached the door to the temple the soldiers cut her down.

Mark Anthony had sent his soldiers for the sister who had plotted against Cleopatra. Eventually the renegade sibling was buried in an octagonal-shaped tomb which looked like the Pharos lighthouse in Alexandria, and forgotten for two thousand years. Mortal sisters. Rivals. Once close, but when it came to ruling Egypt they would do anything for the throne...even kill each other.

Cleopatra was a warrior queen, a woman used to getting everything she wanted. She manipulated, fought, and set her sights on Rome. Mark Anthony lay asleep by her side in his opium dreams but she was far from sleep. Naked, she left the bed and walked across the white marble floor, over to a white vase full of Egyptian Blue irises, and picked one up. She thought of the mother goddess, Wadjet, and prayed for her guidance, and strength. Cleopatra picked up her cloak from the floor, where Mark Anthony had thrown it, and wrapped it around her shoulders. When she stepped out onto the balcony and looked out upon the city she saw that the heavens were black and there was no star in sight. Only the moon cast its light upon her anxious face. She heard a movement behind her and turned slowly thinking it to be Mark Anthony. He would want her back in bed with him, she thought.

It wasn't Mark Anthony who pulled her close. It was the tall woman. Cleopatra had been held by her before, and as Cleopatra offered her the flower, Isis smiled.

Two years before The Aeneid was written by Virgil and fourteen years after Julius Caesar was assassinated in the Senate, Cleopatra and Mark Anthony made their great and triumphant entry into Rome. The battle of Actium had been the turning point. On the Ionian Sea Octavian had been defeated. Mark Antony aided by Gellius Publicola, headed the right flank of the Antonian fleet, Marcus Octavius and Marcus Insteius the centre. It was Gaius Sosius who attacked first from the left, and Cleopatra's forces, strongest of all, attacked from the rear. Malaria had considerably weakened Octavian's men and their smaller ships were rammed and broken into pieces. Mark Anthony went on to win the land battle too with considerable ease. Octavian was killed and the Mediterranean belonged to Mark Anthony, and Cleopatra. An empire was born. With the rise of Cleopatra the legacy of Hellenistic civilisation and Ptolemaic rule continued to have an influence.

Cleopatra sat, back straight with her hands firmly placed on the intricately worked arms of the great golden throne, carried by Nubian slaves. The sunlight glinted off their diamond-encrusted armbands. All gold and glory, and the day belonged to Cleopatra, with her dreams of being empress of the world about to be made manifest. She was already wearing the precious jewels of most continents. Mark Anthony, with their children walking by his side, headed the procession. The children all dressed as great warriors, even the girl. A Romano-Egyptian princess carrying a blue lotus cupped in her tiny hands. Cleopatra Selene 11 of Cyrenaica and Libya. She adored her brothers. Alexander Helios, Ruler of Armenia, Media and Parthia. Ptolemy Philadelphus—his to be Syria, Phoenicia and Cilicia. Her half-brother, Caesarean, son of Julius Caesar was to be struck down not a year later by a mystery illness leaving Roman rule for generations to come to the descendants of Cleopatra and Mark Anthony.

This dynasty had lasted for over two thousand years—a dynasty blessed by Isis and protected by her. Ancient scripts had told of her appearance, to all the rulers, since Mark Anthony and Cleopatra. Isis was the goddess of many names and not all of them good. Her name was understood to mean knowledge by Plutarch but others considered her to be cruel and ruthless. Isis was so powerful or so his script had described her, she was '*the lady of the people, the royal wife, great goddess of the sky, powerful on land, the mistress of Egypt and the desert,*' and according to Diodore, Osiris bestowed the totality of power to Isis. To some Isis was known as the daughter of Prometheus.

During Osiris' absence, Seth never fought against Isis so certain he was of her power. That was all a very long time ago. Osiris and Seth were dead now. Only four gods were left. Isis, her sister Nepythys, and their sons, Horus and Anubis. None had the courage to stand in her way. She had appeared to many of the Romano-Egyptian rulers in many forms from that of protector to a goddess of great malevolence when she disliked the path that the nobility took. When the empire was threatened by the barbarians she had appeared to Mentuhotep, when the great earthquakes had caused famine she had appeared to Semerkhet V, and when the great meteorite had hit the northern forests, to Cleopatra Seneca XlII. And so on down through the centuries, to give comfort and give guidance but she had never appeared to the present Empress Cleopatra or to her father or grandfather. Now, in the time of the great plagues, rumour was spreading through the Romano-Egyptian empire that Cleopatra had lost favour with Isis. The current super-plagues and their effect on the populous seemed to bear that out. Where was Isis now? Had she deserted the favoured ones she had supported down through the centuries?

Clovis Domitius Corbulo was to be the new Governor General of Britanniae. He was cousin to Cleopatra, and a descendant of the Frankish King Clovis who had been married into the royal family in return for loyalty. The Arvernians had helped this Clovis defeat the Visigoths, who had been in the foederati and had been richly rewarded for providing soldiers for the Romano-Egyptian Empire. But this relationship had fragmented, and the Visigoths had rebelled against the empire. Clovis had wanted a Romano-Egyptian alliance, a permanent link to Cleopatra and Mark Anthony, one of blood relative. Most of the renegade barbarian kings did the same over the next few hundred years. A vast empire was now held together by marriage alliances and Isis, but perhaps that was all going to change. That was centuries ago and now Clovis Domitius Corbulo wanted more. Much more.

Chapter 1

16th February 1890.

Ella felt the opium mist in her mind settle and although she felt sleepy she walked steadily. Her hand fell to her side where she could feel the small gun and when she touched it lightly she withdrew her hand quickly, afraid to even come into contact with it for a second now. She had been told to use it by her father, Ptolemy Child, if anyone showing obvious signs of the plague came too close. Ella had used it only the once. She had also been told to wear a surgical mask but rarely did. As Ella walked through the transparent-sided skyway her boots made no sound on the rubber beneath her feet. She had been on an errand for her father and had decided to use the skyway for the journey home to the part of the city called Kares-Bu. Ella had few friends and was a loner. She found comfort away from others, but did tolerate and sometimes enjoy the company of her younger sister, Loli. Rarely did Ella smile, and when she did, that would be when she was with Loli or when she thought of Swin.

It was snowing again, bitterly cold. Yet Ella doubted that even if she were at ground level in the open, she would feel it. Anyway, the skyway was preferable to the dirty streets. Privileged, as a daughter of the Chief Embalmer, she was allowed to come and go freely. The security guards based at the entrance to each skyscraper got used to the pretty young woman with the blonde hair. Ella never saw herself as pretty at all.

She looked down from above. The sound of gunfire echoed around the tall buildings. She was especially nervous as the day before the authorities had tried to contain a riot after a soldier had shot an entire family in broad daylight, all with obvious signs of the plague, in front of many citizens. Ella feared she was about to witness another riot. Down on the street someone shot a plague victim again, and a few bystanders ran screaming and shouting down towards the river. Boxes of fruit were knocked over and peaches squashed underfoot as children ran into a skyscraper entrance for cover. Within minutes, some people took advantage of the chaos. Windows of shops were broken and looters piled baskets high with merchandise, only to drop them a few minutes later when the garrison soldiers hit the streets. For over an hour Ella watched, high up in the skyway partly shielded by the entrance to the building, disgusted at how the soldiers took every opportunity to degrade the rioters. One fell upon his knees and pleaded with his captor. The soldier shot him in the head.

There came a low rumbling sound from somewhere in the distance and then one of the steam tanks came into view. Ella was terrified of these machines. The government had come in heavy-handed. The steam tanks were fuelled by kerosene, and the flamethrower on the rotating top cabin had a range of twenty-seven metres. Mounted on the four corners of the cabin were four machine guns. Ella gasped when she saw a huge plume of flame arc and fall. Flames from heaven and two people fell to the ground, writhing in agony as their bodies burned. She saw horses pound the burnt bodies in an attempt to escape, terrified of the ironclad tortoise. The horses bolted and ran for the river as if they knew instinctively that water would cool their burns. Ella had seen such horror before.

She watched, a silent witness, as the steam tanks rumbled away again and fire engines put out the fire that had caught hold of the store on the corner. By the time it was over, twenty lay dead, either shot or burned. They were quickly taken away. The owner of the store sat in the street with his head in his hands, shouting abuse as the garrison soldiers retreated. Ella closed her eyes, stifled a sob, and moved quickly through the skyway and home.

The next day the newspapers would hardly mention it at all. And nothing of the steam tanks as usual. A steam engine and a flamethrower in the same confined space were considered by most to be a dangerous combination. However the new Governor General, Clovis, would not give up on his steam tanks, even though they often overheated, and more legionaries were hurt than rioters. They had been the playthings of the last Governor General, who had used them in a campaign against concrete pillboxes in the last fighting in the east—a campaign that he'd won, although the casualties on his own side had been high.

The human Y pestis infection, consisting of bubonic, pneumonic and the septicemic forms of plague had been treated with antibiotics successfully years ago. But now some hybrid of the pneumonic had reared its ugly head and had the city of Manceastre in a panic. Day by day new discoveries were being made that kept many pathogens at bay. However the inhabitants were terrified of this new variant of plague, which had already killed many in the city, and seemed so virulent. The wealthy preferred to get about in the high covered walkways or skyways as some of them called them, protected from the weather and disease.

No one dared cough as this was one of the initial symptoms, and a common cold could easily be misinterpreted. Neighbour spied upon neighbour and reported anything that might be plague symptoms; such was their fear of the terrible disease. Clean drinking water had rid the city of cholera a hundred years earlier, but even with scientific methodology and consequential positive practices in hygiene, the people of the city were still attacked by bacterial agents that mutated as quickly as scientists identified them.

In some districts in Manceastre, notably the richer ones, and in particular Kares-Bu, there were more monuments to the dead than there were mansions for the living. Tombs were built around little squares not far from their living relatives who mostly dwelt in the skyscrapers. The small tombs, miniature replicas of pyramids, were linked by underground catacombs to each other, and to the skyscrapers. From there the bereaved could visit their deceased loved ones, safe from the colourmen and from the prying eyes of their neighbours who watched from above. The small pyramids were a constant reminder of their short time on earth. The rich were content in the fact that they had the money and privileges to pay for the right ceremonies to ensure that they progressed to the afterlife when their time came; the poor had to settle for less.

Behind the tombs of the dead the prostitutes called for business, even on the darkest and foggiest of nights. Not all embalmers did their job properly and even the wealthy dead rotted in their bandages not far from the pox-ridden women of Memphis Square.

As it entered Kares-Bu, Ella could hear the shrill call from the whistle of the underground steam train as it passed under a ventilation shaft close by. The square shaft had been clad with bricks. Imitation windows had been painted on, so that it blended with the buildings, resembling an actual house frontage. Ella could just make out the steam rising above the rooftops, soon to get lost in the smoke that drifted across from the industrial part of the city, where the factories tirelessly produced the cotton and textiles that the city was famous for.

At least Ella and her sister had escaped the mills. They might live and work amongst the dead and the artists but at least it was quiet. She looked up at the outer temple building shrouded with frost and then down into the violet darkness, where she knew Loli was hiding from her. Loli was the other daughter of Ptolemy Child, Chief Embalmer. He was the head of one of the few favoured families who embalmed the dead. His was the most important family business because he embalmed the nobility and the rich. Ella helped him to prepare the bodies for the afterlife, and the services of Ptolemy Child didn't come cheap.

The heat from the kerosene lamp kept her hand warm as she looked among the shadows for Loli. Ella shivered. It was a cold January night. She walked quietly through Kares-Bu. Many artists lived in this part of the city not too far from the tombs that they worked in. Ella had buttoned up her long overcoat to under her chin but she was still cold.

As she looked behind each tomb she felt unusually afraid of the dark. Her father had cured her of her fear of darkness years ago, but now each branch of every tree seemed to point at the tombs of the dead, grimly reminding her of the inevitable, and that made her shiver. Here lay generations of Romano-Egyptians, culminating in a society so totally given up to the cult of the dead that children were brought up to look forward to their deaths, for at that point their eternal lives began. There were more burial grounds with houses for the dead than there were playgrounds.

Ella would have to be quick, as she was due back in the preparation room soon. She was to help her father prepare a female corpse. It had been why Loli had run away again. Ptolemy had wanted to teach her the process, but as his knife was about to pierce the grey body of the heavily pregnant woman, Loli had disappeared. Ella had done the same on her thirteenth birthday. Loli was only ten. Ptolemy will be running out of patience, thought Ella, although he sometimes hid that behind a cool smile and a soft voice.

When Ella had first placed a knife on dead flesh, the corpse had been male and her father had never thought about the fact that Ella had never seen a living naked man before, let alone a dead one. Ptolemy Child had told Ella what was about to happen in great detail, but Ella had still suffered. Loli would have to get used to it.

"Loli. Loli," Ella called, hoping for a quick reply. No luck.

It was getting late and she had to get back to her father. Would he be very angry with Loli? Probably not. She knew how to get on his good side, and although Ella was his eldest daughter, she thought that her father loved Loli more. Ella's delinquent mother had run off with one of the artists. Their father had said she had been wild, far too wild, and Loli's mother had left too. Unusually, Ella had no memory of Loli's mother at all, though she had been old enough. The woman had only stayed a year. The daughters of Ptolemy Child had been brought up by slaves and the occasional governess, but they had mostly learnt all they knew from the many books in the family library.

Ella was now eighteen and Loli ten. Ptolemy's attempts to limit their freedom were half-hearted and he quite frankly couldn't be bothered. He was a self-centred creature who indulged his own whims, so Ella and Loli managed to get out into the city without supervision, frequently. Ella glanced at his thin face and drooping lips. They didn't go together, she thought.

"Did you find her?" Ptolemy was about to make the first cut in the abdomen. He hesitated and looked up at Ella. His blonde hair streaked with grey had fallen a little over his face.

"No. I searched in all the usual places but I couldn't. I was a little rough with her earlier."

Ella looked nervously at the heavily pregnant corpse. She knew what was to happen next. She put the red rubber apron over her long dress. She had been careful not to put on any of her better clothes for the procedure, and it came as no surprise to her when her father made the incision from beneath the breasts down to just above the pubis. Ella watched his steady hand. Even though the woman was dead, Ptolemy cared enough about his craft not to be labelled a butcher, as the notorious Master Embalmer of Eboracum had been. For this part of the process he was beyond reproach. Could that be said for all of his work though?

There was a movement behind her and a door closed quietly. Ptolemy looked up and half-smiled. "Ah—Loli. Did you think better of hiding on such a cold night? Come closer, we are about to witness a birthing of sorts."

Loli was dressed in her best clothes and wasn't about to get too close. She wore a full deep pink scalloped-edged skirt with tiny red roses sewn along the hem that came to just above the knee and a ruffled white blouse—just the right outfit for learning the more intricate skills of embalming. She was even wearing pale pink shoes over white stockings, which of course were now splattered with mud due to her truancy. A little mud clung to her dark hair at the side of her front parting, where she obviously had been brushing her hair back off her face with a dirty hand. She seemed unaware of any of that and was all candy kisses for her father. Loli ran over to him and hugged him from behind and then turning to face him looked at him apologetically.

"Sorry, Father, I didn't mean to run away. I just didn't want to learn today."

The look between the girls said it all. One of reproach from Ella, and when her father turned away, one from Loli for Ella—that she'd got away with it again.

"That is fine Loli. You are here now. Put on an apron and come and help."

Loli ran over to the table on the far side of the room and reached up for one of the smaller aprons that hung there. She placed the apron over her head and struggled to tie a bow at the back.

"Ella, help me will you?"

Ella hesitated and seemed reluctant to step forward. She pulled the apron strings tight.

"Hey—not too hard, Ella." Loli frowned and there was a look of reproach in her brown eyes.

A wooden stool had been placed in front of the embalming table for Loli to stand on. Ella and generations of young embalmers had used it before her. It had been made of the sturdiest oak and had been decorated with hieroglyphs recalling the names of the first few of the family of embalmers.

"What do I do, Father?"

Ella stood behind Loli ready to step in if, and only if, Loli faltered. She didn't. Ptolemy pulled the abdomen apart so that Loli could see the baby. Ella could see the head and the sleepy eyes of the small grey creature and recoiled a little.

"Let me. Let me." Loli tottered on the stool, regained her balance and tugged roughly at the head of the baby.

"Not so hard, Loli," said Ella. Loli smiled apologetically at Ella.

"I don't mean to Ella but it is difficult to get out."

The incense lamp did nothing to hide the smell and Ella saw Loli start to retch a little. Ella quickly reached into her pocket, took a tiny jewelled container, put some myrrh ointment on her finger, and put a little under Loli's nostrils. She applied the ointment to her own nostrils also.

"One more pull, Loli, come on, nearly done now," Ptolemy encouraged.

"I've got it. Here it comes," said Loli eagerly.

With a final tug the baby slipped out of the mother, and after Ptolemy cut the cord, Loli cradled it lovingly in her arms.

"It isn't a doll, Loli," said Ella. She looked pale and her hands were shaking.

"Oh it is, look at it. It's beautiful and so very quiet. Can we wrap it in something to keep it warm, Father?"

Ella looked away. Ptolemy handed Loli a white cover with the Child insignia in the corner. He smiled again. "Wrap her in this."

"Oh, it is a girl isn't it? Can I name her?"

"Well the family will name her before the interment."

"Can I name her until then, please?"

"Okay Loli, you can give her a name."

"I'll call her Cleopatra Selene. A fine royal name."

"It certainly is Loli. A fine royal name," repeated Ptolemy. "Give her to Ella now, she will show you what to do next."

Reluctantly Loli handed her over. "Be careful—don't drop her."

"I won't," said Ella grimly.

Loli jumped off the stool, pulled it over to another embalming table and hastily got onto it. "Come on. Let's get on with it."

Ella brought over a small blue bowl filled with cold water—she tried to not look at the tiny form.

With great tenderness Loli took off the white cover and washed the body of the baby. She picked a clean cloth from a pile to hand and gently dried her. Loli picked up a large jar of myrrh. She at first struggled to get the lid off, but managed in the second attempt. She stuck her nose in the jar. Loli thought that the myrrh from the jar smelt a little too sweet and preferred it when they added frankincense. The fragrance of myrrh was one of her earliest memories. She began to rub it on the baby's pale skin. Ella placed her hand over Loli's. Loli turned to Ella with a smile. "I like this bit. It will make her smell nice."

"Not yet Loli, there is more to be done before this. It is a cold night; we will leave the baby with her mother. Can you can help in the morning?"

"Can I take her to my bedroom?"

"You know the answer to that, Loli," said Ella.

"I'll see her in the morning then?"

"In the morning, Loli."

Loli kissed Ella good night and then her father. She swept the hair from her face as she ran out of the room and couldn't understand why Ella didn't hug her anymore. She always used to.

"And Loli. Loli?"

Loli turned on the second call of her name.

"Wash your hands really well before you eat."

Loli shrugged. "Always do."

Ella thought about mothers at that point. Ella tried to be good to Loli but if Loli had a mother, life would certainly be easier, and she wouldn't have to look after her sister so much. Sometimes Ella resented the responsibility and any of her attempts to please her father seemed to be useless. Everything seemed pointless. Then she thought of Sophia's baby and tried to remember something important about it but could not do so. She felt numb when she looked at the little corpse and wondered why.

The embalming rooms were attached to the great house and there were even more storage rooms off those. The house was built of black marble, fitting for the preparation of the wealthy dead. A small courtyard garden lay all around the house. In summer it was filled with many flowers and the most beautiful was the iris. The iris dominated every household in the summer months. Her father had told her the colour of it was Egyptian Blue and belonged to the goddess, Wadjet. In ancient times a messenger from Olympus was called Iris and led young girls to the afterlife. As a child Ella often called it the bruised flower. It reminded her of the colours she had seen on a corpse. Too cold for it to bloom now, thought Ella.

The house had six bedrooms but Ella had promised Loli that they would share one of the great beds that had witnessed the births and deaths of the last hundred years. It was made of solid oak decorated with strange designs that she had never learned the symbolism of. Nine years on and they still shared a room but it wasn't just for Loli's benefit. At night Ella had, many times, thought she had heard the first cries of a newborn and the last sighs of the dying. In the dark she imagined that the dead came back to that room time and time again. Sometimes Ella would keep the gaslight low so that she could see the pale rose-pink face of her sister. That practice, Ella thought, kept them both closer to life than death. She might be an embalmer's daughter but she was still afraid of death...more so these days.

When Ella got in bed long after the night had enshrouded her sister, Ella pulled a dark strand away from Loli's face and wondered if they would both really carry on the business of embalming after Ptolemy was dead. They would have to embalm their own father—a disturbing thought.

Just the two of them to carry on the tradition well into the next century. This was 1890. The 1900's—would they be full of promise or the beginning of the end for the Child family?

Chapter 2

The next morning Ella had many tasks to perform. She knew her history and taught Loli occasionally. Ella read to her about the plagues, especially the one that had spread via The Silk Road, the great trading route that crossed Asia. The planet's population had been decimated. Century after century, as each plague appeared, it seemed more virulent than the last; bottlenecks were created in society where sometimes communities became so small there was even more inbreeding than usual.

Society had seen nothing wrong with incest even though generation after generation had thrown up anomalies and bizarre deformities of the human body. Hermaphrodites were common, although many could not reproduce. To have a hermaphrodite lover was considered a novelty. Inbreeding had a catastrophic effect on the population. Children were born with various degrees of deformity from fewer toes on each foot to infants who could not chew food properly. This was bad enough, but mental retardation had become widespread, and yet the Empress had still not made incest illegal until recently, because of tradition or some such madness.

Not just the hermaphrodites were affected by infertility; lower fertility in general was a widespread issue, too, and many had become barren, leading to a further decrease in world population. And yet it had taken thousands of years before the dynasty had thought seriously about the consequences. In fact if truth be told, the ruling elite didn't want an explosive population, so it had suited them just fine until the plague had taken too many and there were fewer people to work the land, and in the factories. There had been enforced removal of the second and third child born in each family. He or she had been taken to other parts of each country for re-education with specially chosen families, but it had caused riots, so had been stopped. Another measure had been that deformed children were taken away and put into foster homes, and still the Empress said that she loved all the children of her empire.

Through the generations the royal family married whoever they had wanted including brothers and sisters, but in the last century they had considered it a prudent practice to marry cousins instead. Cleopatra wasn't too badly affected by earlier incest in her ancestry. She showed no obvious signs of abnormality. She suspected that many children of the so-called pure lineage had been the offspring of countless relationships outside the marriage bed anyway. She had got off lightly compared to the others.

Children knew all about death at an early age, and then they were usually taught about sex much later. It was a reasonably liberal society, but the legal age of consensual sex was sixteen—a decade ago it had been ten, but child prostitution and sexual disease had become so commonplace that anyone found having sex with a child was taken away by the authorities, and few were ever seen again.

Loli didn't find it too difficult to progress the conversation from plague and incest to sex.

"How is it done?"

Ella more than ever wished that Loli's mother hadn't gone away. After an embarrassing silence Ella finally told her. That explanation led to even more embarrassing questions, "Since it is against the law for you to do it until you are of age Loli—you don't need to know much more about it."

Loli had been disappointed by that and had been even more determined to creep into her father's library and rummage around for more enlightenment. Even though Loli had asked what a hermaphrodite was Ella had managed to escape giving an answer. Ella knew that all she had to say was that a hermaphrodite usually had both male and female genitalia, but Ella couldn't begin to imagine what Loli's questions could be after that.

Loli had the last word. "Fine. I'm old enough to cut up dead bodies but not old enough to learn about sex, let alone do it."

Ella threw the book she was reading from down on the table and glanced at her notes. Her handwriting was clear and precise, unlike her father's, which was nothing more than a scrawl and couldn't be easily read. She felt her mood changing quickly like lightning striking the earth out of a blue sky. It was useless to carry on with the lesson.

"That's all for today, Loli."

After that Loli amused herself by following the servants around and spying on them, wondering if any one of them was a hermaphrodite. Later she played with her dog, Juniper, complaining to him that adults just weren't worth the effort.

Loli, as any normal ten year old would, got caught up in the moment all the time. When bored or frustrated she let her tiny dolls do things that she could not. Loli had a doll's house. When she was angry with Ella once, about helping out in the embalmment rooms, Loli broke every stick of furniture in the doll's house, as she never dared break anything in her father's house. Why couldn't she be angry for once? Why did she always have to 'contain' herself? To ease her frustration she tied a loose silken thread from curtain pole to door handle with a tiny doll, the one that looked most like her, attached to the middle. When Loli slammed her own bedroom door, the doll had been positioned so that it flew out of the dollhouse bedroom window and out of Loli's bedroom window, too. One day she would show them all, thought Loli. Exhausted, Loli sat down on the floor, reached for her hairbrush, which had been carelessly abandoned, and started to brush her hair. Twelve times on the left side, twelve times on the right, and twenty at the back. She never left her room without doing that.

With her governess role out of the way, Ella's mood improved and she was happy to move on to embalmment duties. She quickly checked over the old Governor General, Claudius Ptolemaeus Tiberius. His naked body was almost ready for entombment. Ella touched his arm gently. She tested the latest coat of resin to make sure it was dry. She thought of insects trapped in amber. One had been made into an amulet for her and had been a gift on her fifth birthday, a custom in the houses of embalmer families. This man was ready, except for his robes, for the afterlife. Some of the relatives asked for their dead to have one coat of resin and then to be wrapped in bandages, but not for this body. Amber resin was expensive and what denoted rank and wealth added up to how many layers were painted on the mummy. Claudius Ptolemaeus Tiberius had received six, and Cleopatra, Empress of the world, would have a dozen.

Ella next moved to the drying out room, which smelt of pepper and spice. There were six vats—only one of them was occupied that day. Barrels of natron, a natural form of soda ash, had been poured into it to dry out a body and Ella would, tomorrow, rub it with cassia, a type of cinnamon from Asia, and myrrh from Africa. She didn't mind that part of the process at all. Without it, enzymes eventually got to work and the body would turn green then black. The face and abdomen would swell, the scrotum if male, the vulva if female. Foul smelling fluid would ooze from the mouth and nose, and the nails would fall off. Skin would bloat and split, but never after their work.

Her father was busy in the next room. He hardly greeted her, just carried on with the awful hook instrument that he pushed up the nose of the corpse to puncture the small ethmoid bone between the eye sockets before he could get the brain and viscera out. Ptolemy had already finished working on the abdomen and had removed the internal organs, ready for the canopic jars.

"Come on Ella…pack the chest."

Ella didn't hesitate; she'd done it many times before. She picked up the small linen bags full of natron and started to place them into the chest cavity. It had already been washed out with alcohol and that was preferable to the smell of putrefying organs.

Ptolemy liked his work and was at his most cheerful when cutting up a corpse, "How is old Claudius then?" He looked up briefly.

"He looks marvellous Father." Ella turned her head away. She rarely met his gaze.

"Good. We have to ensure he really does look his best even though he will be in the sarcophagus soon enough. Is the photographer coming this afternoon?"

"Yes father. It is all arranged. I'll go and see that the robes are brought over and all will be finished."

"Leave what you are doing now. I'll finish this one off. Go and see that the dust has been taken off the sarcophagus. I want him photographed and sealed in. Then I'll be happy."

Ella washed her hands, rubbed some myrrh oil into her own skin, and went to the mausoleum where the sarcophagus awaited the body. This sarcophagus was made of wood but the one it would be placed inside, in the tomb, was of the finest marble engraved with funeral spells, poppy flowers (also called the white lotus) and inside it had already been placed the *Book of the Dead*. The custom now was to place it with the body, protected by the heavy lid, not beside the sarcophagus in a jar, because grave robbers sometimes stole the scroll and rich ornaments outside the sarcophagus before they got to the mummy. There was always the hope that the thieves would be interrupted before they disturbed the dead. These scrolls were expensive to buy from scribes, and thieves occasionally stole them for other people. They rubbed out the name of the owner and a new name appeared on the scroll. The scroll was a guidebook to a happy afterlife. The text helped the dead overcome the ordeals of the underworld and find their way to the Fields of Aaru and safety. Some funerary goods had not been added yet. Ella would see that they were packed. They were the little figures called ushabti who were to do the menial tasks in the next world. On returning home Ella went to the library, where she occasionally spent some of her free time.

Ella picked up the *Book of Isis* that they kept in the sarcophagus room. She read out loud the words of Apuleius. *"Isis is nature, The Universal Mother, Mistress of all the Elements, and Queen of the Dead."* Ella hesitated. So many names. Ella knew that many of her friends did not believe in Isis. She had played no part in their lives. Down through the centuries Isis had been worshipped by the dynasty and as chief embalmer, Ptolemy Child, followed the old traditions. But Ella was not so sure about the future and whether she would want to be bound to the old religion.

The next morning Ella dressed with the usual care—black suit, white shirt and black tie, with her blonde hair loose around her shoulders. She looked strangely androgynous but she liked that.

Metal curtain rings clanked together. She pulled aside a little the long heavy green curtains and looked out across the grey rooftops. It was sleeting and Ella shivered at the thought of working in the chapel and tomb in such cold conditions. She thought that she'd rather have her heavy skirts than the male attire she wore for the sake of tradition. Her father had no sons. All adult sons or daughters of the chief embalmer wore male clothing in the tomb. She had no idea where the custom came from, and as she lived in a society where females were almost equal with males, she found it odd. Almost equal. Men still had the upper hand, their boys' clubs and jokes that she didn't find amusing at all. She remembered when her cousin, Aulus, had been mean to her when she had talked about art and then accused her of being oversensitive, which she hadn't been. She had thought him insensitive. Seemed to be par for the course, women being treated as oversensitive, men the flip side.

She was listless and opened the top drawer of her dresser to find the opium. Opium thebaicum, from the Egyptian fields at Thebes. She took out the little black pills that were made up of opium combined with citrus juice and quintessence of gold. She needed opium to face the day with her father—just a little. He wouldn't notice she was under the influence, and if he did, so what—it wasn't illegal. Stealing it was illegal, but eating or drinking opium wasn't. Ella poured herself a cup of red wine and added a pill. When she felt the warm glow within her she felt that she had enough energy to get on with her work.

Ella tugged at the curtains again. The clamour of the steel rings on the metal pole woke Loli. Poor winter light flooded the room.

"Time to get up?" Loli asked, rubbing the sleep out of her eyes.

"Yes, it's time Loli."

"How come you are wearing those clothes today? They look horrible."

Ella looked again into the mirror, but at her pale face and the dark circles under her eyes. She often had trouble sleeping. "You've forgotten. I'm to check the interior of the chapel and tomb with father today."

"I thought it was tomorrow. I can stay in bed then."

"No you can't. You need to help."

"Okay. I'll look after Cleo."

"Cleo?"

"The baby."

"Oh, the baby. I think that the baby would rather stay with its mother, don't you?"

Ella didn't want to talk about the baby.

"Its mother is dead of course—I'll look after Cleo now."

Ella reluctantly sat on the white bed cover and looked at Loli. Ella gave her that pseudo-mother look that Loli pretended not to notice sometimes.

"Loli—you cannot keep the baby. It is dead, too. Now promise me that you won't take her away from her mother."

There was an abrupt knock at the door and her father's voice sounded impatient, "Ella. Come on, we'll be late."

"Now promise, Loli, Cleo is to stay with her mother." Ella fumbled in her jacket pocket. "I have something for you, Loli."

"What is it? A present?"

"I found it a long time ago but now I want you to have it."

"Show me."

Ella held out a closed hand then opened it palm up. It was a funerary amulet, a large Egyptian eye with a teardrop beneath. It had been placed on a silver chain.

"It's beautiful. What is it?"

"It's called The Eye of Horus, also called Wadjet. It wards off evil and father says it enables the dead to see again."

"Is it real, Ella? Is it very old?"

"Very old, Loli—a true antique. Father said that your mother left it behind before she went away."

There came another very determined knock at the door.

Ella jumped and still felt far too irritable to face the day. She hoped the pill would take effect soon.

"Ella. I'm waiting." Her father sounded most agitated, the way he always did before an internment.

Ella opened the door. Her father stood in the hall. He was also irritated because he had to wait for her.

"I'm ready."

As she closed the large oak door behind her she didn't hear Loli say, "Don't cry, Cleo. I'll be there in a minute."

Loli threw off the covers and ran over to the oval mirror. She placed the amulet around her neck, pulled out her dark hair from beneath the silver chain, and admired the eye made up of tiny emeralds and a black stone in the middle for the iris. Loli's hair was dark; a stark contrast to her sister's which was blonde. Loli had been told, but she couldn't remember by whom, that she looked like her mother. Loli smiled at her reflection. In haste she got into her clothes and picked up a myrrh container. These containers were put in strategic places all over the house. Loli dipped her finger into the grey cream and smudged it under her nose.

Cold stone steps led down to the storage rooms and Loli, unusually confident, descended alone to the embalming rooms. The slaves were busy upstairs and were rarely allowed access to the rooms, except to sweep the floor occasionally.

Loli chose a door off to her left. The only sound coming from within was the steam driven refrigeration machine, which pumped cold air into the cabinets. Although the rooms were unheated, Ptolemy Child kept the bodies very cold. The room was lined with the cabinets three levels high, all with the insignia of the Child family on the doors, and each with a place to slide in a card with the deceased's name on it. She had once been punished for changing them around as a joke, but the joke was on her when her father slapped her. Loli hated the noise of the steam machine, so she switched it off for a little while. She looked intently at each name and found Sophia on one of the lower cabinets. Sophia was the mother of the baby. Loli pulled the drawer open carefully. She shivered against the cold. Inside there was the tiny body of the infant. No Mother, only the baby there who gave a weak cry, and tried to suck its tiny hand. Loli cried out and scooped it up into her arms, looking around for something to cover the tiny child.

A loud bang made her jump. It came from one of the cabinets. Startled, she looked down at the baby and then back at the other cabinet. She would not open the other cabinet for anything. Again—the bang. This time followed by a low moan. Terrified, Loli made for the door but heard muffled voices outside. She looked anxiously around the room, then saw the door beside the cabinets and ran towards it. She tugged the handle, being careful not to bang the baby's head as she manoeuvred herself into place inside. The small storage cupboard was just big enough for her and the baby. Loli left the door slightly open so she could see who was about to enter the room.

Two men came into view. They were both big, stocky men and dressed poorly, but not household slaves at all. They started to open the cabinets one-by-one and eventually found one that was occupied.

As they opened the drawer one of the men started back. "I know he said that he would do that, but it still gave me a fright."

"Calm yourself Sleeward. Come on. Between us we'll get him walking a little, and then it won't be too hard to get him out. If anyone sees us it will look like he's drunk. That's it, get him out. Now then," he said, shaking the corpse by the shoulder, "you can walk, can't you? Come on, shake yourself awake. I know it is a stir, and you don't know what is happening, but come with us. We'll take good care of you."

The other man laughed. Loli recognised them as colourmen, the ones who hung around Memphis Square. Unknown to Ella or her father, Loli had bought the paint called Egyptian Mummy from one of them.

Loli held her hand over her mouth to stop herself from shouting out as she watched the dead man helped out of the cabinet. It wasn't because the corpse was naked that she thought him repulsive, but that he should be dead. The dead shouldn't walk. She felt sick.

Unlike any other corpse she had seen, rigor mortis didn't seem to have set in. The colourmen had brought some clothes with them. They managed to get some trousers and a jacket on him. They then stuck a cap on his head, and if you didn't look too closely at his face, they'd get him out without too much trouble. The slaves wouldn't bother, they hardly blinked unless beaten. Nothing had been done to the dead man yet; no organs removed, unlike some of the bodies that had been in and out of the main embalmment room. What if it had been a body where the organs had been removed? She shivered at the thought.

In Loli's mind the baby she held had never really died, but she knew the man the two strangers had taken away was dead. How come he could move? The two men must be body snatchers. Her father had talked about them. Lowest of the low—akin to tomb raiders and hated just as much. Colourmen. Paid by someone to take bodies, he'd said, but for what reason? Surely they weren't going to do anything too bad to the man they just said that they would look after?

She heard the front door slam and managed to get back to her room at the top of the house without being seen. Once there she put the baby in the centre of her bed, a tiny grey-looking thing, too thin, and whose hands grabbed at the air as if trying to hold onto life. A purple bruise had spread across its forehead. Loli looked through all her doll's clothes for anything that would fit Cleopatra Selene. She found muslin in a drawer that she could use for a nappy. Her baby doll was discarded on the floor, a pale copy of the real baby that now whimpered in a dress of gold, and was wrapped in the finest of Egyptian cotton sheets.

Loli put all thoughts of the dead man out of her head. She then put more of the cream under her nose and cradled the baby gently, singing a lullaby to the infant. She cooed to it and kissed the baby's face, and once gently on the lips. Within Loli some memory stirred, and she felt compelled to hold the child to her chest tightly. Too tightly. Realising that she would hurt the baby if she held it so close any longer, she quickly put her down in the centre of the bed once more. Then she forgot why she had been holding the infant so tightly.

"Never mind, Cleopatra Selene. Until we find your mother I'll look after you." Loli wondered if it had been the second time that the two colourmen had visited the Ptolemy house that day.

She made up the little doll's cradle in the corner by her bed and settled the child in it. Once satisfied that she was okay, Loli skipped over to the wardrobe and changed her pink dress for one of the deepest red. She thought about going downstairs to see if Ella had come home. She had lots to tell her. Ella and her father wouldn't be angry with her. Not when she told them about the colourmen, and certainly not when she told them she knew one of them. Perhaps she wouldn't mention that bit; she didn't want to get into any trouble. She was a good girl after all. Perhaps she would follow the colourman next time she saw him and find out where he had taken the body, which would be better. The colourmen hung about Memphis Square all the time. She liked the idea that she should play detective and then she would look really clever in her father's eyes—she wanted desperately to please him.

It was late afternoon already. Loli drew back the heavy curtain and looked into the foggy square. No sign of her father or Ella. As she looked down she saw her cousin, Aulus, leave the building and Ella emerge from round the corner and come inside. The door slammed and Loli heard her father's raised voice. Surely he hadn't been in the house all afternoon? He hadn't been in the library, she had checked. She hadn't looked in his bedroom, it was well away from her on the second floor, in the east wing of the house where she was forbidden to go because her father liked his privacy, he said. In fact she had never seen her father's room. She might take a look some time when he was out. She had been meaning to do that for a while now. On his door hung a slate—on which he usually wrote what time he wanted breakfast or more usually said NONE TO ENTER. On those days the slaves did as he bid and didn't come to change the bedding or collect the leftovers from meals eaten alone or in the company of strangers. Ptolemy rarely ate with Ella or Loli, and although he occasionally pampered Loli, she wondered sometimes why he had ever had children at all.

That evening Ptolemy prepared for a private ceremony in the library. In the old days the head embalmer used to wear the Anubis mask to represent the jackal-headed god whilst embalming. That part of the ceremony had been abandoned, but if Ella was going to take on the role of chief embalmer one day she needed to know of the secrets that had been passed down through the Child family. Ptolemy had decided to show Ella one of those secrets, to stir old memories—that very night. His own father had called it, irreverently, his party trick. Ptolemy thought that at least one of his children should learn about the magic. It was late and Loli was in bed. Ptolemy locked the door behind himself and Ella.

He picked up a scroll from a casket that he had placed on a small table near the window. The curtains were closed. Ella wondered what was in the cage covered with a cloth. She gasped when he took the small dead dog out of the cage. The dog showed no signs of life. Ptolemy stroked it. It was Loli's pet. Ella had seen it running around with Loli a couple of hours earlier. What on earth had happened to it? There was no blood on it at all. Ptolemy placed its cold, brown body on a small stone altar in front of a statue of Anubis. Ella felt nothing for the dog but she allowed herself to feel slightly sorry that Loli would be devastated.

"Ella, come help me a little here."

"It's Loli's dog."

"I think I know that Ella."

"But what happened to it?"

"Ella!"

Ella was then told exactly what Ptolemy was going to do, but it didn't seem right and it didn't seem possible. And she remembered when he had tried to show her the 'magical games' before and she had run away; and there had been that time she had stayed. She'd show him she wasn't afraid.

She gently held Juniper whilst Ptolemy read from the scroll.

"Oh mighty Anubis. Give the power of restoration also to Ella, daughter of Ptolemy Child."

Ptolemy gave her the scroll and told her to speak the appropriate responses.

"Say the words Ella."

"I—follower of Isis," here she hesitated, "utter the words of Dedi given to the family of Child." Ella stopped once more. It all sounded so ridiculous.

"But father...I can't do this."

"It has to be done, Ella. Do you want me to tell Loli what we did?"

"We?"

Ella continued the incantation. It took what felt to her like an eternity to complete the ritual. She grew tired and the words just seemed a jumbled mess on the scroll. She finished with, "I, with the power given to Dedi and then entrusted to his family and descendants, restore this creature to life."

Nothing happened. Ptolemy looked puzzled and he went over the scroll again this time on his own using the same incantations. It had always worked. Isis had always blessed this ritual. Always. Why had she withdrawn her blessing now? It had been a long time since any in the family had performed it but Ptolemy had changed nothing. He had the scroll but if he had the other one—*The Book of Thoth*, he would be more powerful. There had always been a curse on that book: it was that whoever read from it would be punished—one of the reader's loved ones had to die as payment. He looked up at Ella.

"Is that it?" asked Ella.

"I don't know why it didn't work. There is precious little magic left in the world but this ritual has always worked for me. Only on animals though, never on people."

Ella was beginning to wish that she wasn't the daughter of a head embalmer. She'd had some opium before the ritual and apart from feeling ill at the sight of the dog, she felt so very tired. Opium. She wanted more opium and she wanted the artist, Swin. Her thoughts turned to Aulus and she wished him dead, too, and if ever he died she was pretty sure that she would not use the power of Dedi, or rather *The Book of Thoth*, or anything to restore him.

Not long after Ella left, Ptolemy threw the scroll back in the casket, ordered a slave to get rid of the dog and retired to bed. The slave wrapped it in some cloth and placed it in one of the basement rooms. The whimpering could not be heard by the people in the rest of the house. That night the dead dog, Juniper, stirred, rose unsteadily to its feet, and arched its back. The crack of its spine caused the animal little pain.

Chapter 3

Aulus' parents were dead. His mother Claudia had been Ptolemy's sister and had a share of their parents' wealth, but her husband had gambled it all away, leaving the family practically penniless. Aulus had artistic tendencies but rarely painted. He had acted once or twice in a local theatre but the desire to be constantly admired, which he wasn't, caused him some stress. And the lack of other actors' attention to detail, and then them forgetting their lines, had offended his sensibilities so much so that he had abandoned that career. He was given a small allowance by his Uncle Ptolemy, and as repayment he occasionally had sex with him, which didn't bother Aulus too much. He had to think of different ways to supplement his lifestyle. His latest venture, he thought, was a stroke of genius.

The house of Aulus was falling into disrepair and he wanted the best furnishings for the lower rooms. The outside of the house had to be redecorated too—it would make him look important, give him more of a standing in the city. Also the roof needed to be mended as a matter of urgency.

Aulus had planned the unwrapping months ahead. All was in place. The large box had been delivered. The caterers had spread out a sumptuous banquet in one of the lower rooms. There was plenty of wine and the guests had started to arrive. Special invitations for eight, only. Guests braved the severe cold to be there, such was the uniqueness of the event. They had paid large sums of money to be present.

After the guests had finished eating they were led into a room where there were enough seats for all, and Aulus had arranged for a carpenter to build a small raised stage. It hadn't cost him anything, because the carpenter owed him for a small business venture that they had pursued together. On this dais was a sturdy table and placed upon this was a wooden sarcophagus. The sarcophagus was very old. The gold paint had faded in places but the seals had not been broken. It hadn't been opened for over a thousand years. The contents would go to the highest bidder. The colourmen sold whole mummies for unwrapping in private, for great sums of money. People would take part in the process of unwinding the dead, or rather cut the mouldy bandages away to see what gold or jewels they could find. In a society where the dead were venerated, they were still defiled in secret. The excitement in the room was tangible. There hadn't been an unwrapping of a mummy for a very long time in Manceastre, certainly not in the lifetime of the old Governor General. The new Governor General, Clovis, didn't seem to be as reverential about the dead as his predecessor. It was still technically illegal to unwrap a mummy, but not if it belonged to any member of a family outcast by the royal dynasty, and Aulus claimed just that of the mummy before them. Few doubted that the law would be enforced even if he weren't who Aulus claimed him to be. It was said to be the body of Aristos, and had been recently found in Greece. This person had tried to assassinate Alexander VII but failed in the attempt and disappeared; his body then no doubt secreted away by his followers, who were keen that he should have his own name for the afterlife. Although some said that the naming would be pointless, as there could be no afterlife for a man who had tried to kill one of the chosen family. His name had been passed down through the centuries and told to children to warn them of disloyalty to the ruling elite.

Aulus was tall and of medium build—he always wore the best clothes he could afford, not black, for he liked colour far too much for that. This day he wore a mid-blue suit. It wasn't a garish blue but a subtle shade and the colour went with his long brown hair. He always had his hair trimmed to just above his shoulders.

Some of the guests complained that they weren't seated in the right place and shuffled their chairs forward a little.

"Junius stop that; you are in my way now."

Aemilius smiled apologetically, "Sorry. I need a better view."

"Well, move a little the other way so I can see too. Come on Aulus, get on with it. You've had our money."

"Gentlemen, gentlemen. Be patient."

Aulus beckoned two slaves who stood well away from the guests. They both had knives and the audience fell into silence as they started chipping at the seals.

"Are you sure you have the right body, Aulus? You might not have the right one you know."

Aulus looked slightly annoyed. "Come and look. Check the inscription on the coffin. Validate it. Be satisfied that I have done my research properly."

33

The slaves drew back for a moment.

Junius stepped up on the stage and peered at the hieroglyphics on the sarcophagus.

"It's all right. It's him."

Aemilius joined him to take a closer look and peered at the inscription too. "I disagree; looks like it has been tampered with and changed, as if filed off and re-worked."

Aulus began to get frustrated, "Gentleman I assure you the mummy has been authenticated—look at the hieroglyphs, they haven't been tampered with. Who else could it be?"

Junius and Aemilius left the dais and sat down again.

There was a low murmur and work on opening the sarcophagus began again. It didn't take them long to loosen the wooden lid. With a heave it was taken off and removed to one side of the room.

"Now gentlemen, if you would like to come forward one or two at a time. We can begin."

The mummy had been preserved in the usual manner. It was a male, which was obvious because the penis had been mummified. The man had been tall.

"Aemilius, you can start if you wish." Aulus handed him the scissors.

Aemilius rose from his chair and darted forward eager to start around the chest of the mummy. As he made the first cut a cloud of dust emanated from the wrappings. Aemilius coughed a little but carried on. Before long he found a rare prize, an ibis-headed amulet. He wouldn't be able to keep it but Aulus would give him a little of the profit at auction. Besides he wasn't there for the money; he was there because he'd always wanted to help unwrap a mummy.

"Careful Aemilius, you don't want to make too much of a mess."

A ripple of polite laughter emanated from the room. Traditionally mummy unwrappings left the corpse in pieces and the bones sometimes crumbled to dust. Some, however, were sturdier than others. Feeling lucky after his first find, Aemilius wanted to see if there was a scarab beetle near the heart. He was disappointed to find nothing there.

"Come on, Aemilius, give it up for the next person," shouted one of the guests.

Reluctantly he gave the scissors to Junius who ventured further down the body. The mummy shuddered suddenly. "Aulus, don't jolt the table," said Junius.

"I didn't jolt the table. I don't know what you are talking about."

Again Junius thought he felt a shudder and he glanced angrily over at Aulus. "I've paid my money, kindly have the consideration to let me continue."

With a great creak of the table and a cloud of dust the mummy moved again. One guest started laughing.

"Good joke, Aulus. A good joke on us. Now give us our money back," said Junius.

Aulus was dumbstruck and backed away from the table. Some of the guests got up from their chairs; others jeered, and then one person left, after shouting at Aulus. The mummy shuddered once more. This time more violently. That was enough for the rest. They thought that they were victims of an elaborate joke. The room soon emptied, most angry that they should have known better than to give good money to Aulus in return for a cheap trick that Aulus would no doubt find extremely funny in the tavern later on.

"We all expect our money back tomorrow, Aulus, or we'll get the solicitors in," shouted Junius. One guest even threatened Aulus with a visit from the colourmen. A few seconds later and Aulus stood alone amidst the overturned chairs. He stared at the mummy, confused and bewildered by what he had seen. The mummy trembled slightly again and Aulus fled the house.

The colourmen, who could barely be bothered to conceal themselves across the street, watched Aulus' guests leave with some interest. When Aulus had left too, they expertly picked the lock on the front door, which only took a minute, and took in a linen chest. To any passers-by it would look to be a delivery, and no one ever paid too much attention to what the colourmen did unless it affected them.

"What's so special about this one then?" asked Lento.

"Don't know but we have to be careful with it," said Sleeward.

"So this one isn't for sale like the others?"

Sleeward raised his voice. "No, it's special—like I said."

"Okay, no need to be bad tempered. No need to shout. You are worse than my wife, you are."

"There's nothing worse than your wife…"

"I should swipe you for that. I'll curse you instead."

"Curses. Curses. If I believed in curses do you think that I'd be doing this? As for your wife, you swipe at her enough yourself."

"If Clovis finds out that we're taking this to someone else won't he be angry? He likes to know about these things."

"Look. The person who is paying for this is paying good money—more than Clovis gives us for the others. Who says we can't work for both?"

"Just as long as you know what you are doing, Sleeward."

"I do. Trust me, I do."

In different parts of the city the colourmen watched and waited with their overcoat collars turned up against the biting cold. The families of the dead could hide their loved ones, but the homeless and the very poor were taken away by the colourmen, and most didn't even notice

Aulus visited quite a few taverns that afternoon. He ended up at The Temple Inn, which was situated on the Via del Foro. Aulus tripped up over the step going into the establishment, which was unusual as he usually did that upon leaving. There was a man standing in the doorway; Aulus fell against him. Aulus wasn't looking for trouble, so he muttered an apology and half-smiled before entering the low corridor to a room at the back of the inn where there was little light and the smell of opium in the air. A colourman followed him inside.

"So it didn't go well then?"

Aulus then recognised the man as Sleeward. He couldn't understand why he hadn't sooner. Sleeward never appeared ruffled; well, he had never been, in the company of Aulus. He was the man who had obtained the mummy for him. Sleeward smelt of decay. It lingered on him like the foul smelling fog that hung low over the river, but he was an easygoing fellow and pleasant enough company for Aulus.

Aulus pointed a finger at him. "There is something strange about that mummy. I want my money back. Nothing has worked out the way I planned it. I've got to give money back to the people who came to see it."

"There's nothing wrong with that mummy. I'm not giving anything back. Just give them the money back that they paid to unwrap it."

"I can't."

"Why not?"

"Because I've spent it already. Anyway, something scared them about the thing. They're not real collectors, just amateurs with money, superstitious and easily riled."

"But they pay."

"They do."

"What scared them? Wait a minute; let's get that table over there." The colourman pointed to a table next to the wall in a corner of the low-lit room.

Sleeward beckoned a girl, wearing a long blue dress, over to the table.

"Some wine, any will do. A large flask of it."

The colourman sat on a chair and pulled it roughly up to the table. One or two drinkers looked round to see where the noise was coming from, recognised the colourman, and quickly turned away. The girl didn't take long to come back with the wine.

Aulus poured a glass from the jug and then poured one for the colourman.

Aulus took a swig and explained to Sleeward what had happened. "I don't know. Perhaps it did move."

"Perhaps it did but I doubt it."

"Why do you say that?"

"Let us not make any pretence. You know what I do and the many ways in which I deal."

"Yes."

"I deal in mummies and sometimes I have great difficulty in getting my hands on the old ones—the ones behind the door seals, always guarded by temple snakes and such like."

Aulus nodded.

They started to drink quickly and the subject changed to women. It wasn't until they were on their third flask of wine that Sleeward loosened up a little and changed the subject back to the mummy.

"I believe that there is something weird going on in the city at the moment."

"What's that?"

"It will be obvious about the dead, soon, anyway, but if I tell you what happens when Clovis gets his hands on them, if you breathe a word of what I'm going to say, I'll break your arms, right?"

Aulus nodded.

"I've been taking bodies to Clovis, been doing it for years...mostly before the embalming, sometimes after the embalmment process. We come along and take them away."

Aulus nodded again, nothing seemed to surprise him.

"Anyway, lately these bodies aren't dead."

Aulus drew back. "You mean you've been kidnapping the living?"

Sleeward stared at Aulus. "Don't be barmy. No. I wouldn't do that. The bodies are dead all right. It's just that they can move. They don't die. They can't die."

"How do you know that they can't die?"

"Because one of us tried to kill one again. Stuck a knife in the corpse three times and it still kept on walking around as if it didn't know that it should be dead."

"Impossible."

"It might be impossible, but it happened. I was there."

"Where are all these…these walking dead?"

"Well, we got a load of them for Clovis and his experiments, but mostly the families of the dead are hiding them away. They are too afraid for people to see them."

"And this is happening all over the city?"

"All over the city. I'm desperate, Aulus. I've got to talk to someone."

"The other colourmen?"

"They'd tell Clovis."

"About what? I could tell Clovis."

"Not if I offer you money."

"Money, and all you want to do is talk to me?"

"For the moment." Sleeward took a large swig of the wine. "I'm hiding someone who has died."

"Who?"

"The only relative I had left in the world, as the plague took the rest."

"And who is that?"

"My son, Luce. He isn't going to be used in the Clovis experiments." Sleeward thumped the table and the girl stared at him. He controlled himself.

Aulus' face softened a little. Aulus was an opportunist, but even he could see that it wasn't worth a whole lot of crap from Sleeward for mentioning a boy to Clovis for more money. Besides he quite liked Sleeward; they'd had some good drinking sessions together.

"Will you keep quiet about it?"

"I will."

Fifty years had been too long to be alive, thought Sleeward. He would have finished his own life off a long time ago, but his son had needed him. And now, even in death, his son still needed him. Was there no end to the torment and suffering? In his time Sleeward had been a sailor, a prize-fighter, a pig farmer in the north of the country, and now a colourman; settling down again into a life of the lowest of the low. His son knew that he was a colourman, and he knew what that meant. The boy's mother had died a long time ago.

Aulus poured more wine from the flask. He knew that it was going to be a long night.

When Sleeward did get home later he found that his son had gone missing. The woman from the butcher's yard had agreed to look after him, but had fallen asleep. Sleeward grabbed her roughly by the arm and flung her out into the cold night. She slipped and her face hit the stone step. With difficulty and slipping on the ice, she got to her feet, and staggered off into the darkness. Snow fell upon the blood. As the blizzard began to rage it was covered up completely.

When Aulus eventually left the tavern he was totally disorientated as to where his house was. He was too drunk to even think about going with the Wainside Street girls who complained that he was cutting back and not giving them much money any more for their services. One stood before him and lifted her skirts high to her waist. Aulus laughed. She slapped his face before he stumbled and fell into the gutter.

Aulus woke up in the bed of Licinia. She had heaped a hundred curses on his head but had taken him home with her. She wouldn't do that for anyone except Aulus and that was for purely selfish reasons. Licinia had washed him and put him to bed. He was greeted on awakening with warm, red wine. He took a sip, grimaced and swallowed. He tried to sit up, tentatively propped himself up on his elbows, and succeeded in sipping from the glass which she held to his lips. He looked around the low-ceilinged room. It was quite well furnished with deep reds and blues. A lamp, now out as the winter sun streamed through a crack between the crimson curtains, stood too close to the edge of a table. He reached out and pushed it into the middle.

"It seems to me that you are in need of looking after. I was on my way back from seeing Calvi last night," said Licinia.

She was in a reasonable mood now. She had made plenty of money the night before and not behind the tombs in Memphis Square like some of the other girls. She usually was invited back to one of the artists' studios. She had been painted by Calvi whom she had known quite a long time.

"I don't know why you bother with him."

"He pays well of course, for the slutting and the sitting, as does Clovis."

"Well Clovis is just plainly mad, and as for Calvi, I've never met a more deceitful, hypocritical man in all my life."

Licinia was tall, blonde and slender. In fact, her ribs showed too plainly through her skin for Aulus' liking but she had a vigorous nature, which he appreciated at times.

"I think that you are describing yourself," she laughed.

"I've never met a more deceitful, hypocritical man in all my life, other than me...that is."

"Of all the artists around here he has always been kind to me. He actually cried last night. He had been drinking wine, fucking me, painting me, and then threw his brush down and wept. I was embarrassed. I'm not used to tears. He thought that he wasn't a good enough painter."

"Was that the real reason?"

"He kept moaning that Swin was a better painter than he could ever be and that he hated him for that reason."

"Swin?" Aulus always pretended that he didn't know Swin that well.

"You know Swin. Wonderful red hair, he works for your uncle. Swin's wife and child died recently. His wife Sophia had been a good friend to ..."

Aulus became impatient and interrupted. "What has this to do with me?"

"Nothing, just telling you what happened to me last night. I want to learn to paint too—thought you might be interested," she replied. "What led to you getting into such a drunken state?"

"Do I need a reason?"

"No. I just thought that there might be one."

Licinia changed the subject. "Someone is going to have to do something about Clovis one day."

"What do you care? Cleopatra or Clovis—both despots. Barely in control, with two thirds of the empire's people dead, and us probably next. There isn't much to be done."

"She isn't quite as cruel. The lesser of two evils. That is all we can hope for. There is no dignity with death anymore."

"There never was. You die, some get their insides ripped outside, and then you are stuck in natron, and wrapped up—swaddled like a baby—again. Where's the dignity in that? In fact, there is no dignity in anything we do. Ah. You are going to mention art now...as if we can live up to art. All idealised. Our cities are belching out smoke and steam to produce crap for what is left of us. Best to pull down the cities and start again—let's go and live in the country."

"Have you finished ranting on?"

"Seriously, what is the point of art?"

"Perhaps it gives us something to aspire to?"

"There is nothing to aspire to, nothing left worth preserving, certainly not religion in this pox-ridden land. The country is the best place to go—leave the city."

"If this is such a good idea why haven't you gone?"

"And live on what, Licinia? I like nice things," Aulus laughed.

"Is there anything that you would fight for, Aulus?"

"I used to think not, but I've been thinking about what a friend of mine said the other day, and there might just be. Better to go out with a bang than dying of the plague. Do something before I go."

Aulus searched his memory of yesterday. He dismissed the unwrapping of the mummy for the moment and thought of what Sleeward had said to him.

"Do you know a colourman called Sleeward?"

"I do. I know many of those who live in this quarter. Since so many people prefer to live skyward and get about on the walkways up there. I know many of whom are left down here: the artists, the colourmen, the other girls, the men and women who come down from the apartments occasionally. They are all so afraid of catching something down here."

"It's hardly clean," said Aulus, and then he thought that there were more things than the plague to be caught from girls like Licinia. She didn't catch on.

"This plague isn't as bad as the last although the dead Governor General saw that the skyscrapers got all the money for cleaning. The pollution from the industrial quarter is bad at a lower level and you can see why the people choose to walk the skytubes to get about this quarter, rather than suffer the weather and the smog down here. Calvi said that the artists live down here because they'd rather paint real people in real surroundings than paint rooftops and clouds through windows."

"But do people buy the paintings of down here?"

"Well, some do, but more and more frequently the artists go up there and rely on commissioned portraits. Some of those apartments are enormous. No wonder the people never come down here."

Licinia gestured at the table. "Some bread and cheese?"

Aulus shook his head. "More wine."

She poured him another glass and walked over to the dresser. Licinia brushed her hair, readjusted the tie belt on her violet gown and sat down on the edge of the bed. She was quite pleased with her one room flat near the butcher's yard. She had got some cheap silks and other fabrics from the wholesaler down the road and hung them from the walls. They were all shades of red and blue. Above the large double bed was a swathe of indigo, and in her boredom one day she had cut out little golden stars, and stuck them on the cloth so that they were the first thing she saw when she woke up in the morning and the last thing at night. She never let men or women stay over—only Aulus.

Aulus stared at her. He had always been intrigued by Licinia. She was a hermaphrodite. In their encounters he had always been fascinated by the fact that she had an extraordinary libido, and more enthusiasm for sex than even he had. She continued to fascinate him.

"Licinia."

She knew what he wanted by the quiet tone of his voice and she slipped off her robe. Aulus put the empty glass on the table beside the bed.

Chapter 4

It was desperately cold and very quiet. The steam train that carried the dead had not rattled its way up the slope from the other parts of the city by Memphis Square for quite some time. It usually ran night and day; never stopped. Ella noticed that there hadn't been a train for days. It brought plague victims to the large underground mass burial chambers where the priests attended to them. If they were very wealthy they would go to Ptolemy. Manceastre wealth had been founded on cotton and the production of woollen garments, and although many lived in the skyscrapers above the burial grounds more lived in large mansions on the outskirts of the city. Manceastre had always been the dreariest and wettest city in the northern empire, and many of Cleopatra's family refused to rule there, preferring the warmth of the Mediterranean or the eastern part of the empire. Ella shivered as she made her way down the hill. It started to snow once more.

At the tomb of Claudius Ptolemaeus Tiberius, Ella stood in the chapel. She held her lamp up to admire Swin's work. Ella had been in charge of the decoration and had worked closely with Swin. All aspects of life had been portrayed with a fine hand. Nothing had been left out or the deceased would have not been able to cross over and live happily in eternity. There were scenes taken from the dead man's life. He had been a wealthy cotton merchant and the walls were partly covered with pictures of the making of cotton—from the growing of it, through the various processes, to the finished products themselves. The man had enjoyed fishing so on another wall Ella had asked the artist to show him casting a net and catching fish. Standing behind him was the god Osiris with his green face smiling down on the abundance of crops, cotton and fish that were depicted in a huge mound almost as high as the blue ceiling. Osiris had a hand on the man's shoulder. On one wall there were pictures of offerings in case the relatives didn't attend in person.

Ella felt a firm grasp on her shoulder and even as she jumped she knew before she looked that it was her father. He had a fierce grip and she had felt it before.

"Fine work. The artist has done a good job. Where is he?" asked Ptolemy.

"You should know, Father."

The grip tightened. "I don't like your tone Ella, where is he?"

"It is his wife and baby who are in our embalming parlour, Father."

"I was so caught up in this project I didn't realise—she only came in a few days ago."

They heard a footstep on the stone behind them and both turned. "Ah—Aulus. Good that you should come to see the finished chapel and tomb. I'm happy to see you taking more of an interest."

Ella wasn't happy to see her cousin. He had always been mean to her when they were children and his ego and arrogance in his adulthood revolted her more. If it wasn't for Loli, Ella was sure that her father would turn the business over to him. Ptolemy had always wanted a male to continue with his work, even though custom declared females equal to males as far as inheritance was concerned. Aulus never even acknowledged her presence and just leaned against the still drying paint on the chapel wall. Instead of speaking out and having her father chastise him she did it herself.

"Get off the wall," she said in a low voice—her father was too intent on looking at the detail on the face of Osiris to hear her. Aulus shrugged and wandered around the room, selecting a comment here and there that pleased Ptolemy, and praising the artist. Nothing was said to Ella who had ensured day after day that any errors had been rectified, and some scenes had taken many months since the death of the Governor General's wife. Claudius Ptolemaeus Tiberius was now going to join her. He was the latest of the northern royal family rumoured to have died prematurely from poisoning. Members of the royal family regularly killed each other off in the hope of getting nearer to the Empress Cleopatra. Two thousand years of rule by the same family encompassing an enormous empire hadn't eliminated absolute greed.

Ptolemy looked at another of the paintings. "Don't you think that Swin has caught the form of Claudius wonderfully?"

"I think he has captured something of old Claudius," said Aulus, hardly bothering to look at it at all.

"Claudius was the same age as me. I wouldn't call myself old."

"Old. You are not old." Aulus attempted a recovery. "Good grief I thought him at least twenty years older than you."

"Indeed, Aulus."

Aulus smiled at Ptolemy and quickly tried to backtrack. "The Empress will like the work, I'm sure of it."

"Swin is good, isn't he? I must use him again."

"What about that artist, Janus? He's done some work for you, hasn't he? I thought he was better. Use of colour and all that," suggested Aulus.

"Aulus."

"Yes Ptolemy?"

"Shut up. Don't pretend you know anything about art. You don't. You might live amongst the artists and embalmers but you know nothing about art, or embalmment for that matter either. You know about business, sometimes. I'll give you that, but only sometimes."

Ella smiled at Aulus whilst he glowered at her. She then corrected herself and turned to look at one of the paintings. She saw Claudius in the act of giving his wife a gift of jewels on the birth of their son and she thought that Swin's wife, Sophia, should have been suckling her own child right now. The night she was found a thick fog had clung to the streets of Manceastre. There weren't many people abroad that night, and no one could understand why Sophia, with her newborn, were even out in the cold. She'd been found with a bullet through her stomach and it had penetrated the baby within her also. Ella stifled a sob.

All was in order in the chapel. The painting of Claudius Ptolemaeus Tiberius appearing before Osiris in the final judgement was finished. So were all the others, including the opening of the mouth ceremony, and the weighing of the heart. The latter predicted that the Governor General answered the questions correctly in an assumption of a secure afterlife, audacious but not uncommon in the family of Ptolemy. Then there was the false door—where the gods or deceased came and went freely into the world of the living.

Ptolemy and Aulus walked before her. Ella thought she saw something move out of the corner of her eye. She made a mental note to return later to check no animal had got in.

"Get one of the workers to sweep the floor Ella, it isn't good enough." Ella had heard his sharp words countless times before and she caught a smirk from Aulus as he followed her father down into the tomb.

The tomb was arranged or rather piled high from floor to ceiling with everything Claudius would need in the afterlife. The canopic jars had been already put in place. His clothing, food, drink, household goods, furniture were all there—a bed, chair and small table. The funerary papyri had been placed on a small wooden table. All the trappings of life that a dead man would need in the underworld surrounded the sarcophagus.

When Ptolemy was satisfied that all his new instructions would be carried out by Ella they made their way back up to the chapel. There had been no praise in Ptolemy's voice when he said goodbye to Ella. He left to go for a drink with Aulus, and she hadn't been invited. She walked hopefully to the door of the chapel with them, but drew away when she saw her father put his arm round Aulus' waist and pull him closer. In the past, when she had seen that happen, they would retire to her father's bedroom. She had seen him escort boys there before, including the ones of his own family, and when she had to pass his doorway, she would cover her ears as she had done so many times before.

Ella checked for any dogs or cats that might have strayed in from the street. She had always been careful to keep the large door shut but it didn't always stop something from getting in. Ella searched the chapel diligently and assumed that whatever she had seen out of the corner of her eye had gone back out or descended the stone steps into the tomb.

As she entered the tomb Ella fell backwards and searched in vain for something to hold onto as she realised who stood before her. Ella was so shocked her body began to tremble. The dead woman fumbled with the sheet that covered a wooden chest close by. She was instantly recognisable to Ella, for she had helped Loli take the baby from this woman's womb. Ptolemy had sewn the abdomen together later. With pale hands, Sophia, the wife of the artist Swin, tried to cover herself. Ella backed away and tried to regain some control of her weakening legs. She wanted to run but became rooted to the spot. Sophia—her tangled hair, covering her once beautiful face—not dead? How was this possible? The dead woman shuffled with difficulty and turned to seek out the light from the torch. She tried to see through filmy eyes, through eyes that could make out form but could not tell the brain where she was, and what had happened to her and the child. She stumbled. As she collapsed into Ella's arms Ella struggled to stop herself from retching. The smell was revolting.

Sophia tried to speak but couldn't. Ella could see that her tongue had turned black around the edges. That sight sickened her yet she held onto the dead woman, wondering what on earth to do next. This woman needed to pass on to the underworld, and why hadn't she? And how had she found her way into the tomb of Tiberius?

Ella finally commanded her body to move and it responded. It took her some time to overcome her fear but pity became the dominant emotion.

Ella draped the material around Sophia's body and secured it in the best way she could. She led her over to the chair and sat her down. The woman grasped Ella's hand. The iciness of it made Ella shiver but she squeezed the woman's hand gently in reassurance.

"Sophia. Stay here. I don't know if you understand me but you must stay here. I'll lock the door."

Sophia didn't respond. She just put both hands on the chair arms and started rocking silently to and fro.

"I'll come back for you later…"

As she closed the large oak door behind her, Ella thought she heard Sophia moan, and Ella hurried up the stone steps, out of the tomb and made her way back to the house, just as Aulus was leaving. He smirked as he passed her on the threshold. She looked at his flushed face. She had never been bothered by the thought of two men together, but her father and Aulus? And Aulus wanted her, too? He raised the hood of his cloak up around his head and laughed out loud as he disappeared into the night.

Cleopatra Selene made a weak sound in the cradle. Loli walked over to it and rocked it gently to and fro. "I'll have to hide you and keep you just for me. Ella won't understand." Loli picked the baby up and ran down the corridor to the linen cupboard where she hid the infant in a basket of clothes. Closing the door gently she ran back to her bedroom just as Ella was leaving with a bundle of clothes from her own wardrobe.

"Ella. I need to tell you something…"

"Later, Loli. It will have to wait."

"It is important."

"What I have to do is important, too. I'll try not to be too long, Loli."

Ella brushed by her sister and made for the stairs.

"It can wait, can't it, Loli?"

Loli looked anxiously in the direction of the linen cupboard. "I suppose it could, but don't be long. Promise?"

"I promise, Loli."

As Ella stepped into the street she looked up into the tumbling snowflakes. It had been a long time since she had done that. As a child she had loved to but now there was no joy in anything for her. She hurried to the tomb. It all looked so pretty, small pyramids covered in white, but down by the oldest mausoleum she saw a dark form crawling along in the snow. She had enough horror in her life. She couldn't deal with anything else, she thought to herself, as she ran off into the night.

Ella, with great difficulty, got Sophia to the top of the stone steps, through the marbled hallway, and to the front door. Ella had overcome her fear and disgust—she had to. Ella hesitated, pulled the hood further down over Sophia's face, and opened the door. She looked up at the lamps that lit many of the windows in the skyscraper above and down into the street where she saw a group of men who looked to be colourmen.

"We shall go through the catacombs," whispered Ella to Sophia. In her fear Sophia seemed aware of the fact that some terrible pronouncement had been unleashed upon her, and she gripped Ella's arm tightly. The catacombs that led from Ptolemy's house didn't worry Ella too much. Occasionally her father had talked about criminals using them to hide in and even some plague-ridden prostitutes used the waterlogged and stinking corners to trade in the illegal practices. Down the stone steps they went and by the funerary rooms. They approached a door covered by a curtain on which was a faded symbol. She drew the curtain back and twisted the doorknob. She opened the door. Ella picked up the lamp from the side table, led Sophia through and down the corridor, and into a chamber under the house. Within this chamber were six doors, all leading to various places under the city. Her father had talked of them and had once mentioned that one door led, eventually, to the temple of Isis. Sophia moved slowly, took small steps, and Ella searched for the right door with increasing fear that someone or something would find them. She could not find the door that Ptolemy had described to her. On all doors there were hieroglyphs. She sought the hieroglyph for Isis. Isis, in hieroglyphs, she was familiar with and now sought with some urgency.

Cobwebs like white shrouds hung over some doorways but then she found the door that had the Isis hieroglyph upon it. It was free of cobwebs, as if it had been used recently. Supporting Sophia as best she could she pushed the door open and stepped into the passageway beyond. The lamp lit the way well; they only paused occasionally when a rat scampered across their pathway or they were surprised by their own shadows upon the walls. They made their way carefully down the long tunnel. No crossed passageways but it seemed to go on forever. At last, just when Ella felt she could no longer support Sophia, there came into view another door. More stone steps. Halfway up they had to sit down and Ella sought her small container of myrrh. She put some just beneath her nose and wondered if Sophia had a sense of smell, still. Just in case, she placed some on Sophia's grey skin beneath her nose. The process of rigor mortis appeared to have halted in its tracks. The scars on her stomach were covered by the sheet. There was the smell of decomposition, though.

Ella put the small case away, picked up the lantern and once more they attempted the steps. Once at the top there was another door with the same Isis hieroglyph. This door was locked. Ella hoped that she had come to the right place for help. She sat Sophia down again on a step, placed the lamp by her side, and banged on the door. Ella was exhausted. There was no response. She tried again. After a few more minutes she sat down beside Sophia. At that point the door opened.

A priest opened the door wide. He held a knife. Ella could clearly see it by the light of the lamp.

"I am Ella, daughter of Ptolemy, the embalmer. I need your help, in the name of Isis." She knew she looked nervous.

The priest stared at Sophia, looked at Ella's anxious face, and said nothing. He craned his neck to see who else was with them, saw that they were alone, and moved to one side.

"Then in the name of Isis, enter," said the priest.

In Manceastre, in the temple of Isis, they worshipped the goddess of ten thousand names. She was called Queen of Heaven; The One who is All, The Great Lady of Magic and Mistress of the House of Life and Death. The priest would look after the artist's wife, Sophia. Once they had recovered from their astonishment, two of them took her to the purgatorium in the south east corner of the courtyard, and down into an underground room for safekeeping. Representations of Isis stood at the entrance. One was the snake-headed goddess—Thermouthis to the Greeks. A clever device installed within that statue had been made by the priests. As you walked by it a sound was made by the steam machine, and to all intents and purposes it sounded like the snake goddess hissed. Another snake-headed statue was of Wadjet, protector of Lower Egypt. Along the walls were the Roman deities as well as the Egyptian, and some statues, a curious combination of the two. Also, there were other unrecognisable, older gods.

In recent years, by order of Cleopatra, the most brilliant inventors had been found from all over the empire to make the secret machines for the major temples of Isis. There was the one in Manceastre, another in Rome and one in Alexandria. Beneath some of the other statues were special chambers in which the priests could crawl and speak through pipes, which sounded as if Isis was speaking to her followers. These tricks that fooled the people had been used centuries before then fallen into disuse. Recently, since rumour had spread that Isis didn't appear to Cleopatra, these devices had been re-introduced to help restore faith in the dynasty and the religion.

In this temple the priests did their best to protect mummified corpses of the more important families from the colourmen who dealt in the pigment called Egyptian mummy. The colourmen sold it to the artists or it was used for more sinister purposes in ceremonies. The priests guarded the dead in their charge, the underground burial chambers of the rich. The poor usually suffered because they could not pay for their dead to be protected but if a family brought a mummified body to the priests for safe keeping they had occasionally looked after it. In more catacombs under the city lay the dead that had given up the fight against nature, and the damp northern climate, and had rotted away. Some families sent their dead by boat to warmer climates—to Egypt to be buried near the pyramids or even in secret locations in the dry sandy desert to preserve their ancestors. The poor had to rely on the priests or even try to do the embalming process themselves, with little success.

Once Ella was convinced that she had done all she could for Sophia she turned to go. Sophia tried to speak to Ella but couldn't.

"Shh— the priests will look after you. I'll come back. I promise."

As the priests led Sophia away Ella thought about Sophia's husband, Swin. She would have to find him. Whether she had the courage to tell him about his wife, Ella didn't know. Why Sophia? Why had she been resurrected? How could she still be moving after the first part of the embalmment process had been completed? Did she know who murdered her? Ella then remembered the baby and Loli. She had to move quickly. Ella retraced her steps through the passageways beneath the city. As she picked up her pace she fancied she heard the moans of the dead. Ella, although fearful that she would drop her lantern, then ran through the semi-darkness back to the Ptolemy house.

"Don't be angry with me, Ella. I didn't know what to do. I tried to tell you but you rushed off." Loli kept twisting the bone pin in her hair.

"Stop it, Loli. You'll break that. The baby will have to go to its mother."

"Its mother. But its mother is the artist's wife Sophia. She is dead now. How can she look after it?"

"Like the baby, Loli—like the baby. She isn't dead. I placed Sophia in safe keeping and the baby goes, too. But hear me Loli, don't tell anyone about this. Do you hear, Loli?"

Loli heard. But she didn't want to hear about the walking dead. There were more of them now and that frightened her.

"Let me come too, Ella. Father won't notice. He hasn't been near me all afternoon."

"No—you go down to dinner. Say I'm ill and need to sleep. He won't be bothered. Do that for me Loli and I'll see that the baby is looked after."

Ella couldn't face the underground catacombs for another time that afternoon. She made her way above ground through the darkening streets. A low fog hung over the Irwell. The river was polluted by waste from dozens of factories. Beneath that fog there would be a strange combination of green and an oily blue, and more than once she imagined a grey hand coming up through the water.

The priests didn't seem surprised when Ella gave the small bundle to them.

"She's Sophia's daughter. Keep her with her mother." In silence they took the baby from her and closed the temple door quietly.

Ella leant against the door and started coughing. It was the tired cough that came upon her in moments of exhaustion. She would go to the opium den. There, she would lose herself for a time. She might find Swin there too. He had made it his second home since his wife's illness and death, and it was rapidly becoming hers. His wife.... how could she begin to tell him what she knew? Undead. Sophia and the baby, too. Down towards the industrial quarter she went, avoiding the main thoroughfares. More than once she thought she caught sight of a glazed eye and a shambling gait but she hurried onwards, wondering how many families would be hiding their dead before it would become too obvious to conceal. How many more of them, and why didn't they die like they should or remain permanently dead?

Chapter 5

The Romano-Egyptian dynasty had won the Opium Wars with China. Smuggling of the drug into China from parts of the Empire had led to dispute and consequently—struggle for control. China had lost every battle and opium trade continued. Foreign trade grew and Hong Kong fell under the rule of Cleopatra's Empire. But recently there had been assaults on traders and Cleopatra was apprehensive about another war. She hoped that it would not come to that as the plague had depleted her forces.

Ella, on her way to the opium den, shivered and buttoned her long, thick, grey woollen coat high up to her chin. It was bitterly cold and the wind drove the snow against doors and walls as if deliberately locking the population in. Out of the corner of her eye more than once Ella thought she saw something reach out to her from an alley and worse. Strange misshapen things seemed to crawl about in the shadows. On one street near the better houses, she was still careful not to go too close to anyone, not just because she was afraid of the plague, but also because she now knew that at that precise moment in time, death wasn't the end of the suffering. There was more.

The opium den was in the middle of Langsoon, a not-so-poor quarter of Manceastre, and it was one of the better establishments. Open to men and women. Ella paid a monthly contribution to use it and some rooms in the interior were indeed splendid, or would be if not for the yellowing effect of the opium smoke. In summer it had been decked out in fine silks and cotton, but in winter each room was draped in velvet and red wool. The clientele was well enough off to afford it and they made the most of it as an escape from the tedium or desperation of their everyday lives. Where those already badly affected by life could descend into a new madness.

The entrance was down a dark alley. She found it easily enough, she always had. There was a lamp on a hook near the door and by its light she could see some wooden boxes at the end of the alley, piled to shoulder height. Ella thought she saw one of them move and quickly knocked on the door. No answer. She knocked again and was about to shout for entrance. She glanced nervously again at the wooden boxes. There was a small figure, perhaps a boy, standing by the crates. Still. A dog by his side. The bitter wind drove the swirling snow even further down the alley towards the boy.

"Hello," said Ella.

The boy said nothing.

"It's cold. You haven't got a coat. You shouldn't be out on a night like this."

The boy took a few steps closer, and the dog limped along beside him. He wore no hat and his long hair was wet.

He took another few steps, into the light given off by the lamp. Ella gasped and knocked harder on the door. His eyes terrified her. They were not like Sophia's at all. The rats had been at him. What Ella had done for Sophia she wouldn't do for this boy—she couldn't. The dog by his side was Loli's dead pet, Juniper. It started to snarl. The rats had been at its face too. Ella knocked harder and hammered at the door.

"Open the door. Open the door. Now!"

The door opened a little and an old Chinese woman peered into the darkness.

"Who is it?"

"Ella Child. I'm Ella Child. I've been here before. Let me in."

The Chinese woman opened the door and saw the boy in the full light of the lamp. She let out a cry and made to shut the door but not before Ella pushed by her and slammed it behind her.

"What is happening? I don't understand all this. The boy..." said the woman.

Ella didn't want to think about the boy. She knew who she wanted.

"Is Swin here? You know him...the red hair?"

The old Chinese woman pointed to the stairs and Ella rushed by her and ran up, the sound of each foot as it hit the wooden stair echoing the beating of her terrified heart. She looked up through a dingy skylight as lamplight cut through the blizzard. The snow looked like a shattering of stars, and Ella wondered how such beauty could appear alongside such horror.

The boy, Luce, turned away from the opium den and found a way into the catacombs. He found the quiet, dark place amongst bodies whose souls had passed over a long time ago. Deep in the dust and dirt he burrowed until finally he came to rest between rib bones that formed a cradle over his head. He knew that he should be there. In the absolute darkness he didn't move and simply waited. When he and the dog finally came out the colourmen were waiting for them.

Swin watched intently as a young Chinese girl placed a small pill of opium in a pipe-bowl. She guided the funnel-like chimney of the opium lamp. Swin lay on his side as a stream of heat rose from the chimney of the lamp and he inhaled the vapourised opium fumes. The young girl said it was his fourth pill. A session could consist of up to seven and the effects would get him through the night.

The air was so thick with smoke it was hard to make anything out at first. Ella remembered one of her own recent experiences in the opium den. When consumed by the drug she felt that she could unravel far deeper mysteries, but they always lay just out of reach, and her father was a part of one mystery in particular. Neither she nor Swin ever touched heroin or morphine. They were cheaper to get but they would have none of it.

Ella didn't have to look far to find Swin. He was in one of the back rooms on the top floor. A room not as generously decked out as the rest. There were about half a dozen men lying on mattresses on the floor, and there was Swin. His shock of red hair always led her to him. Swin was a small man. He had smoked more than enough. His eyes—the large black pupils. His complete immobility. He didn't even blink. Swin sat on a mattress, cross-legged, and just fixed his eyes on the wall.

Ella stood above him and placed her hand on his shoulder. He looked at her and there was a flicker of recognition.

"I see her, Ella. I see Sophia and the baby—the girl. She looks about ten now. She looks like me."

Swin looked so thin. Sophia used to keep him away from the opium den as much as possible, but since Sophia's illness and death he had practically given up on everything. Such was his despair and his addiction.

Ella was ashamed that she had not spent more time with him. She had wanted to but...

"Never. I'll never paint again. Another pipe! I don't remember killing Sophia and the baby. Did I do it Ella? Do you think I could do such a thing? He started to cry.

The small old woman appeared and began fumbling amongst pipes on a table.

Ella slightly turned her head in the direction of the sound. "No more."

The woman shrugged.

Ella looked down again at Swin. He was wearing a dark green jacket that was covered with stains all down the front and a dirty white shirt beneath that. His black trousers were covered in mud. Ella pulled the cuffs back on the jacket to see if there were any needle marks on Swin's arms, just in case. No tracks.

"Not here. Never in here," said the old woman in the corner.

"Come on, Swin. Let's get you home."

He scowled at Ella. "No. Not home. Not anymore. What if I did do it, Ella?"

"I'll take you home with me. Father will be late back tonight, but you have to be quiet."

"I will. I'll be quiet," he muttered. Then he was far away again, lost in his own nightmares.

With difficulty, she got him up from the mattress. He swayed a little at first but seemed able to walk. One of the men helped her get Swin down the stairs before he disappeared into the snowstorm. Quickly glancing to her right towards the wooden boxes, she wondered if the boy was still about. She didn't want to see him again. She had enough to contend with. Swin was heavier than his slight frame indicated.

As they left the alley Ella saw one of the colourmen. She remembered that she had seen him selling paint to the artists in Memphis Square, no doubt dealing in the revolting brown pigment that the artists valued so highly, made from Egyptian mummies. Ella wondered that if the dead were walking what about those corpses that had been dead for a very long time, would they try to walk, too. And what of the mummies bound fast in their wrappings? Did they try to speak through sealed mouths? The pigment was also used for medicine and spells and Ella knew that the colourmen would have no qualms about cutting up a reanimated mummy. If corpses rose from the mass burial chambers, nothing would keep them from overrunning the city. That hadn't happened yet. She only knew of the recently dead rising. They were easy prey for the colourmen unless concealed well.

Ella also wondered just how many more people she would be carrying about that day. First Sophia and the baby, now Swin. At least Swin's wife and child were out of the Ptolemy house and at the temple. It would be some time before Swin could be told anything, and if all returned to normality soon, she wouldn't have to. Why was all this happening? thought Ella, in desperation.

Once on the main road Ella hailed a horse-drawn cab and managed to get Swin inside of it. As they went down Swan Street Ella looked up at all the flickering lamps in the windows of the skyscrapers and the skytubes which linked them together. She was beginning to wish that she lived up there, too. Away from the cold weather, the sickness and filth, and the walking dead.

Ella put Swin to bed in the small room next to hers and Loli's, and told Loli and the servants not to say anything about him. Loli was fine with that, and the servants would rather remain silent than be beaten or sold off to lesser establishments, by Ella, if they didn't do what she said. Swin was mumbling in his sleep, and Ella wiped his face with a cool cloth to try and calm him down. Later that night, when Loli was asleep, Ella climbed into bed with Swin and held his shivering body. In the half-light he sobbed and called out for Sophia.

Loli also slept fitfully. A veiled woman came through the false door. She drifted through the snowstorm. No one saw her face. Not the colourmen, or the prostitutes in Memphis Square who cocked their heads to one side and looked at her strangely, or the lamplighter as he made his way over the cobbled stones.

The veiled woman leant over Loli. Loli whimpered and tried to open her eyes. She couldn't. Loli felt a cold hand on hers and still she could not open her eyes, try as she might. Her eyelids felt so heavy and something deep within her told her that she didn't want to see. The woman removed the veil. Her tongue flickered next to Loli's cheek. Then, with the speed of something that was used to finding its way in the dark, she turned her attention to the occupants of the room next door.

The door opened silently. Ella's arms were wrapped around Swin. Her naked stomach pressed hard into his back to keep him warm. She caressed his leg. Gently. Careful not to awaken him. Even when the veiled woman leant over her she did not open her eyes. She was exhausted. Her thoughts were of Swin, and that before he awoke she would remove herself from the bed, and he would only know her as a friend again. The veiled woman looked closely at Swin and then stepped back into the shadows.

When Ella opened her eyes there was a dim light shining behind the curtain. It was dawn and she knew that in a minute or two she would have to leave. There was the smell of jasmine in the room. From a childhood memory she tried to form the image associated with it, but failed.

After he left Licinia, Aulus thought about going home but couldn't face it. There would be people banging on the door for their money back, or worse. His Uncle Ptolemy would be good for a bed for a night or two, even if the lecherous old sod expected payment of the sort he wasn't in the mood for.

"I need a place to stay, just for tonight. I've some good reasons not to go back home just yet."

"In trouble with someone I suppose. The old Governor General's entombment is soon. There's much left to do."

"Can I stay? I'll help."

Aulus bit his lip and waited.

From looking at the thin face of Ptolemy Child you could hardly ever tell what he was thinking—anything could be going on under that veneer of self-control. Aulus never knew if what Ptolemy said matched what was in his mind.

"Well. Just for tonight. But stay out of my way. I have a lot to do. Take one of the rooms next to Ella and Loli."

Aulus half-smiled.

"Aulus."

"Yes."

"Leave Ella and Loli alone. Right?"

"Of course, Ptolemy. How can you think…?"

Ptolemy was unusually abrupt. "I don't trust you, Aulus. Never have. Now go."

Ella was surprised to bump into Aulus on the landing.

"Aulus. What are you doing here?"

Aulus wasn't about to be questioned too closely by his cousin.

"I'm not staying long Ella. Your father said I could have one of the rooms next to you. Will you show me?"

Ella looked anxious for a moment. "Er—yes. Follow me."

She led Aulus by the room she shared with Loli and the room where Swin still lay in a deep sleep, to one at the far end of the corridor.

"Is this close to your room Ella?" He touched her arm.

"Not that close, Aulus."

She turned to go and get some food and water for Swin.

"Any food going?"

Ella didn't like the thought of Aulus wandering around the upper landing. She needed to lock the door to Swin's room, but she couldn't in front of Aulus. It would look suspicious. She needed to lock Swin in and keep Aulus out.

The main door downstairs closed with a loud bang, and she knew that her father had left on business.

The door to her bedroom opened, and a sleepy-eyed Loli came out.

"Loli. Take Aulus down to the dining room. Father has just left and you can keep Aulus company. I have something I have to do."

"What? Go downstairs in my nightdress?"

"Go and get into some clothes quickly."

Ella remained rooted to the spot engaging Aulus in trivial conversation until Loli's return. When she was sure that they had both entered the dining room she checked on Swin, locked the door to his room, and joined them.

Aulus was his usual cocky self over breakfast, but it was more forced than on other days. He looked tired, but that wasn't unusual knowing what she knew about his lifestyle. She had never liked him, ever since he had stolen some of her books and sold them on Dallow Row, and he favoured blackmail.

"How long are you staying, Aulus?" Ella tried to keep the impatience out of her voice.

Aulus tore the crust off the nearest warm loaf and stuffed it in his mouth. He tried to answer but raised his hand to indicate he would speak soon.

"Not sure Ella. For as long as possible, perhaps."

If her father liked him just a little more he would, thought Ella.

Loli brought down her cup a little too hard on the table as she put it down.

"Loli!"

"I couldn't help it."

Her younger sister frustrated Ella sometimes with her clumsiness and Ella was in no mood for any backchat today.

Loli opened her mouth, looked at Ella's frown and thought again.

"When I grow up I will be an artist like Swin."

Ella shot her a glance, which Loli ignored or didn't notice.

"What makes you think you have the talent, cousin?" said Aulus.

"I know all the colours. Naples yellow, made out of lead antimoniate. Kings yellow out of arsenic trisulphide, cadmium yellow."

Aulus wiped honey from his lips with a napkin and laughed. "Is yellow your favourite colour by any chance? What a bright little mind you have, Loli"

"Stop laughing at me, Aulus. I know more colours. They were the first to come to mind. There is cobalt blue and…and Egyptian mummy."

Aulus stopped laughing. "Have you been buying that from the colourmen?"

Loli bit her lip abruptly.

"What if I have?"

Ella looked horrified. "You know that you shouldn't, Loli. You know where they get it from."

"Yes—from dead bodies. So what?"

"What if it was one of your ancestors that they ground up to make the pigment?"

Loli shrugged.

"What if it was your mother?" laughed Aulus. He spat his food out and laughed again. "That is precious."

Loli burst into tears and ran around the table to find comfort with Ella.

"Tell him to stop! I hate him. I hate Aulus!"

Ella held her close and told her that it was all right, but Loli still wasn't too happy. She hugged Loli, a little. Then, as the minutes passed, Loli cheered up and started to irritate her. Ella finally pushed her away.

"You know. You can be nasty too, Ella," said Loli. She looked at Aulus and thought of the most impolite question she could ask him. One that would really annoy Ella, too.

"Aulus—are you a hermaphrodite?" That set Aulus off laughing even more and Ella couldn't help herself laughing, too. When it went on for longer than a minute, Loli tired of the company of them both, went off to find some slaves to torment.

Aulus moved over to the chair next to Ella's and placed his hand over hers, which in turn rested on her knee. Ella stared down at the long skirt that she was wearing, thinking that she would rather be wearing boy's clothes at that moment. That would never stop Aulus' advances. He always tried for something. Moving his hand swiftly from hers he quickly pulled up her skirt and placed his hand between her thighs. Ella's tried to stop it venturing any further.

"We've been over this before. It isn't going to happen between you and me. Are you crazy? After what you do with my father?"

"Different altogether. I do that because I have to. What I would do with you is what I want to."

"Well, I don't want to do anything with you." Ella tried to move his hand away.

"Not even if it meant that I would be quiet about whom you have hidden upstairs? I'll say it was Swin who killed his own wife."

Ella looked shocked. She was taken off guard and didn't understand what Aulus knew.

"Why would you do that?"

Aulus did not answer.

She looked confused. What did Aulus know about Sophia's death?

"I'd make something up," said Aulus.

Ella was close to tears but she would not cry in front of Aulus.

"I think that it would be better for all of us if we formed an alliance. Don't you?"

She took her hand away.

"You are no virgin, Ella. We both know that. I'll be quiet about Swin and what we do."

Sex didn't mean much to Ella. When or if she married there would be none to accuse her of anything, not in Manceastre, where sex and death were tended to in equal measure. And yet, to have sex with the same person as her father? To be blackmailed into it?

Aulus locked the door. All keys were kept in the keyholes in the Ptolemy house. He gently pulled Ella by the arm over to one of the three settees that lay against the cold, blue walls. Ella didn't resist. She let him do what he wanted. When he had finished, Ella picked up her glass of wine from the table and emptied it quickly. One drop fell from her lips and onto her red skirt where it blended in with the rest of the colour.

He walked over to the door. Before he left he turned to Ella, who still lay on the couch, and looked at him through half-closed eyes.

"What could a young girl know of life?"

"I know some. I get enough freedom to find out about most things."

"Your reality is determined by your past experience."

"Yes."

"Then you do not know of something that you haven't experienced. Do you like your life, Ella?"

"I'm left alone to do what I want."

"Don't you think though, Ella, that we would all benefit from a little restraint?"

"What do you mean?"

Aulus smiled. "Mankind is the lowest of the animals, and animals shouldn't pretend to be something else." With that he left.

Ella looked at the blue-black irises in a vase on a table in the far corner of the room. She then wondered how soon the bruises would appear on her body.

Animal skins covered the floor, laid upon large intricately woven rugs. A statue of Isis stood on a table made of Thya wood. Ella looked at the tapestries that adorned the walls. Some were of hunters killing their prey and some were of men and women looking to the gods for their salvation. The gods looked down indulgently. Mankind had always aspired to be godlike. As a child, Ella had been so full of awe before these representations. Had the gods chosen to rise above what had gone before them, or had they always been divine? Humans killed, maimed and destroyed their fellow man. What could be less divine than that? People were still animals. The so-called civilised man. How much longer would it be before Aulus treated Loli in the same way? The way he had treated her? She thought of Aulus with her father. Her father. They were wealthy but what did it matter alongside poverty and disease. And now the dead could not die. There was no peace—just torment. How could they all survive?

Ella rose from the couch and went to see how Swin was. She hoped that she didn't bump into Aulus again, for if she did she would swear to him that she might kill him one day. She quietly climbed the stairs and went into Swin's room.

"How long have I been asleep? Have you got any wine, Ella?" Swin half-sat up wearily.

"Shh. Rest a little, Swin."

Ella sat on the bed beside him.

"Rest? I can't rest...haven't been able to since Sophia..."

Ella placed her hand on his arm. "I know."

She tried to think of something, anything to take his mind off Sophia. "Tomorrow is the Governor General's entombment."

Swin looked confused for a moment. "What? I've finished the work and I don't want to go anyway."

"It is the custom for you to attend."

"I don't care about custom, Ella. Have you got any opium pills?"

Ella lied. "No."

"Am I in your room?"

"One of the rooms in our house."

"Your father."

"Out."

"I'd better go before your father gets back."

"You are going back home?"

"No, I'll go see Calvi. I'm not going home yet."

"I understand." Ella put her hand up to Swin's cheek.

Swin abruptly pushed it away. "I can't bear to be touched."

"I'm sorry, Swin."

"So am I. I'm thirsty, Ella."

"You get dressed. I'll get you something to eat and drink before you go."

As Ella locked the door behind her she heard the door at the end of the corridor close. She had to get Swin out before her father came back. Aulus wouldn't keep his mouth shut for long. As a child he could never keep a secret. When Swin was strong enough to leave she would have a long, hot bath, and forget Aulus for a while. She would think of Swin, of Sophia and the child, and what could be done. Then she would go to the temple of Isis and pray to her for understanding and guidance.

She wasn't long in the bath before she descended into an opium dream, a false happiness that would take her away from her troubles; and for a little while time seemed to stand still. The effect of the drug was different, occasionally, and instead of inactivity it drove her to the streets, where she found even small groups of people intimidating and too loud. When she took just the right amount of opium, she could study something for hours and wonder at its very essence. When she felt like that, she made sure she bought some flowers from the hothouse market—they were expensive, and of course heated by steam, too. Orchids were her favourites, but lately she had become attached to the flower, nymphaea lotus, the Egyptian water lily. Believed to give strength and power—she needed that now. White petals tinged with pink. She had placed three in the bath and watched them float around each other, exquisite little white ships that beached on her stomach, and then floated away under the bridge, the tilted arc of her leg.

Her reverie was interrupted when one of the female servants knocked on the locked door and asked to speak with her. She got out of the bath, wrapped herself in a large white towel, and opened the door.

The slave looked worried. "I know not to go there mistress, but the steps were dirty and needed to be cleaned. And..." here she hesitated.

"Yes?"

"The refrigeration system for the embalmment chambers. The valve has been turned off."

"Not more trouble." Ella tried to remember how many bodies were in storage and wondered if they would still be there. She got dressed quickly, put some myrrh under her nose and went down to the embalmment rooms. She checked the drawers. Two had cards on the front. They said the date and name of the occupants. She knew the drawer that had held the body of Sophia was now empty. When she opened the second drawer she found that empty too.

Ella went to the central system and turned the valve on. It didn't seem sensible without any bodies in the cabinets but she wasn't feeling sensible. The old machine stirred itself, and the pump finally got under way. She knew better than to disturb her father at any time, but she would have to tell him about the missing bodies. She would tell him that they were gone, but she wouldn't tell him she had taken Sophia to the temple. She had no idea where the male corpse was.

Reluctantly she knocked on the library door.

"Gone? What do you mean gone?" Her father was furious.

"What do you mean gone? Doesn't anyone see anything happening in this house?"

The answer to that was always no.

"No one saw anything, Father."

"The colourmen. It must have been the colourmen."

"Could be."

The colourmen, even though they dealt with the ancient dead for the pigment, also doubled as body snatchers and had been known to steal the recently deceased for Manceastre University, or more recently, Clovis. They always managed to produce documentation saying that a family or individual had given permission, which was unlikely in most cases, as some still held on to a belief in the afterlife. The staff at the university kept quiet about it. Fresh bodies were a rarity.

Ella wasn't about to tell her father where Sophia and the baby were.

"The entombment of the old Governor General will be a big day for us, Ella, and now we have this distraction. The artist's wife and the baby disappeared. What was the wife called again?"

"Sophia."

"There's nothing that can be done at the moment. I've got too much to do, anyway. If we can't get Sophia back we'll find another body when her time comes to be interred."

Ella had known her father to go to such extreme measures before, and no one ever named or openly accused the colourmen.

Chapter 6

The next night, Ella decided that she'd escape the heavy atmosphere of the Child house and go to the theatre with Loli. It had been suspected that as the latest epidemic spread, the theatres would be shut down. And some had, but not the Theatre Macabre. The fog weaved its way through the street, searching out the lost corners of Kares-Bu. Much like the colourmen, who crept through it on the business of the Governor General. Most of the people in the skyscrapers looked down upon the foggy streets and stayed put, with their lamps and their heavy locks on their doors. Safely away from the plague.

Ella made sure that Loli was wrapped up warmly against the cold, put on her own cloak, and took one of the lamps from the shelf near the door.

Loli looked nervous, "Are you sure we should go to the theatre tonight, Ella?"

"I'm certain of it, Loli. I need to be amongst people again, and you know that Licinia is in this play…you do want to see her perform—don't you?"

"Well, yes but…"

"Tell you what Loli, you stay here and I'll go. I need to go. I can't stay in tonight."

Loli grabbed hold of Ella's hand, "No, I'll come, but will you hold my hand all the way? I'm afraid of getting lost in the fog, and I'm afraid of what I cannot see."

"Most things that you should be afraid of, Loli, can be seen in broad daylight. Think of the fog as a shield, a safe place to hide where people cannot see you."

Loli thought about that for a minute and nodded. As they left the house, it was Ella who saw the colourmen skulking in the fog. Recently, besides the dead disappearing, she thought that perhaps the living had been taken, too. She held on to Loli's hand tightly.

The theatre was in the nearest piazza, they could see the torches that surrounded it dimmed by the fog, but they were still lit, so the play would be performed. The billboard announced it in the usual perfunctory way;

blunt and to the point, not how Ella would describe each play at all. True, they were always bawdy, but there had to be leeway for a little decorum, thought Ella.

Loli peered at the billboard. There were two posters above them. They both said for one night only. Then, with the usual notice pasted over, saying 'and for another night,' which covered whenever they wanted, really. The season's favourite was called *Pantalone's Lament* and Loli couldn't help but smile, because she knew it well, and some of the responses in the comedic parts. The poster showed Pantalone's costume, a red vest, with baggy breeches, black cassock and a large mask with prominent nose. He wore an enormous codpiece. Loli giggled, and for one moment Ella felt the strain of the last few days leave her, too, and she laughed out loud. Loli then pointed at the figure next to Pantalone. The clown wore loose fitting trousers, and the jacket was covered with alternating blue, green, and red diamonds. This was Arlecchino. He held a wooden slapstick in one hand and a glass of wine in the other. Loli had last seen that stick slapped across the face of a butcher, who had apparently sold the clown bad meat the last time he was in lodgings in Kares-Bu. All stared up at a monkey on top of a ladder, which seemed to teeter a little. A character Loli couldn't remember the name of held out her hands to catch the monkey, who stared wide-eyed at what the clown held in his hand.

He had felt that slapstick before, thought Loli.

"Come on, Loli,' said Ella. 'You can see them for real inside."

People, their collars turned up against the cold, appeared out of the fog, like ghosts from half-remembered dreams. Some silent, some exchanging comments about the plays that they had seen before at the theatre. Most of them braved the plague to show the world, or rather themselves, that they were not afraid of anything.

Traditionally, there would be the play within the play. And it amused the director-manager to change this around night after night—so you might have the serious play within the farce one night and the farce within the serious, another, and any amount of switching between the two for effect and comedy.

The second poster proclaimed a play called *The Judgement*, set to anger the gods themselves. A Greek play about the gods before the deity of Isis, and therefore just for entertainment, although some thought performing on the subject of the gods strayed into dangerous territory. Not many stayed away because of that though.

As they entered the theatre, Loli marveled at the statues around her. If the Egyptian influence in the empire rules religion, Rome has the theatre for itself. No mixing of culture here; it is Roman, taken from the Greek, or a later interpretation of it.

Ella likes the theatre with the plush red velvet seats and the smell of the oil lamps along the front of the stage. The actors know to keep well away from them. Rushes cover the stage floor, well away from the lamps. The prologue for the first play, as tradition dictates, is performed by the slave, Arlecchino. Ella recognises it, although it sometimes changes, much to the amusement of the audience. He says that his rich master has a secret that only he knows, and under no circumstances could he be persuaded by the audience to reveal it. Except…if perhaps the stunner in the fourth row would step up and help him roast his onions. That sets the mood for the comedy. The woman, as usual, goes up the steps, and he gives her his onions…he whispers into her ear, and she takes the secret back to the audience swearing she will not tell. No sooner does the woman get back to her seat than…

"Dear lady please help me tend to my apples, too."

There is laughter from the audience, as he asks her to polish them with a cloth he hands her. She blushes and he places his apple next to her cheek as if comparing them. Each time she sits down he calls her back, racking up the laughter with some other extended metaphor. When he picks up the large root vegetable, the woman puts her face in her hands and refuses to come on up to the stage. He begins to descend the side steps to get to her and sits on her knee with the vegetable peeping out from his waistband. The audience becomes hysterical at this point, as Arlecchino clutches the woman to him. The actor who plays his rich master shouts at him from the stage, and Arlecchino, clutching his root vegetable, regretfully leaves his newfound love.

"Go to the market and buy five slave girls."

So off goes Arlecchino. He buys the girls and brings them back, telling the audience that he's been very quick. But…he has had to leave them off stage, much to the amusement of the audience. He says it is his choice and he doesn't have to obey any rules, especially if it halts the pace of the story. Ella remembers how the plot would play out: Arlecchino falls in love with one of the girls, and the audience eventually realises that they are sister and brother. They both wear identical lockets given to them by their mother, and they were separated at birth. And, of course, that throws up a new dilemma for the young couple. To make matters even worse, it turns out that the rich master has lost two children when *they* were just babes in arms.

The rich master looks at the slave girls. "You have the five slave girls bought from the market."

"Five, master? You asked me to get four."

"No Arlecchino. I have plans for five."

"Dear master, when you asked me, you clearly, well not so clearly, asked for four; so here are the four, and a monkey."

"Are you sure? And a monkey?" Pantalone opens his mouth as if to ask further about the monkey but decides against it.

At that moment a pretty young girl pops her head out from the theatre wings and steps forward.

Pantalone tries to see who it is, over Arlecchino's shoulder. "My, you've done well with one of the four, though. She looks familiar. Do I know her?"

Arlecchino gestures behind his back to Arlecchina that she should leave the stage. She moves quickly, backing away from the monkey who makes a grab at her. The audience bursts into laughter as the monkey tries to look under the girl's skirt. She runs off with the monkey in pursuit.

"Where has she gone?"

"Who?"

"The girl the monkey tried to grab."

"The monkey?"

"The monkey…never mind the monkey. Where's the girl?"

Arlecchino turns around to look for the girl and the monkey. When Pantalone's back is turned he makes a gesture to his own head, whirling his finger around. The audience laughs once more.

"Never mind, bring the four girls in."

It isn't the girls that make an appearance next, but Arlecchina, Arlecchino's mistress. Both Ella and Loli had known that Licinia would be on stage that night. Ella always liked this part the most—she had seen it many times before, but the actors changed the routine many times depending on the monkey's mood.

Arlecchina pretends to be indignant, as she knows that Pantalone, who usually pursues her with little success, now has turned his attentions elsewhere. However, Pantalone then decides to pursue Arlecchina instead, and chases her around the stage. The audience is reduced to hysterics when she runs down the steps and up the aisles amongst them with her diamond pattern skirt over her head, and displays a codpiece covering her most manly parts. Loli taps Ella's shoulder and points. Ella hasn't forgotten

Loli's all-consuming interest in the hermaphrodite. Loli wonders if her friend, Licinia, is indeed one. Ella nods, and Loli laughs even louder, not because of what Licinia is, but because Licinia plays the part of the pursued virgin very well.

Pantalone runs excitedly around the stage and nearly knocks the monkey off the ladder, which has been expertly placed while all the commotion is going on. And the monkey keeps on clambering up and down it, banging it against the scenery until even the cast thinks that the monkey is going too far. They try to calm him down a little, but to no avail. The monkey becomes hysterical, and starts chattering over the dialogue, causing Arlecchino to forget his lines. Then the monkey starts to throw apples at the audience, which is amusing for the first minute. But a couple of boys start to throw them back, and that way lies madness, as the monkey then picks up a melon. And yes, the monkey chucks the melon. It soars high in the air and comes down on the head of the butcher from two streets away, covering the women on either side of him with melon seeds. The butcher takes it well enough. The manager calms him down and offers to give him a free ticket to the next play. Loli thinks that the butcher must have a hard head to split a melon.

"A free ticket for the next performance, Sir?"

"Not if that bloody monkey is in it you don't."

There isn't a person who has any sympathy for the butcher—no one likes him. His contempt for all mankind, when he serves them at his stall, has always been barely concealed.

The play recommences, and the monkey seems calm for a few moments on his ladder; but then he gets excited all over again. The manager moans, and then sighs, as the monkey starts mucking about again. It seems in control of the ladder. But then the monkey moves the top half of his body to try and get the ladder to sway a little: slightly to the left one minute, to the right the next, and then the ladder faces the audience, tips, and hovers above the first three rows. Slowly the inevitable happens, and the ladder lands with a thump…on the head of the butcher. The monkey screams and the audience howls; until one woman, who clearly should not have been out on such a damp night, starts coughing—either because she is chilled to the bone, or because she's laughing too much. The butcher looks stunned and remains silent. Leaving him, thankful that he is quiet for a moment, the manager brings her a glass of wine. This she drinks with relish, and assures the audience that she hasn't got plague symptoms. Ella sees a few hands go into pockets, and she wonders how many carry guns.

She hasn't hers with her. Ella looks down at Loli, who holds a handkerchief to her face as she has cried so much with laughing. The crowd breaks out into cheers as the monkey tries to rub the poor butcher's head, and the manager offers him a glass of wine, too.

Soon the audience settles, and on the play goes, Pantalone dismisses the girls and he summons Arlecchina to him and sits her on his knee. He kisses her passionately. It soon becomes clear that Pantalone is getting very excited, as Arlecchina keeps rising and sitting repeatedly, and giggling. They kiss again and Pantalone begins fumbling under her skirt, just as the monkey appears again, runs across the stage, puts his head under her skirt, and screams. The audience explodes into laughter once more.

Arlecchino appears and sees Pantalone chasing the monkey around the stage. "Don't slap the monkey," says Arlecchino.

"Don't what?" Pantalone peers into the crowd looking for the monkey.

"Don't slap the monkey. He *will* bite!"

Meanwhile the monkey snuggles up to the bosom of a lady in the sixth row and attempts to put his hand down the cleavage of her dress.

There comes a resounding slap and a scream, and the woman flees her seat followed by the monkey. The manager judges the mood of the crowd to be still with them, but thinks it prudent to call a halt to that part of the proceedings as soon as he can.

The audience is still in an uproar. The monkey speeds down the aisle after the woman, and he has somehow managed to acquire the slap stick. As he passes the butcher, he belts him across the face. The manager swears and takes after the monkey, pursued by the butcher. The monkey leaps onto one of the hot oil lamps on the wall, screeches, leaps to another, and screeches again. This monkey doesn't learn very fast, thought Loli, stifling a giggle as the troupe leaves the stage.

The next act comes on quickly and stands in front of the curtain. It is the reconciliation scene between Arlecchino and Arlecchina. To the audience's amusement, Arlecchino has to do all the hard work of making up and coming up with excuses, one after the other, while Arlecchina scolds and reprimands. Then the dialogue moves on to each trying to get the advantage over the other with puns. Neither actor can completely annihilate each other with their rhetoric. The audience is most satisfied that the performance that night is even better contrived than usual. Just as the crowd is becoming complacent, the two in front of the curtain leave abruptly, and an actor wearing the royal vestments of the Governor

General appears. He wears a full-length purple tunic with trousers of the same colour underneath, for warmth. His short black hair is meticulously combed, and on his chest, on top of the tunic, he wears a large gold disc studded with precious stones. It is obviously meant to be Clovis. The audience mutters and someone shouts a rude comment. The actor puts a hand up to quieten them.

"I will tend to this world and not leave it to a female to rule my life or religion."

The actor pauses to let the words sink in. He knows that the people of Manceastre are rapidly going off Clovis as well as Cleopatra because of plague, and that they have not seen her for years, until now. It is a common thing to blame whoever is in power for some calamity beyond their control.

"You surely question the divinity of the gods and their absolute power, but to what end? What could possibly happen to any who challenged them? I will show you what could happen—what happened. Is there anyone here brave enough to challenge the gods? I thought not. Look on, fellow people of Manceastre, look on…"

And then the curtain rises as the actor backs away to the side of the stage and disappears into the wings.

As the curtain goes up there is a swift intake of breath from most. Prometheus stands defiant, bound to a rock face. The scene is almost a tableaux vivant. The nymphs, Panthea and Ione, silent, close by. There are no screams from the girls as a gigantic falcon swoops down and attacks Prometheus. He does not scream. He just turns his face away slightly and raises his eyes to the heavens. Only the audience cries out. The falcon seems so real, but no blood falls from the wounds on Prometheus as the falcon repeatedly swoops. It can't be a real falcon then, thinks Ella. The falcon flies a few times around the theatre. The people cover their heads and hide their faces with their hands, but they do not leave. They are used to the theatrics in this particular theatre. There is the usual shock and then the disclosure that nothing is as it seems. The falcon attacks Prometheus once more, and seems to penetrate the abdomen properly this time, flying away with something in its beak. But still there is no blood. A screech and the final flap of its wings, and it is gone.

Prometheus screams out in anguish. "Is there no curse that can be shouted to the heavens?"

A woman appears on the stage dressed in a long blue dress and a green cloak. She stands before Prometheus. "I will not speak the curse, but you can call upon the Demogorgon. Ask the shadows of the ghosts themselves to help."

The orchestra plays the strangest of music, high pitched and elongated notes from violins, accompanied by the percussion section. The music stops as Prometheus calls upon the ghost of Jupiter to help him. The latter appears—a giant of man, his namesake to be cursed. He utters the words.

> Fiend, I defy thee! with a calm, fixed mind,
> All that thou canst inflict I bid thee do;
> Foul Tyrant both of Gods and Human-kind,
> One only being shalt thou not subdue....
> Thou art omnipotent.
> O'er all things but thyself I gave thee power,
> And my own will....
> I curse thee! let a sufferer's curse
> Clasp thee, his torturer, like remorse;
> 'Till thine Infinity shall be
> A robe of envenomed agony;
> And thine Omnipotence a crown of pain,
> To cling like burning gold round thy dissolving brain.

Prometheus hangs his head. "I wish no living thing to suffer pain."

Ella and the audience can read between the lines. They know that the play is about tyranny. And a warning, or rather a statement to all, that Clovis is the tyrant. Ella looks over her shoulder. The audience shifts restlessly in their seats and Ella half expects Clovis' guards to enter the theatre and arrest the director and actors. But she also knows that tomorrow night the play will be changed, again. However, a colourman could be in the audience and report back...

Panthia and Asia, now on stage, call upon the Demogorgon for help, and eventually Prometheus is freed by Hercules. Jupiter tries to take on the Demogorgon but fails, as the elements refuse to help him.

> Gentleness, Virtue, Wisdom, and Endurance,
> These are the seals of that most firm assurance
> Which bars the pit over Destruction's strength;
> And if, with infirm hand, Eternity,
> Mother of many acts and hours, should free
> The serpent that would clasp her with his length;

These are the spells by which to re-assume
An empire o'er the disentangled doom.

To suffer woes which Hope thinks infinite;
To forgive wrongs darker than death or night;
To defy Power, which seems omnipotent;
To love, and bear; to hope till Hope creates
From its own wreck the thing it contemplates;
Neither to change, nor falter, nor repent;
This, like thy glory, Titan, is to be
Good, great and joyous, beautiful and free;
This is alone Life, Joy, Empire, and Victory.

The curtain comes down and the audience seems not to understand what they have seen, but they clap all the same; hesitant, at first, then it builds up. Loli looks at Ella. Ella shrugs and claps, too.

There is a short pause and the curtain rises again. A woman lies on a bed—a royal bed it seems, with all the regalia one would expect for that, and the crown of the Empress Cleopatra emblazed on the wall hanging at the head. There can be no doubt that the woman lying on the bed is supposed to be Cleopatra herself—a knife through her heart. A man stands above her, the Clovis character, and another woman joins them on the stage. She is dressed as the goddess Isis herself, wearing the white and red combined crown of Upper and Lower Egypt. She moves around the side of the bed, takes the knife from the heart of the body, and plunges it into the lower abdomen of the dead Empress. She rips through the skin and plunges her hand inside to draw out something small—something so small that it cannot be easily recognised and then she puts it to her lips. Blood drips down from the tiny form and onto Isis' dress. The symbolism of the scene isn't lost on Ella, although Loli has no idea what is going on. It is clear now to Ella, that it means that Isis has abandoned the line of Cleopatra, and that no child of that lineage will have the blessing of Isis.

How did they do this? It looks so real, thought Ella.

Then Ella lets out a small cry, and Loli reaches for her hand. Loli knows she is thinking about Sophia and the baby.

Loli leans across to her. "Shall we leave now?"

Ella doesn't answer.

The audience stay silent as the curtain comes down. As the lamps are turned up the audience remain silent. They are a hardy lot—used to the scenes in the Theatre Macabre's repertoire. Ella and Loli rise from their seats. Ella thinks about what she has just seen—Prometheus and the falcon—it all looked so real. It then strikes Ella. She—she has just watched a real performance. Some of the actors are, in fact, the undead, and the very recently deceased, perhaps, which accounts for blood from the person who portrayed Cleopatra. And Prometheus has been undead for quite a while. Only, these undead aren't like Sophia. The make-up and masks are used to hide any corruption of the skin, and they are much more aware and responsive than Sophia.

When all the audience has left the theatre, the cast and the theatre manager stand over the actress who plays Cleopatra and wait for her to rise again.

And what the audience didn't see, either, was that the falcon turns into a young boy of about fourteen years of age, and that boy smiles at the theatre manager about their little secret, before he goes off to find his mother—the real Isis.

In her opium dreams that night Ella cried out for Swin, and for her dead friend, Sophia. Then the ghost of Sophia seemed to hover above her, and a knife came down upon Ella. She woke suddenly and looked at Loli to see if she had been disturbed. Loli slept on. Ella turned her face to the pillow and cried.

Chapter 7

It took well over an hour to finish the last part of the journey through the ship canal. Cleopatra saw the great temple of Isis, in the distance, on the embankment. Six golden sphinxes, three on each side of the canal, stood sentinel over it. Sphinxes dusted with a sprinkling of snow. Steam poured from the funnel as the steamship, *The Alexander*, chugged slowly along the grey water like an iceberg searching for open sea. The sky darkened and the snow fell heavily. Cleopatra had never seen snowflakes so large before.

The Alexander prepared to dock. Two grey gun towers were manned by her guards, each gun trained on the crowd, in case of trouble. It wasn't expected but it was better to be cautious, her advisors had said. Britanniae was small, but important, nonetheless. Cleopatra was usually far more preoccupied with the lands to the east, which prospered and were rather warmer to visit. Still, she was here now and would try to make the best of it. The steamship was decked out in the finest gold and red flags that ruffled in the cold wind. A sailor fixed the eagle and insignia to the prow that proclaimed *The Alexander's* status as an important vessel.

Cleopatra, cloaked in ermine, raised her hand and waved with little enthusiasm at the crowds who craned to see the black haired diminutive Empress who rarely left Rome. Cleopatra smiled, but she was in a bad temper, and could hardly be bothered to hide it. Her cousin Flavius, the one person whom she had wanted as emperor by her side, had died, suddenly. All her close cousins were dead. She didn't care for the rest of the relatives. Who would she marry? Cleopatra shivered. She had and would have many lovers. If she wasn't so particular, she would rather use a slave to get pregnant by.

She decided that she would only leave the ship for the internment and the subsequent swearing in of the new Governor General, Clovis, and always sleep on board *The Alexander*. She would return to Rome as soon as possible. Overnight, the ship would take on fresh supplies, and fuel.

Cleopatra still felt the cold even though she wore the ermine over the thick golden gown. She wasn't in the mood for celebration. Besides, the biting wind stung her face. She went below. It was too cold to stand about the deck. Although she hadn't been back to Britanniae since her childhood, when she had visited with her father Septimus, she doubted much had changed. A few new buildings, perhaps. One or two more dissenters. Nothing much that was new.

Once below deck, Cleopatra removed her coat and drank some mulled wine. It fortified her a little. How she wanted to be back in a warmer climate. It was winter in Italy too, but nothing ever seemed as bad as the bitter climate of the more northerly cities. Gaius Anthony Sosius was waiting for her in her room.

The wood panelled cabin was quite a reasonable size. In one room that led from it there was a large brass bed in one corner, and a small room off that contained a bathtub and luxuriant oils from all over the world. It was a bathroom fit for an empress. The fine clear glass bottles contained a myriad of coloured liquids, from the deepest shade of red to a pale azzurro blue, all on shelves and held fast by metal grips, so that they could survive intact in the roughest sea. Rugs made from various animal skins adorned the floor throughout. The soft glow from red wall lamps comforted Cleopatra on such a dismal day, and she was always pleased to be in the company of her general, Gaius Anthony Sosius. Gaius was a big man, his light brown hair was kept short, and his dark brown eyes studied everything in minute detail.

Gaius always got straight to the point. "I don't think you should have the open carriage in the procession. There have been a few rumours that the population is less happy to see you than when your father visited ten years ago."

"Why should that be?" said Cleopatra.

"Under Septimus, there was a period of stability. In the last few years there has been less wealth, less food, the great plague…"

"Less food you say." Cleopatra was thoughtful for a moment.

"There will be many people watching the procession?"

"Yes."

"Then get the new Governor General to buy food for the people, say it is from me, but not just bread. Give it out the night before and on the day."

"But, that will hardly sort out the long-term problems."

"No, but it will make me look good, generous, just for now."

"And after that?"

"I'll speak with Clovis. Perhaps the taxes of the more wealthy will have to be increased and decreased for the poorer."

"Not a popular move. You would want to keep the rich on your side."

"Gaius, we have had the rich on our side for almost two thousand years. Nothing is going to change now."

"But ..."

"But nothing. I am far more concerned with what the ordinary people could or would do without food. See to it."

Cleopatra paced the floor. She was worried about some other information she had received. For the first time, in a very long time, someone had tried to remove the hieroglyphs of Isis, which had been placed in prominent places. It had happened first in Gaul, now in Britanniae. Cleopatra was beginning to worry.

She would never form a union with Clovis. He was too old, too repulsive. She thought about her relatives, who ruled parts of the empire in her name, and decided that she'd think about marriage when she returned to Rome. She'd choose someone who could command respect, but not be more popular than herself.

After the boat had been moored safely, Cleopatra retired. Although the furnace of the great steamship blew the heated air into the cabin, Cleopatra began to shiver. Once warm again she slept well enough, at first.

The veiled woman stooped and looked at Cleopatra. In her dream she saw the woman lift up her veil to show her face. Cleopatra screamed. The woman, from the waist up, had the upper body and head of a large cobra. Following her cry the guards ran into the cabin and Cleopatra, kneeling and trembling on the bed, bade them search the cabin. Gaius was awakened immediately. He searched with the guards, but they found nothing; no one was in her cabin.

"There is nothing here and we have searched everywhere. And as for snakes—if that triggered it, there are none worth mentioning in Britanniae. Never have been—well not unless someone imported them in illegally. Only a few of the temples are allowed them, you know that."

"It wasn't a snake as such," said Cleopatra.

Still shaking from the nightmare, Cleopatra dismissed the guards and wrapped herself in the fur rugs on her bed. She had always been afraid of snakes. What had terrified her most was that in the nightmare the cobra-woman had opened her enormous jaws and bit deeply into her stomach. She could almost still feel the pain as she pumped her venom into her. Had she offended the goddess? Was Isis about to turn on her? Before Cleopatra went back to sleep she prayed to Isis. Cleopatra asked for forgiveness for whatever she had done wrong, and also prayed to her for strength to rule the empire well. Most of all, she begged for Isis to appear before her and support the dynasty once more, perhaps for the next two thousand years. A dynasty without the support of Isis was unthinkable. It had already been three generations since Isis had appeared before Cleopatra's forebears, and the people had begun to question her power and authority. There had been no magic in the world for far too long, but then something happened which couldn't be explained away very easily.

It had been hailed as a supernatural event. The ship canal had frozen to a depth of a few metres so very quickly. It would have been impossible to take the royal ship out. Just before it happened, one captain told of how the day before he had seen the sea freeze and thaw in quick succession. He reported terrible snowstorms and rogue waves that had sunk fishing vessels. Cleopatra's soldiers worked all round the clock chipping away the ice from the hull of the great steamship, so that the pressure of the ice didn't damage the vessel.

Cleopatra didn't want to stay around too long after the ceremonies, but it looked like the weather, and it seemed, the gods, would dictate the departure date. Whilst in Manceastre she declined Clovis' offer of staying in the palace and decided to stay on board *The Alexander*. Although she had sanctioned his appointment as Governor General, she had no intention of getting too close to the man. When the celebrations were over she would have to wait for the ship canal to thaw. She prayed to Isis that it wouldn't be too long.

From the deck of *The Alexander*, Cleopatra looked down at the canal. The local people were excited by the snowfall, and as the ice thickened, the beginnings of an ice fair could be seen. It usually took weeks for the ship canal to freeze and support so many activities but miraculously it had only taken a short while. People needed to do something in times of crisis, anything that would take their minds off plague, and poverty. Within a few days, people were travelling on foot and by sleigh from all parts of the city to the various stalls and attractions that had been set up around the royal ship. On the banks, braziers were lit and a whole ox was roasted to the delight of all. There were puppet shows and actors put on performances beneath the great hull of the vessel. The banks of the ship canal were slightly inclined, and children slid down on anything they could find, and right out onto the ice. They used boards, wooden crates, sleds, doors, babies' prams with the wheels off, anything that they could get their hands on. Cleopatra smiled. The children came up with increasingly unusual ideas to have fun with. One group of children used shovels as toboggans, and another took the metal sign from the man who sold chestnuts before he caught up with the lad, and sent him off with a flea in his ear.

The heavy smell of roasted meats hung in the freezing, foggy air. Fruit pie and cake sellers, whose biggest crowd were the children, competed for business. People could also buy spiced apples, hot pudding, cream buns, gingerbread, and nuts. Mulled wine and ale were on sale, and all seemed happy enough, even though many of the delights on offer could only be purchased by the wealthy and their children. All thought of plague had been set aside.

On the far side of the ship canal the tower blocks stood like silent grey guards against an iron sky.

One enterprising businessman brought glassware to the ice fair. He dealt in the rare obsidian glass of green, black and orange, the earliest of the glasses that people still valued. Not to be outdone, a rival glassmaker had brought his more modern glassware too, of the thinnest finest glass. These two vendors always had one eye open for the children who bumped and jostled between the stalls with their homemade sleds. Some children tied animal leg bones to their feet and picked up planks of wood and tried to propel themselves along. Others used metal skates and circled the stalls, with more children running after them, trying to catch their coat-tails, laughing and joking, red-cheeked and freezing cold. But they would not go home.

Of course the artists came out and with cold hands did quick sketches for the people who gathered around them. Between each sitting they'd amble over to a brazier and warm their hands. They wore the thinnest of gloves so that they could handle a pencil and suffered because of it. Still, they made some money to spend on food and wine and even took home a little to pay the rent. Printers set up, too, selling commemorational scrolls, with the name of the purchaser and the date, so they could have a personal record of the event. One woman did a roaring trade knitting scarves, putting in names and love messages as she finished, before delighted onlookers. Another entrepreneur built a row of three swings on the ice, which delighted many of the women and children in the ever increasing crowds that chose this part of the ship canal to play on. There was a little controversy about what would happen if the ice couldn't take the weight of all the activity and all fears were allayed when some bright spark brought an elephant from a local menagerie to test the weight. The grey ship canal ice remained intact, no cracks, and even more stallholders set up, saying a little of the old magic had returned. It had all frozen over too quickly.

People came down from Temple Bridge in horse drawn sleighs to catch sight of Cleopatra and have fun at the ice fair.

Cleopatra loved every moment of it. She either looked out of her window or climbed to the higher deck wrapped in furs to see what each new day brought to the frozen canal. She would not leave her ship even though Clovis had asked for the pleasure of her company, twice. When Julia, her companion, had helped dress her for bed the night before they both laughed about the boy who had asked the captain if he could use one of the lifeboats as a sledge. Children clamoured around the ship all the time and it was a constant distraction for the crew, who after the first day no longer found their attempts at getting on board amusing.

Cleopatra watched her general, Gaius, as he wandered the deck issuing orders and making sure they had and were being carried out. He had served her well over the years. The legions had been badly affected by plague, and the last campaign had been halted by severe weather. In the spring, new soldiers who had been recruited recently, would be ready to strengthen the depleted ranks. The immune class, the elite ranks of specialists in engineering, architecture, surgery, and other fields of expertise, had recently been bolstered by the arrival of some Chinese mercenaries. They had been generously paid because of their skill and knowledge of explosives, but Cleopatra was eager to learn if they knew of new weapons, perhaps more efficient than dynamite, and use of the cannon. The army had their own experts but joint efforts could produce a radical innovation. The Chinese were being integrated into the army as quickly as possible, and Cleopatra had no doubts that they would learn much from them about the people, and leader of China. She was always eager to listen to her interpreters for anything to do with the country whose population had grown to such a large extent, even though they were affected by the new super plagues, too. Cleopatra wanted to keep one step ahead in the race to find even more efficient ways to kill any enemy.

In her empire, Cleopatra had retained power by sheer force, but subterfuge had played a part too. Her spies kept her well informed, and her generals were more than capable of putting down any rebellion in most countries. She'd have to keep her eye on Clovis. She didn't entirely trust him, but he did keep the people under control. The man she trusted above all others was Gaius Anthony Sosius.

Cleopatra looked at the lights of the city. Gaius stood behind her nervously looking up at the many skyscrapers. It would only take one shot, only one.

"I was wary of coming here anyway, but now we could be stranded for weeks and not be able to get back to Rome. There's too much to do for the spring campaign. We shouldn't have come. "

"I wasn't going to come here without you, Gaius."

"You chose that backwoods cousin of yours to be Governor General. Why Clovis?" He was annoyed with her again, but she didn't mind. She never did.

"There aren't a great many candidates of the European noble families left, Gaius. I think he will be able to keep the population in order."

"You've heard of his reputation. You should have got someone from the east."

"The plagues haven't spared the east, Gaius, you know that. There isn't anyone."

"No, but Clovis? That man is a cunt-eyed bastard. He's never fought anything except ill health all his life."

"For now he'll be fine."

"For now? He'll eventually marry and you'll have more of the same. Is that what you want?"

"For now he'll be fine, Gaius!" The tone of her voice was dismissive. Cleopatra knew about the rumours concerning Clovis.

Gaius winced. He was troubled by an old back injury inflicted when he was thrown from his horse during battle. For his thirty-five years, he was in good condition, except for the back trouble. He looked at Cleopatra. A tiny woman ruling a massive empire. He admired her for her tenacity and single-mindedness, but he thought that she could be rather foolish, too. It was a shame it was against the law for him to marry her. Her line was pure enough. If he were emperor he would never allow Clovis to come to power—he didn't like or trust him at all. In fact, the more he thought about Clovis, the more he wished that the plague had taken him and not the other, more stable members of the nobility. Stability was what the empire needed now or it would fall apart in the aftermath of disease and famine.

Cleopatra was tired. Gaius left her and went to put more men on duty. He told them to watch the skyscrapers carefully. He also checked that the soldiers still worked hard to chip the ice away from the hull of the steamship. Above all, he wanted to keep Cleopatra safe, and he wasn't confident about that at all.

"We never should have left Rome," he muttered and then barked more orders at the guards. Reluctantly he left the deck and went below.

Cleopatra felt cold all the time, even in summer. As a child she had

read about bliss and passion, but as an adult she had never found it. She
drowned day after day in a dead sea. A sea that contained none of the
vitality of life. Her sea bed was littered with creatures that had the hardest
of shells. She felt like them most of the time. The current occasionally
battered them against a rock in an attempt, perhaps, to crack the shell.

That night Cleopatra dreamed of the snake-headed goddess again. It
had happened many times. The cobra head. Viridian green with silver
eyes. This time, the goddess was less angry, and as she hissed close to
Cleopatra's ear, the snake's tongue lightly touching her skin, it seemed to
Cleopatra that she was trying to tell her of some great secret. Cleopatra
awoke with a start, and spent half the night praying to Isis for guidance.

In the morning she sent for Tjuya Meresamun, the oracle who was
never far from her side.

"The dream is a warning from Wadjet. She warns you of some danger
and you must heed the warning, especially whilst you are here, and the
dream has become more frequent."

"Here in Britanniae? There is little we can do until the canal thaws."

"I can only interpret the dream. Wadjet— the old one, who came before
Isis, tells you of the danger. Go to the temple of Isis in this city and pray.
As soon as possible it would be better to go to Alexandria. I could do a
reading for you?"

Cleopatra had become rather dependant on the readings from her
oracle; she hardly ever made a decision before having Tjuya Meresamun
read the cards for her. Gaius had criticised her for the practice many times.

Tjuya Meresamun gave the cards to Cleopatra. "Take a card that
represents the question you most want guidance on."

Cleopatra chose The Magician. It represented her search for
knowledge. Tjuya Meresamun knelt on the rug and began to place the tarot
cards on a low table. When she finished she pointed at the first card. It was
The Empress and the picture depicted was Isis seated in the centre of a
radiant sun and a crown of twelve stars. Beneath her feet was the moon. In
her hand a sceptre in the other an eagle.

The oracle hesitated, "To me she represents you as perhaps you see
yourself—a leader unsure of a direction, a true course to follow, to find the
knowledge you seek. We have discussed before how you feel Isis has
abandoned you."

She pointed at another card, "Here, The Chariot of Osiris. I sense some
success but also there is the danger of defeat."

"So we go to Alexandria?" Cleopatra suggested.

"We've talked about that before. I think so."

"There is also this one, the card that represents fortitude and strength. As you see the card shows the picture of a woman holding the jaws of a lion, whether she is prying them open, closing them or simply holding them it is difficult to say."

Tjuya Meresamun pointed to another. "This is a difficult one. It can denote the strength of purpose or the coming of danger. The Tower is an important one for you as it can represent the punishment for being presumptuous or too proud concerning the pursuit of forbidden knowledge. You must act with humility lest it may destroy you."

The turning of cards went on in silence until Cleopatra became impatient. "None of this means anything. It leaves me more confused than when we began. Should I go to Alexandria, or not?"

"I rather think that you have to." The oracle seemed resolved as she pointed to the last card. It was The Judgement, called by some The Awakening of the Dead. It had upon it the depiction of a spirit blowing upon a trumpet over a half-open tomb. Rising from the tomb was a man, a woman, and a child, half-wrapped in the bandages used in mummification. "It means the end of all things good and evil—a time of punishment or reward."

A look of concern spread over Cleopatra's face, "I'll think about what you have told me. Go now."

Tjuya Meresamun left the cabin and Cleopatra picked at her breakfast. She couldn't eat much; she was so worried about what the oracle had said. She ate a little bread and fruit. Shortly her dresser came to show her the new furs that had just come in on a trading ship before the canal froze. Cleopatra had no time for the clothes; her mind was preoccupied with the images in the dream. She should have never left Rome at this time of year. Now her ship was trapped by the ice, and she wondered just who she could trust. Gaius, of course. She'd never trusted Clovis. He was a relative, but perhaps she should have never given him high status. She thought that perhaps to give power to Clovis might be a mistake, but between them they could, if everything went to plan, keep the other noble houses of Europe in order. Cleopatra decided that she would take a walk on deck to clear her head and Julia went with her. Her companion knew when to be silent.

Cleopatra didn't hear the shot that brought Julia down. Gaius rushed up from below, pushed Cleopatra into the shadow of the huge steam funnel, and then got her down below as soon as possible. The crowd screamed and pointed. People slipped and stumbled, trying to get off the ice as fast as they could, or they cowered under stalls or behind cart wheels looking for some shelter. The guards carried Julia away to the deck below, and Gaius despatched some of the soldiers to look for the sniper. Gaius knew it was useless, too many apartments where he or she could be hiding, and a quick exit through the skyways. More soldiers were sent to search the high apartment blocks, but no one was found and no citizen had seen anything.

Cleopatra bent over Julia and tried to reassure her that she would be fine. Cleopatra's personal physician was called for and he did all he could to stem the flow of blood. It was a futile act.

Julia died in the next hour and Cleopatra wept over her body. She loved Julia—trusted her.

"I'll find out who did this. I promise, Julia."

Cleopatra swore that when the canal thawed she would go to Alexandria. She would pray to Wadjet. Why had Isis deserted her? Cleopatra would still have Clovis for Governor General, she had little choice, and she would still attend the ceremonies. Her people must see that she was not afraid. As soon as she could do so she would send Gaius to Rome to get the legions ready, just in case.

Six hours later Julia rose from the dead.

Cleopatra heard the rustle of cotton close to her arm. Julia grabbed Cleopatra's hand as she turned away.

"Julia! Praise Isis—you're alive."

Julia tried to speak, "Not alive..." she tried again to speak.

It was evident that Julia had great difficulty in sitting up. Cleopatra helped her, and then sat down on the bed a little way away. She looked nervously at the cabin door.

"I'll call for my doctor," said Cleopatra.

Julia shook her head and started to become more agitated. She stared frantically at Cleopatra and then down at her own pale arms and hands. Julia dug her fingernails into the flesh on her own arm. Cleopatra gasped and tried to stop her, but Julia pushed her away and started tearing at her own arms again. No blood ran from her torn skin. Julia began to whimper and looked desperately around the cabin. She saw a knife on a nearby table, quickly reached for it, and began cutting across her arm, time and time again. Cleopatra tried to stop her.

"Julia! Julia!"

Julia shook her head and cried. "No blood...no blood."

Suddenly she stopped and stared hard at Cleopatra. With one lunge she tried to drive the knife into Cleopatra's stomach. Cleopatra screamed and caught at the knife, blood spurted onto the blue cover of the bed. She screamed again and the legionaries came running. One burst through the door and threw himself upon Julia, knocking the knife to one side. After a struggle she began to calm down and seemed to be unaware that anything had happened. She just stared blankly at the ceiling of the cabin.

The doctor and Gaius were quickly called for. Cleopatra winced in pain as the doctor tended to her hand. She had never felt pain like this before. No one had ever dared to touch her without her permission. How was all this possible, she thought? Julia was dead and yet she was alive. She started to speak again. Most of what she said was incomprehensible but Cleopatra caught a little of it. She was calling for her father and mother. They had been dead for ten years now. How could this be?

"I'll put her somewhere else where she can do you no harm," Gaius said with concern in his voice.

"No. She will stay here in her cabin. Just move anything that will be a danger to her."

"She will be a danger to you and others. She was dead and now she walks."

"I'll get someone to sit with her. She's calm now."

"At least tie her up."

"No. Just put a guard on the door. One of the slaves can stay with her."

Later, when some sort of calm had returned to the ship, the guard who had just come on duty answered a knock on the door from inside the cabin. He simply assumed that the young woman, wrapped in a warm cloak with a hood up and then over her face against the cold, was the slave, and let her pass by him. He saw another woman asleep on the bed with blood on her gown and thought her to be Julia.

Julia left *The Alexander* and wandered around the quayside. The guards didn't stop her. They were more bothered about someone boarding the ship than leaving. As she walked by one guard, he noticed how pale she looked, but he didn't recognise her. Then, he found himself thinking about how bitter the night had become, stamped his feet to get some feeling back to them, and promptly forgot her.

Julia held the cloak tightly about her—so tightly the knuckle bones threatened to split skin. She didn't know where she was going at first, but then she instinctively made for the temple of Isis. To search for the goddess who had broken faith with Cleopatra. Her thoughts never fully formed. Just as she caught hold of something familiar, it was gone and another incomprehensive image flickered through. She did feel—a little. She heard wind howl, and shrank back if any came too close to her. As the snow fell, her feet left light steps in the snow, although her heart sat heavy as a stone in her body. She looked at her pale hand before her and felt for the bullet hole in her head, through the cloth. She pulled the hood down further over her face and shivered ever so slightly, like a moth in a shimmer of light. A child screamed when she saw Julia's eyes and the mother pulled her away. Julia took a step back, and turned to go back to *The Alexander*. Once on the quayside she wandered along until she found a pile of bricks, some rope and a sack. Slowly she put the bricks in the sack, tied it with rope, and then tied the rope around her waist. Julia stood on the side of the ship canal, the ice broke up to reveal black water —and then she jumped. Hardly anyone heard the splash, and if they did they didn't care. People were always committing suicide there. It was probably someone with the plague anyway, thought the guard who had turned his head slightly on hearing the sound. He never left his post. As poor Julia was dragged down by the weight of the bricks she had a sudden moment of clarity. She saw Clovis try to destroy Cleopatra. She saw the brass bull. She saw the end of it all. Her tears mingled with the water and she wanted to go back, go back to Cleopatra and warn her—but it was too late. Far too late.

Chapter 8

The ceremonies would take place in Manceastre. Tradition decreed that all investitures were carried out in the cotton capital of the northern empire, and that was Manceastre. Clovis was getting over excited, and had already begun the celebrations that would lead up to his appointment. He kept his black hair short, which looked strange with his florid complexion. Dismissing any help, he wiped the sweat from his brow and adjusted his clothes numerous times. He was short, pugnacious—he had put on far too much weight for the last suits made on Menser Row, and even now he still felt uncomfortable in one of the new ones.

The large brass bull was to be the centrepiece of a magnificent private party, and was mounted on a brass frame and wheels. It had been pushed in by the slaves and placed over a pit in the stone floor. Well away from it was the top table, raised on a dais where Clovis sat with some favoured friends. He made constant eye contact with one or another as if to stamp his authority quite forcefully. He never looked at anything else except the bull or his friends, and he always controlled the conversation.

Some were in on the secret. The other guests sat on lower tables, not too close, but around the brazen bull, which was decked with white orchids from the palace greenhouses. White silk from China had been hung in broad swathes across the ceiling and tied to the enormous columns. Tables were covered in a violet material. White orchids were everywhere, filling the palace with their fragrance. There were exotic fruits and expensive wine from the Mediterranean, too. Clovis had ordered the chefs to cook the finest delicacies. Swan—cooked in honey, minced and put back inside the carcass, and its neck wired, and tilted at an angle so it looked that it would peck at the grapes that decorated the next platter. It was decorated with feathers. There was duck, boar, even baby, stuffed starlings in chocolate nests. Course after course of elaborate offerings fit for the new Governor General. The tables were set well back from the bull. There was a good reason for that. There were more incense lamps than usual, too, placed close to each person, and the slaves moved carefully around them as they served from gold edged porcelain plates. Then, a new fragrance of jasmine wafted around the pink marble pillars. These Doric pillars held up the magnificent glass ceiling to a black night sky, which was rapidly being blanketed out by the snow. The snowflakes became heavier, fell rapidly and swirled faster. The palace made of limestone and marble was heated by steam from the massive underground pumping station, which groaned loudly every now and then as if it were Atlas, carrying the weight of the world on his shoulders.

The musicians played the pipes, delicately at first, and all the while they did so Clovis smiled, until one of his friends patted him on the shoulder and asked what was so good about them.

"You'll see …you'll see, and I hope that it will create some amusement for you in this dreary winter," said Clovis.

Wood, soaked in a little oil, had been placed in the pit under the bull. The place was warm enough as it was, and one of the nobles looked puzzled when a servant put a torch to the wood and the flames reared up readily. The slave backed away nervously and bowed to Clovis, who laughed out loud and bent forward eagerly in his seat. It took a while for the fire to get going, and the pipers played their happy little tune to the clapping of the guests. Some of the young women left their seats and danced around the tables, fawning over the men and feeding them with their own pretty little fingers, and still the fire grew fiercer, and the pipes played more loudly. The noise of eager conversation, dancing, and the heady incense in the smoke coming from the bull's nostrils, gave one or two an excuse to leave. Clovis refused permission without taking his eyes off the golden bull for a moment. The glow of the fire reflected in his staring eyes. He couldn't take his eyes off the glowing belly of the bull. He dismissed the young men and women who came to him. Clovis couldn't be distracted. It soon grew too hot for more of his guests and one or two others wanted to leave. Clovis made them sit down. As the fire roared the musicians put down their pipes, and the guests couldn't understand where the other, louder sound came from. Then the bull bellowed again. Its underbelly was now red hot. The terrible noise echoed around the room changing in pitch and tempo. Occasionally sounding like a muffled cry, and then the bull bellowed again, as if at the height of great excitement. More smoke came from the bull's nose. The servants brought the jasmine lamps even closer to the guests, and still Clovis would not take his eyes off the bull. The bellowing became louder, less rhythmic, wilder in its tone, and then it stopped, suddenly. Finally, there was one last cry. Then silence.

Silence from the guests and then laughter from Clovis—a hideous laughter that echoed around the palace.

Clovis dismissed all the guests except for those from the top table and told the servants to put out the fire with the large ceramic jars of water that stood near each pillar. Then he dismissed the slaves too and he picked up a metal poker that had been on the red tablecloth. The brass bull was glowing red on the underbelly, and steam rose from where the water had splashed its body. Careful not to stand in the embers, Clovis put the tip of the poker into a socket and gave it a sharp turn. There was a grim sliding of metal and something black fell from the belly of the bull. The remaining guests burst into laughter too, and Clovis stabbed at the thing with the poker. The face was pulled back in a grimace, and the fists were clenched tight to the chest. The swollen body, perhaps, was that of a man, but curled up it looked like that of a blistered pig.

One guest got to his feet. "You've gone too far this time, Clovis."

Clovis just smiled at him.

Two slaves were brought back into the room to remove what was left of the man. At this point, one or two of the favoured guests wanted to leave, but Clovis made them stay. The guests drank and ate more than they truly wanted that night. Clovis couldn't stop laughing and making jokes about the man. He wanted to share the joke with Licinia. Clovis scoured the drunken faces, and then remembered that she wasn't there. Perhaps he would send for the prostitute later.

Fire-eaters, jugglers and dancers came in as Clovis steadily got drunk. Girls had been brought in from Constantinople. They were young, clean, pretty and eager for the pleasure of the guests. Happy though he was, Clovis' mood changed quickly. He went too far with his games, making one girl sing over and over again. He became angrier with her performance, pushing her back against one of the columns, until she fell heavily against the knife in his hand. The dead girl meant nothing to Clovis. She wouldn't be missed by anyone. He thought about killing the rest of the girls, too, but his guests were enjoying them far too much, and he had promised they could take them home. A favour. Gifts given out after a party. He laughed at that thought.

After the celebrations had finished, the slave Amar was told to clean the inside and outside of the bull. He had been summoned from the kitchens, and had heard all about what had happened. Nervously, he stepped close to the bull. It was cold now and the metal flap was still open underneath. The servant's hand trembled as he took a jasmine lantern from a stand and looked inside the bull. There was a terrible stench, but he was determined, had to out of necessity, look inside. Something was stuck to the inside of the belly of the bull. It looked like burnt leather. There was some sort of contraption which led up to the bull's head. It looked to be a metal funnel, also the remains of a harness put in to secure something tightly, and a long pipe from the funnel to the bull's mouth. It was a pipe not dissimilar to the ones he had seen being played by the musicians in the hall earlier. The servant suddenly started to retch when he realised who had made the bellowing of the bull.

Later that night Amar told his friend Sleeward of what was in the bull. He had gone to look at the body, later. "I've never seen such a sight, and I swear on the immortal soul of Isis I hope I never do again."

Sleeward put his head close to Amar. "You are never to tell anyone again about this. It's bad enough you've told me, and I should turn you in for even mentioning it. Clovis doesn't like news of what he does to get out of the palace."

Amar sat bolt upright. "You wouldn't do that to me, would you?"

"No, of course not, we're mates. You've done favours for me often enough and looked after young Luce. I owe you."

"For a minute there, Sleeward, I thought I saw something in your face that said you would."

"Not I …Not I."

Sleeward was different from the other colourmen who naturally saw themselves a cut above the slaves. In fact, they could leave the palace on Clovis' business, which really didn't amount to much freedom at all, and when in the city they conducted a little business of their own. After more wine and beer Amar tried to explain to Sleeward how the inside of the belly of the bull had looked and smelt. Sleeward placed his hand on his friend's arm and shook his head.

Sometimes there isn't a reason for cruelty. Some people weren't treated badly as children, or started off torturing animals, or took great delight in spying on their parents having sex. Some people are just cruel, and one such person was Clovis Domitius Corbulo. Rumour had it that he had killed off some of the royal family, blood relatives closer to Cleopatra than he, but these rumours were only whispers in the great courts of the empire, and were treated with derision by his supporters. Jealousy was said to be the cause of the accusations, and Clovis didn't even feel the need to protect his reputation by saying anything about it—ever. There were some of Clovis' relatives who, however, refused to visit Britanniae because of the fear of assassination. Clovis was to be honoured with the appointment of the post of Governor General of Britanniae. But, there were precious few of his European relatives in attendance, not just because of fear, for none of them actually liked the man.

Gaius—Oppian padding along by his side, and escorted by his own personal guard of six men, set off to see Clovis. Gaius' guards had never seen him so angry. Before any campaign he had always shown great restraint, and although he rallied his soldiers to arms, it was his cool head that was most admired about him. Gaius was far from cool-headed now. Clovis' slaves tried to explain that he was bathing and could not be disturbed. Gaius pushed them aside and continued on to the Governor General's private rooms.

Clovis was being bathed by one of his female slaves, who knelt down on the side of the huge sunken pool. The surface was covered with white lilies. She stopped rubbing soap onto Clovis' shoulders as Gaius burst in.

Gaius shouted at the girl. "Get out!"

She looked at Clovis.

"Wait. Get me a robe," said Clovis.

Clovis got out of the water. His skin hung in loose folds, and Gaius was repulsed by how flaccid he looked. The girl moved quickly, eager to be away from both of the men. After placing the white robe around Clovis he dismissed her and she left.

"What is it that is so important that you could not wait to be announced?"

"An attempt on Cleopatra's life."

Clovis looked genuinely surprised, because it was too soon. She hadn't sworn him in as Governor General yet.

"Her maid was shot. A bullet that was clearly meant for Cleopatra."

"That's awful—did you catch who was responsible?"

"Those skyscrapers are all linked together by skyways not to mention the underground catacombs. I've sent some men to search, but no one will be found. You know that."

"Indeed I don't. Only a few months ago someone took a shot at me. We got the bastard, too. These are hard times, Gaius, and they call for harsh measures."

"So what are you going to do about this latest attempt?"

"It's just another isolated incident. Some madman afraid of the plague, and so he should be. He just wanted to take his fear out on someone, nothing more."

Clovis took a step towards Gaius. Oppian growled, and Clovis stepped back. He hated dogs, especially ones the size of Oppian.

Gaius couldn't hide his contempt. He felt Clovis to be too dismissive about the assassination attempt. "And what if it isn't an isolated incident?"

"Do you want me to put every fanatic in prison? Not a practical solution—is it?" Clovis waited for an answer.

Gaius knew that although Clovis would need the patronage of Cleopatra until his investiture, he wasn't so sure what he would do as Governor General. Gaius thought that if the plague hadn't wiped out over three quarters of the legions, he would be in a far better position to defend the empire. Gaius doubted that Clovis could find enough soldiers from any of the other noble houses to openly challenge Cleopatra. But, if another assassination attempt was successful, Clovis might make a bid for total power. There were only a few of royal blood left before him in succession.

"I can assure you, Gaius, that there will be maximum security at the entombment of Claudius Ptolemaeus Tiberius, and at my investiture. If you are still afraid, might I suggest perhaps a closed coach for Cleopatra?"

"I'll be by her side. There will be no need of that."

"Gaius, I can assure you that there will be many of my personal guards there, but I can't promise that it won't happen again. We have so many skyscrapers, so many windows of opportunity."

Clovis tried hard not to smile.

Mustering great control, Gaius had to restrain himself from punching him full in the face; instead he turned abruptly and left the room followed by his guards. Clovis clapped his hands and the slave returned. He beamed at her. "I'm in such a good mood you know—lucky for you," and he pulled her by the arm to the couch by the side of the pool.

After his meeting with Clovis, Gaius went straight to the commander of the garrison and barged into the quarters belonging to Vibius Laenus. Gaius found him sitting behind his desk, informally dressed, and very much not the man of action he needed to be speaking to at that moment.

"How many men will you be deploying in the streets for security at the ceremonies?"

Vibius quickly rose to his feet; the chair behind him fell to the floor.

"I…I have as many men as can be gathered…the plague, you know?"

"Damn the plague. I want more action from you. Do you plan to have men in plain clothes in attendance in the crowd?"

"Well, I wasn't planning to…they're busy on the Governor General's business.

"Business? What could be more important than the safety of the Empress?"

"Er—none sir but the Governor General…"

"The Governor General has not been sworn in yet. You answer to me…got that? I want men in the crowds and on the rooftops. I want men dressed in plain clothes at the ceremony and want, most of all, for you to do your job properly, or I'll send you to some back-end of the empire. Have you got that?"

Vibius swallowed hard and tried to speak. "Yes I've got that, Sir…" he swallowed again, "I'll try to do as you say."

Gaius brought his fist down hard on the table and bit his lip. It was all he could do not to punch Vibius in the face, too. "You will do what I ask. If anything happens to her, I'll tear the skin off your back myself and feed it to the dogs. Do you understand?"

"I understand, Sir."

"Good. Now. Get me a street map showing the route and how you propose to deploy what few men you have."

Oppian settled himself down under the desk and sniffed the air. He could smell the oil from the kerosene lamp and that always made him sleepy. A slave came in with some food for Gaius and Vibius. He placed a tray on the desk. Gaius looked up.

"Bring some food for the dog. He likes it raw." With that Gaius went back to the map, ignoring the food. Vibius reached out for the jug of wine on the tray. Gaius dashed the jug from the table and the wine spilled to the floor. Oppian never moved a muscle. It wasn't the first time his master had done that.

Clovis was deep in thought as he walked around his palace and made his way to the cellars. In those cellars had worked some of the best scientists he could find to carry out new work on cryopreservation. The steam pumps worked very well and could attain temperatures of -196 C. Cells were preserved to a certain extent but they had experienced many failures in their condition approaching that temperature. Clovis, although outwardly a follower of Isis, secretly wanted (when, or rather, if he was near death) to have his body preserved until such a time when medicine had developed to a stage where he could be made immortal. If he knew how to prolong his life in this world, what would he need of the next? Gods had never appeared to him. He thought of himself as godlike, and surely, if they really existed, they would appear to him?

He needed more bodies to experiment on. None had been brought in for some time. There had to be more tests carried out involving the freezing and thawing out of tissue, without permanent damage. He still hadn't absorbed the full implications of the fact the recently deceased did not remain dead. The colourmen had brought him someone, but he needed more to work on. He'd used animals, but it just wasn't the same. Then, more bodies were brought in last night...the walking dead...how could that be? There was much to be done if he was going to make any progress. It wouldn't be long before more were brought to him. Would he find out why they didn't truly die?

Clovis' first wife had died childless, and now it was time to take a new wife. He needed heirs. He wanted children that looked just like him. As the slaves put the final touches to his regalia, he tried it on and thought how wonderful he looked. I'll have a wife—the right wife— Cleopatra herself perhaps. His harsh laughter could be heard echoing around the palace.

He did not have a peaceful night, however. In his nightmare, Isis moved silently towards him and with each step she seemed to sway a little. Her black eyes fixed on his, and mesmerised, he could not take his eyes away. She transformed into Thermouthis, and she slithered over the marble floor to him. He could not move. Her serpent tongue flickered over Clovis' stricken face, and then she sank her fangs quickly into his neck, pumping the poison into his body. He fought against the venom. He tried to move his legs and failed. Clovis could not scream.

Clovis wrestled with the nightmare, trying to escape. Somehow he knew the nightmare was just that, and when he awoke he wiped his sweating face upon the pillow. He rose from his bed and called for a slave to dress him. He bid her stay and follow him into his studio. His foul mood quickly changed as he appreciated the artwork before him. His artwork— all painted by Clovis.

The paintings were dominated by the colour red, and it had in some cases been mixed together with the blue to make violet. Some of the paintings were of men and women having sex, some were more 'exotic' to Clovis. The one he was working on at the moment was one of a woman— full-breasted, riding a mythological creature, a centaur to be exact, half man half horse. The violet hair of the woman trailed around through the trees and climbed the lower branches stirring the serpents as they lay asleep. The snakes rained down in the background as the woman pressed herself close to the centaur's back and urged him on. The body of the woman was a strange crystal white, as was the upper part of the centaur.

The slave looked nervous. She had heard about this room before, and seen the scars upon the other slaves. Most, when chosen, didn't last long. He made her sit on a chair and remove her clothes.

Clovis picked up the knife and held her left shoulder. She was new to him and he liked her. She looked like the woman in the new painting, but with bronze tinted hair, not violet, which trailed down her back.

"Hold out your arm."

She held out her arm to him, palm down.

"Not that way—palm up." He smiled at her as she shrank away.

"You aren't going to die."

Clovis looked at the painting and decided what part of it would be red this time. He chose the soft fleshy spot above the elbow on the inner part of her arm and cut deep.

The woman screamed as Clovis dipped his paintbrush into the wound and applied the strokes to the lower part of the centaur's body. It was going to be a long night.

Chapter 9

In the Hall of the Gods Nepythys stood over the dead body of Isis. Nepythys showed no emotion, no thought for the act she had committed. "This is where the years have led you—to nothing. No eternity for you. I will have every image of you removed from the earth and mine put there instead. Your name shall be forgotten."

Nepythys—wearing the white crown of Osiris, brought the flint knife time and time again down on her sister's neck. When muscle resisted she hacked all the harder until the blood pooled under her feet and covered most of her own dress. Red on gold. A hand grabbed her wrist—her son, Anubis. He stared at her eye to eye—his great jackal-head, the colours of rotting flesh.

"Enough! How can you do this to your own sister?"

"She means nothing to me."

"I can't believe what you are doing. She's dead. You killed her before and now you come back to make sure?"

"I have to be certain. Behead her. And when you have done that, let me know."

Anubis resisted for a short time but as usual his mother got her own way. She knew exactly how to get him to do what she desired. When Anubis had carried out the terrible act and informed his mother, Nepythys suddenly felt so weak—as did Anubis. As he lay in her arms she realised that only Horus, Anubis and herself were left now. Thoth was dead also, but she suspected the words of his book still held the great magic. Osiris had been dead many centuries. Seth and Horus had battled for many years before Seth was killed by Horus. It was Isis who then became ruler of the underworld. And it was Isis who had turned Horus into a boy-god. He would always be dependant on his mother, not unlike Anubis. Nepythys would control his every action from now on, and at least he would never be a threat to her. Nepythys, Seth's wife, had always seen herself as queen, and now she had acted upon that wish.

At first unseen by Nepythys, from a dark corner of the chamber, a serpent slithered towards her. It rose up in anger, and hissed at her. It was the black-necked cobra that could spit poisonous venom that could blind. Nepythys threw a knife at it, which clattered against the stone floor, and the snake vanished quickly into the violet darkness. Nepythys stared at the body of Isis and thought of her many representations. Could something of her have transformed into the snake goddess Isis-Thermouthis? In the last moments of her life could she have managed to change into that form of her that she had seen her become in the past? The serpent-goddess of the field? Nepythys looked at one of the paintings on the wall of the chamber. She had seen it often enough. The depiction was a cobra crowned with the headdress of Isis. Isis-Thermouthis. Cobra-goddess, guardian of the Pharaoh alongside the mother Wadjet, the woman with the cobra's head. Her gaze had vanquished all enemies. Wadjet had disappeared many years ago.

Nepythys couldn't stop looking at the painting. Would it be the end now that Isis was dead? Was it over once and for all time?

Nepythys swayed a little and found it difficult to think. She had to make sure that Isis, no part of Isis, could manifest herself in another form. She would need *The Book of Thoth*. The last person she had heard who had sought it out was a mortal.

"Get me the chief embalmer, Ptolemy Child."

"What? Bring him to the underworld?"

"Yes. Here—now."

"Can't you be content with what you have done? You are now Queen."

"Yes, I am Queen. But I can't rule like this. He is the only one I know who may be able to help. Bring me one of his daughters, too. If I am to get him to do what I want I'll need someone to bargain with."

Anubis left without a word. The jackal-headed god reluctantly did as his mother ordered.

Nepythys left the chamber and walked along a passageway to her left. She peered into the shadows for any sign of movement. Her step quickened and she entered another chamber, smaller than the last. In the moss-laden walls, cracks appeared where there had been none before. Nepythys then turned her attention to the son of Isis, Horus. Bound by his mother to remain a boy. The gods, being gods, could choose whatever image they wanted, but not Horus. He would always be his mother's boy. Horus sat, helpless, on an old throne that had lost its lustre for all time.

With a wave of Nepythys' hand Horus found that he could move his head and speak. He tried to move his arms and legs but nothing happened.

He might have the body of a boy of around fourteen years of age, but his mind was far older, and he could see far beyond his emotional reaction, to what had just happened. He knew his mother was dead. He had no need to be told of that.

"What have you done? There are so precious few of us left, and now you do this? Why?"

"I don't have to explain myself to you. You, who murdered Seth for your mother, who repaid you by making you a boy, forever. If Seth had lived, I would have been Queen, and now I am."

"He killed my father, Osiris."

"Are you so sure it was him who killed your father?"

"You know it was Seth. And why do you turn on my mother after all these years?"

"Exactly. All those years in my sister's shadow."

"I'll have my revenge, Nepythys."

"And what could a boy do? You have no strength. That is why your mother had you remain a boy. She trusted no one, not even her own son."

Horus knew that Nepythys spoke the truth. He had always resented his mother for taking his life away from him. To be trapped in such a way. Perhaps now she was dead, he thought, the spell would be broken. He could only hope that would be the case, and he could fight back against Nepythys. But if that was possible, why did he feel so weak? Horus lowered his head and then lifted his eyes to meet the hard stare of Nepythys. She blinked, and in that brief moment he thought she saw fear. As she left the chamber he saw her stumble, but she quickly regained her step.

On the west wall of the offering chamber, in the tomb of Claudius Ptolemaeus Tiberius, was the false door. It was made of limestone and painted red and with black flecks all over it to resemble granite. Above the door was the inscription...

As for those who will do something against this,
it shall be protected from them.
I have constructed my tomb with my own means.
It is the god who will judge my case
along with him who does anything against it.

~*~

97

Anubis went through it as if the door didn't exist at all. He kept to the shadows as he made his way to the Ptolemy house. All were still asleep. Anubis, now in the full form of a man, silently walked up the marble steps to Loli and Ella's room. Ptolemy was not at home again. Ella was fast in her opium dreams. Anubis looked upon the face of the sleeping Loli, waved a hand in front of her face as if to keep her locked within her dream world, and gently picked her up. Just as silently as he had entered, he left the house. Loli did not wake—she could not wake.

Back at the tomb of Claudius Ptolemaeus Tiberius, solid stone became insubstantial once more, and Anubis went through the false door. Loli was aware of the rhythmic movement of the great god and she saw strange creatures in her dreams, or rather nightmare world. Things that should not live and yet did. Creatures larger than men sat like squat green toads, tearing the flesh from forms similar to that of her own. One creature tried to take the meat from another and it attacked, biting into the neck of the other until the luminescent, green blood, for that is what it must have been, splashed the walls of the cavernous world she seemed to be in. Vapour eeled its way across the ground and slid up the walls. She knew it to be the way to the underworld but it wasn't the way she had been taught about from books. This was far more terrifying.

In the great hall of the Palace of Isis, Anubis placed Loli on a couch and left her in her dreadful dream world. Not long after, Loli woke up. Gone were the slimy walls, and in their place she was in the most beautiful of chambers. There were tall statues of gods she remembered seeing pictures of—most were broken. Isis remained intact. Loli recognised the solar disc on the head of the witch goddess. Bastet, the war goddess, lay on the ground, sand piled up against her broken limbs. Her lioness head was still on her body. Loli recalled that at home they had a small statue next to the urns, which held the sweet smelling embalmment oils. Bastet came to be not only the goddess of war, but perfumes, too, which Loli always thought a little odd.

At the base of six enormous marble pillars there were more couches and a huge mosaic covered the floor. The mosaic was an underwater depiction with many bizarre sea creatures she had never seen in real life. Strangely coloured fish—pink and mauve and many that looked to be almost translucent. There were those with fleshy appendages that hung over their heads with little yellow lanterns at the end, painted in such a way as to illuminate the immediate area around them. Loli got off the couch and went across to an enormous gold table. Engraved into the top was a city, and with the symbols of fish and shipwrecked boats around it— it looked to be a city beneath the sea. Loli struggled to remember something about a lost city beneath the sea. A city that was often talked about as being so beautiful, and had been lost.

Paintings adorned the walls. Some captured the god in various stages of change from the human-like form into that of animal and serpent. Isis the serpent. Bastet the lioness, and many more adorned the round chamber walls. Loli turned away from some. Humans having sex with animals. Ella had never said anything about that in the lessons back home. At various points around the enormous chamber were arched doorways, which lead into gloom and darkness where anything could be lying in wait for her. She wondered if she wasn't dead, why she was there at all. She was convinced that Ammit was waiting in the shadows to devour her, even before she had her heart weighed by Ma'at. She had seen pictures of Ammit, the devourer of the dead—a frightening sight, a hybrid of crocodile, lion and hippo. She'd had nightmares about her when she was younger, when she had first been instructed about the *Book of the Dead*. In the great hall of Osiris Loli began to cry, quietly. Someone entered through one of the doorways far across the hall and as the figure came closer to her Loli was convinced it was the goddess Ma'at, and Loli felt her hands begin to shake. She hardly dare look up to see who or what it was.

The goddess Nepythys, mother of Anubis, stood before her. She was the daughter of Geb and Nut, sister to Isis and Osiris. She had olive skin, black eyes and lank hair that hung like dark bandages. Loli looked at her feet and saw that they were covered with blood. Loli didn't want to know where it came from.

"I am Nepythys."

Loli thought of all of what she had learned of the demons and gods of the underworld and of the terrible trials. If she had died suddenly she would not have anything to protect her from the dangers of the afterlife. Anubis entered the hall, still in human form, and moved towards her.

Loli, although terrified found her voice. "I don't remember dying. Are you going to weigh my heart? I've tried to be good but not always managed it." Loli well knew that if her heart weighed more than the feather of Ma'at she would be eaten by Ammit, the devourer of souls.

Loli covered her face with her hands fearing the worst.

"You didn't die," said Anubis.

"And this place isn't the underworld then?"

"It is."

"I don't understand?"

"You don't have to. You just have to be here." Nepythys walked up to Loli, cupped her face, and tipped it up towards hers.

"Who are you?" Loli didn't feel afraid, strangely enough, just curious.

"I am Nepythys, ruler of everything."

"Of everything?" Loli repeated. "Will you let me go home?"

"For the time being, child, this will be your home."

Loli looked around her once more. "I want Ella and my father."

"You will see your father soon. Sleep now, you are very tired."

Loli tried to stay awake. She had to get back to her father and Ella. She would get up. Try to walk. Any effort to rise from the couch resulted in Loli slumping back into the soft cushions. She fought so hard but within a moment or two she was asleep.

Loli did not know how long she slept but when she awoke Nepythys led her down a dim corridor to a bigger, lighter chamber. Loli hesitated on the threshold. She paused and Anubis gently nudged her forward. She could feel his hot breath on her neck and would not turn her head to look at him just in case he didn't look the same.

Loli began to shake. She felt like she did when her father first called her to the embalming table. Her palms became sweaty and she wiped them on her pale-blue nightdress. Nepythys beckoned her to enter. She could see Nepythys more clearly now. She was dressed in a golden gown, her crown encrusted with pearls and diamonds. Loli looked down at the hem of the golden gown. It skimmed across what looked like blood on the floor.

On a dais there was a body. That of a woman in a long white dress smeared with blood. The corpse was headless. On a small table there was something covered with a red stained gold cloth.

Nepythys fixed her kohl black eyes on Loli's face and drew the cloth. She picked up the head by the black hair. The head hadn't been separated from the body long. Loli knew that. She started to shake uncontrollably. She couldn't take her eyes off the grisly sight yet she was filled with awe as she stared at the face.

"A little late for anything meaningful now but this is or rather was, Isis."

Loli felt afraid. Why was she in the underworld? Where was everyone? Where was Ammit? Loli, her mind—confused, was this really the underworld? Could this really be real? Where were the dead to be judged? Could Isis really be dead?

Nepythys placed the head carefully back on the table and covered it up again. She smiled as she did so.

"I don't understand. How can a goddess die?" asked Loli.

"We are as you are above. We can die."

"But who would kill Isis?" If indeed the woman was a goddess. She didn't look much like one. She would have expected one to be more magnificent for one thing and immortal for another.

Loli could smell incense but beneath it she could detect the acrid metallic smell of blood. Nepythys pulled at Loli's arm and then dragged her away from the body.

"There's more to see. More that you should see."

Loli was led into another dimly lit corridor and into another chamber. There was little light in this room. Sitting on a throne was a boy, not yet a man, his head slumped to his chest.

"Have you ever heard of Horus?"

Loli nodded, she had learnt all about him, too. She usually knew him as having a man's body and head of a falcon. That is what she had been taught. A hunter's god and this boy before her… he couldn't look less like a god; he looked more like the hunted. If this is true, thought Loli, it would be impossible to live and see all this. Loli was to be left with the boy they called Horus. As they left, Nepythys called over her shoulder.

"Be kind to him. He doesn't have much time left, either."

Loli looked at the boy with pity in her eyes. Was he going to be killed? Was she?

Horus opened his eyes. He tried to focus on Loli. Loli wished Ella was there. She'd know what to do. Without thinking she gently pushed his black hair from his face. She touched his cheek gently as she did so. Horus reacted as if he had been struck by lightning. He trembled horribly and then seemed fully awake. He tried to move his hands and seemed surprised when he could do so.

"Are you hurt?" she said.

"Not if you count being bound by magic being hurt. What did you just do to release me?"

"Nothing. I just pushed your hair from your eyes."

Those same eyes looked at her, bewildered, and then he got up from the chair.

"I have to get away from here. I have to get my mother away from here."

Did he know? thought Loli. "Isis is…" she didn't have to finish the words; she saw the sadness in his face.

"I know, but that isn't the end of it. What do they call you?"

"Loli."

"We'll leave here, Loli, get you home and take Isis from this place until I can work out what to do next. I am weak now but we have to get her out of here. Will you help me?"

"Help you and I get out of here?" She glanced around nervously still looking for Ammit. "Of course I will."

Loli looked at the weakened boy in front of her. Could he really be a god? She doubted it. There was a great sense of emptiness about the place. Where were the rest of the gods? Where were the dead waiting to be judged? Isis was dead. Was that why Sophia and the baby hadn't crossed over? There would be no judgement, no afterlife anymore. Without Isis the dead could not cross over to the underworld?

Horus and Loli made their way back through the corridor to the room where Isis lay.

"I need you to be brave for me, Loli. We're not leaving without Isis. I'll take the body but you will have to carry her head."

"What! I can't do that."

It took a few minutes to persuade Loli but she plucked up the courage to carry the severed head wrapped in the cloth. It wasn't too bad she thought. If she didn't think about it too much.

Horus turned to pick up his mother's body. He stepped back. The black-necked cobra was coiled on her chest. It reared up, seemed to think better of it, slithered off the body, and silently left for the darkness once more.

They didn't come across Nepythys or Anubis and once through the false door they rested for a moment. Horus looked exhausted, but he mustered the extra strength or residual power to carry the body of Isis. Loli didn't understand how this god thing worked. If he was immortal how could one of them kill another? Or, perhaps it was true that only a God could kill a God. In the catacombs they rested for a moment. Loli tried to think what Ella would do. Should she take the body of Isis to her father, or to The Temple of Isis? The latter seemed more appropriate but what would they say—that they had the body of Isis? The priests would laugh. Isis had never manifested herself to them. They believed in the power and magic of her that had kept the empire together for thousands of years, but they wouldn't believe in her in mortal form, especially her corpse. Horus slumped against a wall.

"For a god you don't seem to be very powerful."

"I'm not powerful."

"This is all so strange to me. I thought that the gods would be immortal, could never die."

"We can die, Loli, and do."

"Then what is the difference between mortals and gods?"

He half smiled and shrugged. "Immortality."

"But you just said you could die?"

"I said die when I should have said killed."

"We can be killed by each other, not by a mortal hand."

Loli was thinking of the awful thing that Nepythys had done to Isis, if it was Isis, whether she was a goddess or not. Tears fell upon the blood soaked bundle in her arms and she held it even closer.

It was time to decide where to go. One passageway in the catacombs led to her home, and the other led to the temple of Isis. Loli thought hard for a moment. They would take the body home. Loli wouldn't know what to say to the priests, but Ella might. Perhaps they would know already being the followers of Isis. She would find her sister and get her help.

It took them a long time to get to the Ptolemy house. Horus struggled along and had to keep stopping to rest. She wished he could hurry more.

Once in the lower embalming rooms Loli dashed over to the cabinets. She turned the valve a little and a whoosh of steam rose from an outlet pipe. She'd been told not to meddle before but she just wanted to make sure that they were set to the correct temperature. Horus put the body of Isis in the nearest drawer. He took away the bloodied cloth and gently placed the head in the drawer, too. He looked at his mother and moved the hair from her face. He felt tired—tired of his own immortality. He had no strength to continue. He knew where his power came from. Horus fell to the floor.

Loli knelt down beside him. "I'll go and find Ella. I think I know where she will be. If you hear anyone coming down the stairs...hide."

Horus tried to smile at the girl, mindful of the fact that she was so much stronger than him at that moment.

Chapter 10

Finally the day to entomb the old Governor General arrived. As embalmers they would wear the black. It was traditional. Only the family of the chief embalmer wore the colour at ceremonies. It denoted their status as favoured servants of the Empress and the Governor General. Ella looked in the mirror, adjusted the black tie against the purest of white shirts, and tied her hair back in a tight knot with a black ribbon.

Ella looked around the room to see if Loli's dressing gown was there. It was. Funny, she thought. Loli didn't usually get up before her and if she went to the bathroom in the middle of winter she usually wore it. Loli wouldn't be wearing the black. She was too young. Not too young to learn the embalmment processes, but too young to wear the black. Any minute she expected Loli to dash into the room and start pulling out her clothes from the wardrobe. She had many fine dresses. Ella would have to make sure she wrapped up warm. She didn't want to nurse her through any more horrible viruses. Last winter Ella had looked after Loli when she was ill, and through the week after that when she was awake at night with a cough.

Ella looked out of the window and down into the square. The wagon was there. She was always excited to see the one they kept for the best families. It was decorated in gold leaf and inlaid with semi-precious stones given by the Governor General himself, well the one who had been Governor General about twenty years ago. The sides of the cart had been given a face-lift by Swin, beautifully re-painted, and the lapis lazuli, turquoise and jasper looked very splendid under the watery winter sun. It was a strong wagon. It had to be to take the weight of the sarcophagus, although it was made of wood. It was the custom to have two sarcophagi. There was the wooden one for the body to be placed in and blessed at the embalmer's house, and a heavier stronger marble one in the tomb. The wheels were sturdy and would bear the weight of the first.

The slaves brought out the six black horses. They chipped at the cobblestones—skittish and nervous. The horses dropped their heads sharply as if trying to rid themselves of the enormous scarlet plumage on their heads. You could see their breath as they snorted into the freezing air. Bad time of year for an entombment, thought Ella. Her suit was of thick wool but it would be freezing out there. She would sit up front next to her father and he would handle the horses. Ptolemy handled horses well. They behaved for him. He often commented that they behaved for him better than his daughters did. Ella hated her father. Hated him because she had to do what he said, and for him having anything to do with Aulus. She hated him for driving their mothers away. That is the way she saw it even though she couldn't remember her mother leaving at all. Her father was a handsome man, physically appealing, but that didn't make up for his arrogance.

Where was Loli? Ella would check the bathroom.

As she stepped out onto the landing she saw Aulus' door open. Ella didn't believe it. Aulus was wearing the black, too, as if he was a son of the house of Ptolemy Child. Her anger finally flooded to the surface.

"Have you got over your little troubles, Aulus? Don't you think that you should go back home and check that your house is still in one piece? You don't want anything stolen do you? The colourmen might get in. They'd clear the property quickly—overnight in fact."

Aulus saw the look in Ella's eye.

"I'll go back when I'm ready to."

Forgetting Loli, Ella rushed downstairs to find her father. Ptolemy was in the middle of supervising the lifting of the wooden sarcophagus onto rollers and then they would get it into the lift. It was the largest object that he'd put in it before, and he wondered if the steam-powered system that worked it could handle it.

Ella burst into the room. "Father, what is Aulus doing? How could you let him?

Ptolemy looked agitated. He swept his grey hair back from his forehead and didn't look up. "What do you mean, doing, Ella?"

"Aulus is wearing black."

"What of it?"

"But only sons and daughters wear black at such ceremonies."

"He is family, Ella."

"But he isn't your son, Father."

"He's your cousin."

"That doesn't make him your son."

"But a marriage between you would."

"A marriage between me and him—never, Father!"

"Ella. If you want to inherit, I'll have you do as I say."

She would not let her father see her cry. Ella held her tears back just long enough to throw a look of sheer hatred at him and left. It was only when she was halfway up the stairs that she thought about what Aulus and she had done—would do again. He was her cousin...there had been a rumour once that he was her brother. She went back to her room to finish getting ready. In the process of buttoning her jacket she buttoned down her feelings, again, too.

Ella wished Aulus and her father dead. She thought again of Loli, the one person in the family she truly loved. Then there was Swin, too, of course. After searching the house for Loli, Ella sat down on her bed, and finally burst into tears. On their bed she found the Eye of Horus pendant. Loli must have run away again, not wanting to be a part of the ceremony. Ella would have to go alone with Aulus, and her father, and she hoped that it would be over quickly so that she could look for her sister. Ella looked down at Aulus from her window. He was sitting on the first black horse and joking with her father. When he saw her looking down at her he waved. Ella backed away from the window and repaired her make-up. The black kohl had run and she quickly wiped it off with a cloth. As she picked the eye pencil up she thought about her future. She smoothed back her blonde hair, went to the window again and waved, trying to attract the attention of her father.

Clovis donned the royal robes of office. He was Governor General in waiting and would soon be known as Governor General Clovis Domitius Corbulo when Claudius Ptolemaeus Tiberius was entombed. It couldn't happen quickly enough for him. It was a shame that the Empress Cleopatra was going home as soon as possible. Soon he would get a new coin in circulation in Britanniae with himself on it and have the statues of Claudius Ptolemaeus Tiberius torn down. There would be many more statues of Clovis than that of the old governor, who Clovis had considered to be weak-willed and dull. Custom dictated that when the old Governor General was entombed after the forty days of preparation a new Governor General would be sworn in that same day, and he had been looking forward to that for so long. The royal vestments suited him well. Conforming to tradition, he wore a full-length purple tunic with trousers of the same colour underneath, for warmth. He would put on later a black cloak over the top for the same reason.

His short black hair was meticulously combed, and on his chest, on top of the tunic, he wore a large gold disc studded with precious stones. He had banished all the servants from upper rooms in the palace. Although this day was the most important of his life, he wanted to be alone.

It was then time to leave for the temple and tomb of Claudius

Ptolemaeus Tiberius. Clovis had his own royal carriage and would travel by himself. His carriage was pulled by four white horses from Spain, rare and quite beautiful, their harnesses trimmed with gold. Clovis, as usual, was pleased with himself. He waved to the citizens and they cheered; those paid to do so. He waved back as the carriage proceeded down Via Lorenzo. High above him a falcon circled. No one took any notice.

Cleopatra headed the procession in an open carriage. She thought more about her choice of Clovis as Governor General. Claudius Ptolemaeus Tiberius had been well liked by the people and Cleopatra had seen no reason to replace him whilst he was alive. It had only been in the last years that food supplies had become scarce and the population restless, terrified of the plague. That last summer had been the latest of a series of bad summers, more rain again, and the grain crops had suffered once more. Farmland at low level had been swamped and had yielded little, and then there were even more cases of the plague.

After Cleopatra and Clovis' carriages there came the representatives of the legions, headed by Gaius on horseback, with his war dog by his side. Gaius wore the light ceremonial amour so that it was easier to control the horse. Behind him there came the Legio III, the legion famous for its victory against the Parthians, two thousand years ago. Then behind that legion, the Legio IV, formed at the same time. Julius Caesar had levied them against Pompey at Dyrrhachium and Pharsalus in Greece. Pompey's army had suffered two thousand casualties and Caesar only twenty. X Equestris. The gold of the harnesses shining brightly in the winter sun. On the helmet of the aquilifer was an animal head—a bear. This Roman soldier carried the symbol of Rome, which was usually taken into battle, but was used in other parades, symbolising the strength of the empire, and to remind the provinces who ruled.

The sarcophagus, once at the place of entombment, would be placed inside a larger, marble one, which had been beautifully decorated by the artist, Swin. A dozen wailing women followed close behind, tearing at their hair, and howling to the somber sky. Not one tear was shed by anyone in the sparse, silent crowd. In fact, some cheered, but were hastily silenced by their friends or relatives. It seemed they had all come out of simple curiosity. Most had never seen their Empress and if recent past history was anything to go by, they would never see her again.

Only Cleopatra, Clovis, the close family of Claudius Ptolemaeus Tiberius and the embalmer family were allowed into the tomb. As the steam-driven equipment struggled to move the marble lid of the sarcophagus into place, the Empress said a few words. Cleopatra, covered in a finely embroidered cloak of deep saffron, raised her hand for silence. She also wore the pschent, the double crown incorporating the red deshret crown of Lower Egypt and the white hedjet crown of Upper Egypt.

"Sleep now noble Claudius Ptolemaeus Tiberius, you have served me well. May Isis receive your soul for judgement and that you pass safely to the fields of Aaru to be with your ancestors. Isis will watch over you with her sister, Nepythys, her supporter, and Anubis will weigh your heart. *The Book of the Dead* will guide you to safety. Rest assured, Claudius: you will have eternal life."

Clovis suppressed a laugh. He wanted his eternal life on earth. He doubted if he'd ever believed in an afterlife, although it had suited his purposes perfectly. His Queen, his Empress, believed in the supernatural, the promise of life eternal. He would go along with it for now.

Cleopatra looked intently at the richly decorated chamber. Her eyes fell upon a particular set of hieroglyphs on a wall. She knew what they meant, had seen them many times in many temples around the world. But they held more meaning for her now. She had first encountered them in her childhood in Alexandria. Royal children were sent there to be schooled in the great library and then back to Rome where Latin was commonly used. The hieroglyphs: a cobra crowned with the headdress of Isis. Isis-Thermouthis: cobra-goddess, guardian of the Pharaoh alongside the mother, Wadjet; the woman with the cobra's head. Cleopatra shivered. After the ceremony she hardly remembered what she had said. Her astonished scribe reminded her. It was unusual for the words to be changed from the readings in the *Book of the Dead*, but Cleopatra had insisted, and spoke as if in a trance. She had pleaded with the goddess on her own behalf.

"All hail Isis-Thermouthis. Serpent goddess of the field, protect me now and in the afterlife. Fight my enemies and vanquish them to the dust. Assure me of my rightful place beside you in eternity and continue to secure my position on earth." Cleopatra had said nothing more of Claudius Ptolemaeus Tiberius.

The steam pumps were working flat out at the palace. All the rooms were heated to practically subtropical temperatures. Exotic, cobalt blue birds fluttered around the throne of Cleopatra. A throne backed by dozens of peacock feathers framed her. Her gold sheath dress was studded with rubies and sapphires. Empress of most of the world, she dressed in the style of her illustrious ancestor—the Cleopatra, revered above all, dead these last two thousand years. Clovis knelt before her descendant. Again, traditionally, male nobles wore almost the same clothing as Mark Anthony would have worn when he was made emperor of Rome and the ancient world. Clovis wore the toga picta: purple, embroidered and decorated with gold. The robe might have been traditionally Roman, but his crown was Egyptian. Clovis kissed her hand. She drew it away quickly, thinking that he had grown even more repulsive since the last time she had seen him, and that had been a very long time ago. Sweat poured down his brow and he had one more double chin than she remembered. No. She would never marry Clovis.

All through the banquet that followed Gaius ate little and watched anxiously to see that Cleopatra ate what Clovis did. Gaius doubted that Clovis would do something as obvious as poisoning her there before the other nobles, and yet what could anyone do if he did? On looking around, he wondered if those present might be divided—some would be for Cleopatra…others, paid off by Clovis on a promise of more power.

One of Cleopatra's informants had brought news that Clovis' legions had moved camp from the south and were making their way north. Perhaps Clovis was getting too ambitious. Cleopatra made her excuses and left quickly after the banquet. She complained that she was ill and needed to get back to *The Alexander*. She thought that she had made a mistake in allowing Clovis to have power. Gaius had been right. Julia was dead from a bullet meant for Cleopatra, and the sooner she left and had Gaius raise a fully equipped and trained army, the better. She also wondered if what was happening to the dead in Manceastre was happening in the rest of the empire?

The image of the tarot card, The Judgement, The Awakening of the Dead, had said it all. It had upon it the depiction of a spirit blowing upon a trumpet over a half-open tomb. Rising from the tomb was a man, a woman, and a child, half-wrapped in the bandages used in mummification. Tjuya Meresamun's words haunted her constantly. *"It means the end of all things good and evil—a time of punishment or reward."*

Chapter 11

Since she killed Isis, Nepythys had also realised that she had become a little weaker. Perhaps it was because she had killed Isis she was losing her power? She tried to push that thought out of her head. Anubis and Nepythys both went through the false door this time to find Isis, Horus and Loli. In the real world the gods could look human enough. Anubis: without the jackal's head. Nepythys: a young woman but of no real determinate age.

Nepythys and Anubis found an inn down by the ship canal. They paid for a room and talked long into the night about how they would find the body of Isis, and somehow get their strength back.

"This has to do with her death. We are as mere mortals all the time now, no strength—powerless. We have to find Isis. Find out where Horus and the girl have taken her, and work out just what is going on."

Anubis looked at his mother. "Perhaps the old stories are true. How did we become as we are? Who was the first? Whoever made us what we are, gave us power, has simply taken it away. Perhaps we have had our time. We have fought amongst ourselves. Gods killed by gods. Whoever made us might just have had enough. We have killed ourselves off, anyway. With the death of Isis, patience has finally run out, and we have been left to die like mortals."

"You are such a fool, Anubis. There are only a few of us left. How can there be a greater power than us?"

Anubis became irritable. "To put it bluntly, from the Latin futuere, or using the common vernacular of the last few hundred years—fuck off!"

"You know, I'm surprised that we haven't killed each other by now. Would that same mouth kiss your mother?"

They both laughed. Anubis grabbed his mother by the waist. He still had some strength in him.

"Aut futue, aut pugnemus—either fuck me, or let's fight," said Nepythys.

~*~

In the temple of Isis the supplicants walked the pathway through the chamber of snakes. Honoured by the goddess, they had done this, unbitten, for thousands of years. One called Ati, a pale girl, hesitated on the way through. It was a banded cobra that reared its head and struck in her direction at her naked feet. The first time it missed but on the second strike it sunk its fangs into her ankle. The other priests refused to come to her aid. Sophia, upon hearing the girl's screams, made her way across the floor covered with snakes. The banded cobra reared once more and then sank low to the ground and slithered off. Other snakes took its place and struck at Sophia repeatedly, hissing and lying close to her feet in an attempt to block her way. Although sickened by the sight of the writhing serpents to her left, that heaved as if one mass, she took another step forward. At the end of the path, coming towards the young girl, was the largest snake of all. Sophia groped for the memory she had of this snake…someone had told her that it was fed goats by the priests. Sophia had difficulty in walking, her legs did not now work as they once did, but she ventured further. She was aware of the snakes' fangs, but then Sophia felt no pain. The giant vermilion snake slithered towards the terrified young priestess, who was already feeling the effects of the poison within her own body, and could hardly move. Finally Sophia made it to the girl. Not without some difficulty, she picked her up, and turned to go back on the perilous journey she had just made. Again the smaller, faster snakes threw themselves at her, biting and snapping at her feet and legs, but still she moved forward. When she got to the door the other priests opened it, hauled them both through and slammed the door on the snakes. Some of the priests were trying to comfort the young girl as they carried her away to attend to her wounds. Sophia looked down at the red-black swellings on her feet and legs, and then found a dark corner to sit and nurse her baby. It would be a long time before anyone ever ventured close to the snake-room again. The snakes in their anger, and then eventually their hunger, turned upon each other.

Clovis was very much aware that he thought he could do anything he wanted. It didn't matter to him if more people knew that the colourmen were now openly taking the undead away. People were demanding answers as to why the dead didn't die. As Clovis was getting ready for yet another celebration of his appointment as Governor General, which also took his mind off his immediate problems; two richly dressed people were ushered in to see him. They claimed that they were of noble birth and had come from the mother city of Rome.

"Why are you in Manceastre in winter? It is a terrible place at this time of year. Why now?"

"We have come to pay our respects, Governor General."

That pleased Clovis. He never tired of anyone visiting him and he needed new company. He had in the past made them stay.

"And besides, Governor General, I like winter," added the tall, charming woman before him, "the cold doesn't bother me much."

Clovis liked the look of them. "Stay for the celebrations then. I'm sure that you will enjoy yourselves."

He beckoned a slave to him. "Find room for them in the east wing. Not too far from me."

The woman called herself Nepythys, which made Clovis smile. A goddess indeed, and named after one. She was indeed beautiful and the man, even more so. He would allow them to stay. Clovis was happy. The wine was particularly palatable and he was in a good mood.

"Before you go—you say you came to pay your respects to me. Is that the only reason?"

Nepythys laughed. "I can see that you are a clever man, but even a clever man needs help to work out why the dead do not die."

"I am Nepythys."

Clovis looked her up and down and decided he might as well see where it all would lead.

"So, why do the dead not die?"

"I said I'd help you, but before I do I want you to strike off all the images of Isis from the walls and in the temples and replace them with mine. Dedicate all the old shrines to me. And in return, I'll help you find out what is going on." Nepythys almost said the next words as an afterthought, "I'll also help you get rid of Cleopatra. That is what you want, isn't it?"

"It's a trick. You'll get me to agree, say that I did, and return to Cleopatra. She'll have me killed."

"I won't do that Clovis. And although the dead walk, Isis is truly dead. I need to find her body."

Clovis had no idea why he should take anything of what she said seriously, but he felt compelled to go along with it. "I want to believe you. And I would have thought it obvious where the body of Isis has been taken, if she is Isis, which I don't believe for a minute she is—bloody obvious."

Nepythys looked at Anubis. If she were Loli or Horus, where would she take the body? To the Temple of Isis; of course. Nepythys put her hand on Clovis' arm. He liked the feelings that flooded through his body, and shivered a little.

She smiled warmly at him. "If you want to take power from Cleopatra, do it swiftly, without a second thought, whilst she is at her weakest. With me on your side, anything is possible. Whilst the city and her empire is at its weakest."

Clovis felt that he should have this woman on his side. He was also vain and mad enough to think that at last the nobility were on his side, and that would strengthen his case as the new emperor. Soon he would be rid of Cleopatra. In his next thought, he persuaded himself that there was perhaps something he didn't understand about life and death; perhaps magic could be used to extend life. Perhaps he could become immortal that way, instead of through science, and he should believe. Perhaps he would have a 'pure' race. He hadn't made his mind up yet on any of his bizarre plans, but through them he thought that the new world he would create would be a wonderful place.

"I'll think about what you have told me, meanwhile I'd like to have you close by me." Clovis smiled.

Nepythys could see that he liked her. She wouldn't be too bothered about getting very close to him whilst she worked out what she was going to do next.

Cryogenics had become slightly boring to him. He knew that the other distraction was more fun. He couldn't wait to use it again. As he ambled off to bed he chuckled to himself and thought about what the two strangers had said. Still, it could be possible that gods walked the earth in mortal form—he hadn't believed before, but why not? He loved his life so much he didn't want to leave it. His world had a little more to offer now than the realm of the dead. With that, he laughed out loud as he climbed, fully dressed, into bed. He thought about who he could put inside the brass bull, and dreamed of all the people he would like to put in it. All his family were dead, he was the only one left, and he was happy with that. Happy he was Governor General; happy he had wealth. The only thing he needed was a wife, but with what science could achieve, why would he need to? Clovis laughed in his sleep. Perhaps he could copy himself, and then he would be a god and have tiny gods: little miniatures of himself. Oh, how he would adore that.

Clovis woke up suddenly…he was now too excited to sleep. He rose from his bed and walked down one of the marble corridors of his palace. He looked up at the giant, pink marble statues of the old deities he had never really bothered about, turned his head away quickly and went into a side room full of books, maps and a large bronze table engraved with the whole of the empire upon it. He was delighted with himself, the woman who said she was a goddess, and the brass, brazen bull. He was like a child with new toys to play with. Into the early hours of the morning he thought about how magnificent his new empire would be.

Clovis eventually fell asleep in a chair, his hands placed firmly on the arms, as if to keep himself steady. He awoke with a start when someone coughed close by. It was a slave who looked rather nervous. He had told the slaves that if any of the archaeologists had news of the translation of *The Pyramid Texts* he wanted to know immediately. But, on some days he seemed to forget that and fly into a rage at being disturbed. On those days, he had the slaves flogged for giving him the news he had asked for.

"Well! What is it?"

"Gaston Maspero has something he wants to show you."

Gaston Maspero was one of the archaeologists that Clovis had a fondness for. He disliked the others.

"Where is he?"

"In the room next door."

"Well, bring him in here."

It was not long before the slave returned with the archaeologist.

"Have you found something, Gaston?"

The man smiled and placed the parchment on the table. He pulled four books down from the shelves, blew the dust off them, and started to place them on each corner of the old document.

"Is it worth my time?"

"I think so. It's all interesting to me, but I don't know if you will find it so."

Gaston pointed to the papers. "See this, the cartouche of Unis or Unas, the great Pharaoh? This was written over four thousand years ago. Here is my translation." Gaston handed Clovis one of the papers. "I've called it the Cannibal Hymn."

For Pharaoh is the great power that overpowers the powers.
Pharaoh is a sacred image, the most sacred image

of the sacred images of the great one.
Whom he finds in his way, him he devours bit by bit.

"And here…"

The King is the Bull of the sky,
Who conquers at will,
Who lives on the being of every god,
Who eats their entrails,
Even of those who come with their bodies full of magic
From the Island of Flame.

Clovis became very excited at this point. "Are you saying that they believed that if you consumed a god you would become one?"

The archaeologist laughed. "No, I'm not saying that. I'm saying that they *might* have believed that. And there is evidence that the very early Egyptians did perform cannibalism."

"Where is your proof?"

"Well we know that in times of famine it happened. They certainly sacrificed for the Predynastic burials in the south of Egypt, dated to the Naqada II period, five thousand years ago. Also, human sacrifice was not only performed at Abtu, but at Saqqara too."

"I'm more interested in what you said about the gods at the moment. Tell me more about that."

Maspero pulled some parchments out from under some others before him.

On that day of slaying the Oldest Ones.
The King is a possessor of offerings who knots the cord
And who himself prepares his meal;
The King is one who eats men and lives on the gods

"The ancient Egyptians sacrificed bulls, too."

"Bulls you say?"

"Then there is the cult of Mithras where the ceremony of the tauroctony was central to the religious rites. Two thousand years ago, before the Isis cult became well established, Mithraism was popular with the Roman soldiers. But when Mark Anthony married the Egyptian Queen, Cleopatra…the rest, you know."

"All very interesting. I want to know all about that, but first tell me more about this Cannibal Hymn…"

Much later, Maspero left Clovis to his thoughts of what he could achieve without Cleopatra. He could declare himself a god if he could not become one. He might even announce that he was Mithras himself, but he would not kill bulls. No. He wouldn't do that.

Chapter 12

This time it was Swin who found Ella in the opium den. He'd heard of Loli's disappearance and was keen to help console Ella. The old woman indicated that Ella had only had a few pipes. Money exchanged hands and Swin took a pipe too. Ella sat slumped against a faded blue cushion. She looked up at him as he sat down on the mattress besides her.

"I looked for Loli as long as I could, Swin. I looked for hours in all the usual places. I even went into the catacombs, checked the locks and seals on some of the doors. Nothing. Father sent the slaves all over Manceastre. We always let her do what she wanted. We didn't find anything. I need to go back out now..."

"You need to get something to eat and get warm, Ella. Let me take you home. In the morning, Ella, we'll search again. It's been two days since her disappearance and you haven't rested at all. In the morning we'll look again together. I'll go down by the river and ask around the warehouses. She might have been seen."

"Oh Swin, you don't think she's fallen in under the ice do you? If she has, she'd be swept away."

"I don't know, Ella. Until we get any word we can always hope that she's alive."

"It's my fault, Swin. I haven't spent any time with her recently. I've been caught up with other things—with other people."

Swin put his arm around her. "I know Ella, and one of them has been me. I feel bad about that, too, but I'm going to change. I'm going to spend less time in this place and rebuild my life again. I promise."

"Tell me you'll start painting again, Swin?"

"Yes."

Ella was sleepy and lay back on the mattress. "Swin?"

"Yes."

"You do know that if I kept a secret from you, I'd have a very good reason to, don't you?"

Swin was puzzled. "Yes, Ella."

"It is a terrible secret. A secret that you might never forgive me for not telling you."

"It can't be that bad."

"Oh yes, Swin. It can." A tear fell from the corner of Ella's eye before she succumbed to sleep.

Once outside the house, Loli made for Langsoon and the opium den, too. The old woman wouldn't let her in, but the front door hadn't slammed shut as it usually did, and Loli sneaked in when the old woman's back was turned, as she was filling a pipe for someone. Ella had told her all about the den, but had never admitted going there herself. She had told Loli of Swin's addiction, but not of her own. Loli couldn't see why Ella hid it from her. She was trying to set a good example she supposed.

Loli kept to the shadows and peeped into each of the rooms, although it was difficult to see, and the smell was awful. She found them in the fourth room, just as the smoke was making her feel queasy. Loli smiled down at Ella and Swin. Ella opened her eyes and tried to focus.

"Ella," Loli said. Swin grumbled in his sleep.

Ella was suddenly quite taken out of her opium dream. "You've never been gone this long before, Loli. I've looked everywhere."

"Clearly."

"Well, up until last night. I was so tired."

Loli looked around the dismal room. "I'm hungry, Ella. Let's go back to the house and see father. He must be worried."

"Probably not as worried as I was," said Ella.

Ella struggled to her feet and got off the mattress. She hugged Loli tight and drew her towards the door.

"Aren't you forgetting someone?" said Loli.

Ella remembered Swin. "Swin, move yourself!"

"Huh? What? Loli? Good to see you…must sleep," he muttered.

The old Chinese woman gave Loli a disparaging look and offered Ella a bowl of water to wash Swin's face. She handed her a small towel.

Loli insisted that there was someone she needed to help, and that they would have to pick him up from her father's house. Ella was too sleepy to argue and Swin agreed to take a look at this person and decide whether he could stay at his house for a day or two but only after Loli began to cry.

They called in at the Ptolemy house and thankfully, to Loli's relief, Horus was still where she had left him, and there was no sign of her father. Ella tried to remain patient with Loli.

"Who's this?"

"I'll tell you later. You'll have trouble believing the half of it, but it is all true, Ella. All true."

To anyone in the street it just looked like they were all drunks, although with a child, which one or two raised an eyebrow at, making their way home from a heavy drinking session. Not that anyone really cared, anyway.

Once inside Swin's home, they helped Horus over to the couch. Ella seemed more herself and kept on staring at the stranger.

Loli stared too. He had a fever and looked pale. How could a god be so ill? Surely they were beyond what afflicted mortals? He was helpless in the underworld and now here, too.

Loli told Ella and Swin everything in great detail. They shook their heads, looked at Horus, and then back at Loli.

"I didn't think that gods could be so weak."

"I didn't think a goddess could die, before I saw it with my own eyes."

"What did you really see, Loli?"

"I saw Isis, dead." Ella shook her head, not understanding.

"Could you be ill, Loli? A fever, too?" Ella constantly worried about the plague.

"Are you mad, Loli? Isis? She has only appeared to the descendants of the first Cleopatra...."

"Horus said she is Isis."

"And we are to believe that this is Horus?"

"Yes."

"He told me gods have lived amongst us from time to time."

"Why would they want to?"

"Why not? Believe me, Ella, the underworld is no holiday. What is the point of eternity if you have to stay there?"

"You expect us to believe that this boy is a god? No offence, but I've no reason to believe you are who you say you are," said Ella to Horus.

Horus sighed. "Fine."

Loli looked around the room, saw some canvasses under cloths, and peeped beneath one. Swin had his back to her. The first was one of Sophia before she was pregnant, in a green spring dress, all life and colour. She quickly put the cloth down and turned to the other beside it. She only took a glance before Swin noticed.

"Loli...don't." Swin had turned from trying to move drawings around the room.

"You didn't see it, did you? I don't like anyone to look at my paintings until they are finished."

"No."

Loli lied. She'd seen all right, and she was puzzled by what she saw. It was a snake-headed woman.

Oblivious to the cold, Ella went out for some food from the Temple Inn. Staple food: just some stew and dumplings that she was able to reheat upon an old range in the kitchen. Horus refused to eat. It took a while, but soon the place felt warmer, and the rooms too. They were all tired, but except for Horus they ate anyway, in silence. Ella refused to believe that the young boy who sat by her side was a god. He looked, well, too human. Loli insisted that he was Horus. Soon, this Horus lay fast asleep, breathing deeply beneath the blanket.

Impossible, thought Ella. She liked his manner, though. He was easygoing and looked thoughtful. So unlike Aulus, and more like Swin in some ways. How could this boy be a god? Utterly ridiculous. They all had been brought up to believe in the splendour of the gods. That you would be awestruck in their presence. Ella sniffed. All she felt was the first signs of a cold coming on. Just where had Loli been for the last two days? She had blood all over her dress, but no cuts. And she still insisted that the boy was a god. Had Loli experienced some sort of breakdown? Could a child have a breakdown? Ella thought that she shouldn't have left Loli with Sophia's baby, a baby that would not truly die, or the mother for that matter. That, alone, would be enough to tip anyone over the edge.

Horus had one couch, Loli another. When they were both tucked up in blankets and asleep, Ella and Swin went to his bedroom together. They undressed in silence and got into bed. Swin was far from sleepy, and as he gently cupped Ella's face in is hands, as he kissed her, Ella closed her eyes and could only see the pale face of Sophia staring at her with dead eyes. Ella had finally got what she wanted, but all her hopes were in ruins because Sophia and the baby, who were not truly dead, haunted her. Ella hadn't told Swin about them. She hadn't known how to, and now she certainly didn't want to. She did what she had desired to do for a long time, but there was little pleasure in it for her. Soon Swin was asleep, too, no doubt disappointed by her lack of passion. And when she slept, the visions of decay and death filled her mind, and would not be vanquished. Swin turned in his sleep and put his arm around her. Ella awoke and thought she saw something move quickly away in the room. She couldn't sleep for the rest of that night, and she knew there would never be any chance of peace unless she told Swin of his family.

Loli didn't know what to do. If Ella didn't believe her about Horus, how could she possibly believe her about Isis? When they had all slept, well, some more than others, they discussed what they were going to do about Horus.

"He isn't our responsibility."

"He hasn't got a place to stay."

"I don't understand and I've had quite enough of hearing about gods appearing as men."

"Why can't that be?"

"Why would it? Who would want to be mortal when they have all that power? It's rubbish, Loli. Look at him; he's clearly a boy."

"What's the matter with you, Ella? Why are you so angry? I can't help it if Anubis took me away."

"Anubis. The gods do not kidnap children in the middle of the night, Loli. Men do." Ella was thinking of how much she despised Aulus.

There was no change in the expression on Loli's questioning face. Then she suddenly started shouting at Ella. "He is Horus. It was Anubis. Isis is at home."

Ella took a deep breath. Through all this Horus said not a word, just looked up at Ella now and again and shrugged. Ella shook her head.

"Are you still insisting that he is Horus?"

"I am. Well. What if I show you the dead body of Isis? Then perhaps you will believe me?"

"Why would that make me believe? Where is she then?"

"In the cabinets."

"At home?"

"I don't know of any other cabinets."

"Swin, can he…" Ella pointed at Horus but couldn't bring herself to say his name.

"Can he stay here with you whilst I go with Loli?"

"Yes. He can stay. I'll get him something to eat. You do eat, don't you?" Swin half-smiled at the stranger, who smiled and nodded in return.

Loli put on her coat and followed Ella out of the door.

As they left, the colourmen followed. The name was ironic. They were in fact colourless. Pale men in long black coats who usually huddled together in doorways in the artists' quarter looking for a deal to be struck, or something to take to Clovis, or news of a mummy that was at least a few decades old. They were always on the lookout for the living dead for

Clovis that wouldn't be too difficult to smuggle away. One colourman slipped on the ice as they followed the girls down the street. The other did nothing to help him retrieve his footing. Another of the colourmen looked up at one skyscraper in particular. One where he could see faces pressed against the window, and he wondered just how many families were hiding their dead.

Ella knew the colourmen were following, but Ella and Loli were acting innocently enough just walking back to their own home. She knew that people dealt with them to buy paint, the pigment called Egyptian mummy, and although Loli had told her that all the other colours didn't come from a body recently dead, she wasn't sure about that. She wasn't sure about anything anymore. Her relationship with Swin was what she wanted, but the horror of knowing that Sophia and the baby were still partly alive...Aulus was untrustworthy, but there was something about him that she was drawn to, and she had no idea what that was. And now the revelation that the gods were amongst them on earth. Horus was so weak—how could he possibly be a god?

Ella was relieved to find that their father wasn't home, which was nothing unusual, so they went directly down the stone steps to the cabinets. Ella was thinking about Sophia, and that perhaps the same would happen to this newly dead body. She was in the cabinet just as Loli had said; only Loli had neglected to say that Isis had been decapitated.

"I should have warned you about that, but we've seen worse." Loli was thinking about the time they had been given a body to put back together that had been injured by one of the steam trains. They had managed to cover up the worst of the damage with various materials and quite a lot of make-up, for a public viewing.

Loli carefully took the head out of the bloodied cloth. Ella felt suddenly saddened by the thought that the head once belonged to a beautiful woman.

Ella nodded. "I find this difficult sometimes, Loli. When I look at the dead I imagine them as we are now, thinking and feeling. I'm finding it hard to believe that she was a goddess."

Loli burst into tears.

"She is. Why can't you believe that she could be?"

"Shush, Loli. I'm sorry."

Sophia came to Ella's mind. She could believe the dead could walk again and perhaps she could be pushed to believe that the gods walked amongst them, but not that this was Isis. It was just too much.

"How can we make sure that the colourmen won't take her, and what about father if he hasn't seen her already?"

"The colourmen have taken from us before, but as you are so upset, Loli, we'll take her to the priests. If it is, or isn't Isis, they'll prepare her for burial.

"So, we'll take her to the Temple of Isis where Sophia and the baby are."

"Yes, Loli."

Loli closed the cabinet quietly. She didn't want Ella to shout at her, not now. Ella wondered why the woman Loli called Isis didn't show the slightest sign of reanimation, even the movement of a hand. Ella decided that they would go through the catacombs to get to the temple.

"You stay here, Loli. I'll get Swin and Horus to carry her."

"What if father comes back?"

"Make sure he doesn't come down here. He has no reason too. We haven't been asked to pick up a body all week. He won't come to the cabinets if no one has been brought in, but if he returns home, stay near the door upstairs and divert him with some reason, even if it means you leaving the house with him. Tell him you've been asked to go to a house or apartment to talk about embalming arrangements. Lie. Make an address up if you have to and go with him. Pretend it was a mistake when you can't find it, or when someone answers the door. Do anything, but give me an hour to get Swin and Horus back here, and the body out."

"She isn't a body, Ella. She's Isis …not just another body."

"Yes, Loli. Will you do what I just said?"

"I don't want to—you know how angry he will get with me."

"I need the time, Loli, to do the best by her. Understand?"

Loli nodded, "Yes, Ella. I'll do it."

Chapter 13

There were no starving children on the streets of Manceastre. The colourmen always grabbed them as the lay shivering in dark doorways, and carried them away for sale. No one ever seemed to report a missing child. Ella had been kind to one or two of the children. Ella, who had gone hungry occasionally to give her own supper to them, was becoming indifferent to their suffering. Out of the corner of her eye she thought she saw two colourmen carry a child off, near Yoldar Street, but she put the hood up over her lowered head and hurried off into the night. Ella was now so caught up in her own problems that she had no time for the plight of others—she had too much to worry about, Sophia, the baby and now this.

On her way out of the house, Ella bumped into Aulus. He was the last person she wanted to see at that moment. She needed to distract him.

"Aulus." Ella had no idea of what to say to him.

Aulus grabbed her by the arm. Ella winced, as he had his hand on top of recent bruises.

"I fail to recognise any enthusiasm for my company, Ella. You didn't seem all that excited the last time we met, either."

Ella pulled away from him. "Father isn't home again."

"Then, my sweet cousin—you will have to do, won't you."

"I don't want to, Aulus." Ella pushed him away.

"You really are warming to me these days, aren't you? I wouldn't get too excited. It all means nothing."

Ella was tired of sex with Aulus, disgusted too. His threats about Swin were what she constantly worried about. If he did tell the authorities, would they be bothered anyway? She wouldn't take that chance. She was tired of always trying to get rid of him by compliance. Taking her silence as consent he dragged her over to the alcove near the door. There was no way she was going to complain and take him into any rooms where he could fall asleep or dawdle about leaving. As he pulled up her skirt, she closed her eyes and tried to think of anything but Aulus. He was always excited enough. As he backed away, she briefly saw anger on his face, and then he pushed her back against the wall before slamming the door behind him. That is the last time ever, swore Ella—the very last time. If she got pregnant, she'd deal with it like she had done before, but she would never go near him again. She'd have to take the chance that he was bluffing over Swin.

It was just under an hour later that Ella could get back to the house with Swin and Horus. Loli ran up to her almost in tears. Swin was quiet and that was understandable, as he was thinking about his wife and child, who as far as he knew, were in a cabinet in the embalming chamber, so close by.

"You've been so long." cried Loli.

"I got there and back as quickly as I could, Loli. You go and get the small cart out from the side room, we'll use that."

The cabinet door made a slight grating sound as she opened it.

"You seem a little stronger now." Ella looked at Horus. He stepped back from the cabinet door as it opened.

Swin stared at the cabinets. Horrified.

Ella placed a hand on his arm. "Wait over there, Swin."

She had no time to hesitate now. Ella brought a box from one of the other rooms, partially filled with straw, and gently placed the head of Isis in it. Horus didn't move and he showed no emotion. Whatever he felt at that moment seemed to be bottled up deep inside him.

"I'll help Loli with the cart," she added.

It didn't take long to get the body on the cart, and with great effort they got it down into the catacombs, which led to the temple of Isis. They tried to get through the dark passageways as quickly as they could. Ella couldn't help feeling that something was watching them from the shadows; she thought she heard the sound of rubble, as if something was stumbling over it and then it stopped. She heard a sob.

"Quickly, we need to move more quickly."

"What was that sound?" said Loli.

"Nothing. Hurry up, Loli."

The boy hung back in the shadows and reached out. Loli thought she saw a movement.

"Ella."

"Come on, Loli." Ella grabbed Loli's hand and pulled her along.

Ella was thinking about Swin. As soon as they got to the temple she would send Swin away, and she was trying to think of a good reason why she should, so he wouldn't find out about Sophia and the child.

Once at the entrance, the same priest opened the door that had let her in with Sophia and the baby. He looked surprised to see Ella again. After a moment or two of explanation he let them all in.

"The very last, I promise. I won't be bringing any more to you."

Ella turned to Swin. He looked tired and was slumped against a wall looking so exhausted. "Swin, we can manage from here. You need to go back and get some rest."

Swin nodded and looked back towards where the Ptolemy house was. "I'd rather go back through the street. There is no need for me to go back to your house, Ella."

"Of course, Swin," said Ella.

She asked the priest for Swin, and then they were led up some steps, through a passageway that led to another door that then exited to the street, well away from Sophia and the baby who lay in some dark corner of the temple.

Swin didn't want to go back through the catacombs to the Ptolemy house. He knew that Sophia and the baby were in Ptolemy Child's embalming parlour for the final forty days of the embalmment process. All those nights in the opium den when he should have faced up to what had happened. All that hiding from grief when he should have been thinking about them and mourning with some dignity. He'd been looked after by Ella. All he had left was the painting of Sophia when she was pregnant with their child, and numerous sketches of her when they had first met. He had loved to draw her, although she didn't readily keep still. In fact, the only time he could get her to sit still long enough was when she was heavy with child, and very tired.

The priest then led Ella, Loli and Horus to another room and told them to go in. Horus went in first, followed by the girls. The priests carried in the body of Isis. Ella gasped as she looked about the torchlit room. There were dozens of people there now: men, women and children. All looking to being in a state of desperation and only showing a few signs of decomposition, the grey colour of the body being one of them—the living dead, trapped in hell on earth. Some moaned and others cried. Most stared at their hands in silence. One woman faced the wall, not knowing who or what to do. A few hardly showed any signs of a life once lived at all.

Ella could hear a baby cry. Loli looked around her and moved closer to her sister, putting her hand on her arm. "There are so many of them."

The priest explained. "We are hiding them from the colourmen. All over the city they have been taking the dead away. These poor people are the ones that families have asked us to take in. The colourmen wouldn't dare come here. "

"Ella," said Loli. "I think I know the reason why these people aren't properly dead."

"And why is that Loli?"

"Because Isis isn't alive anymore. Think about it, Ella. If this is really Isis, and I'm saying she is, then perhaps the dead cannot pass over—somehow they cannot truly die. That would explain all this wouldn't it?"

"That can't be so, Loli."

"I think that she is right," said Horus. "My mother was a goddess. Her death might have caused this. Isis isn't ruled by the natural order of things; she is above all that and has lived for thousands of years, ensuring that the souls of the dead are saved for all eternity."

Loli spoke to Ella earnestly. "And she isn't like these people, Ella—you would have thought that she couldn't die but she has, and for her, her death is final for some reason. Couldn't it be that she is a goddess?"

"I'm finding it hard to believe."

"And yet you believe the dead can walk again, as you have seen?"

"Yes."

"Then for me, Ella, could you try to believe that this woman could be Isis? What would it take to get you to believe?"

The followers of Isis were trying to comfort the dead. Attempting to explain to them why they were the way they were. It was futile. The dead just stared at them. Ella couldn't understand why some of the undead were capable of understanding, even acting, as the theatre players did, but others showed no recognition of anything.

Two priests, heads bent together, were talking in excited voices. One looked up and then went across to speak to Horus, who still had the box in his arms. He looked at them blankly.

One priest came over to Ella. "The body you brought to us isn't moving. Even if the dead cannot walk, they move a little. There isn't the slightest movement as we've seen in the ones brought in by other people. She is different."

Horus was reluctant to let anyone look upon the face of his mother. His grief finally caught up with him and he held the box even tighter. The priest gently tried to persuade him, but he walked over to a corner away from them and sat on the floor, wondering what he could ever do to bring his mother back.

Ella put a hand on his shoulder and looked into his eyes. "You are staying here?"

"Yes. I'll help look after them all."

"And you?" he asked.

"I have no idea of what is going on, and no one to turn to for help except our father."

Loli joined them and caught Ella's words. "You can't tell him about Isis. What can he do?"

Loli looked surprised.

"For this, Loli, he might be just the right person to ask. He knows the ritual magic, Loli—he's even consented to teach me and has, a little. But I don't know what is going on, so I can't even begin to put it right. I don't know if he can or will, but he might be able to help."

Ella didn't mention Loli's dog, Juniper.

"Will? How do you know he will? Perhaps he won't care at all?"

"His life work has been preparing the dead for the afterlife, and now they can't pass over. I think he will help, Loli. I still don't believe she is Isis, but I really think that it is time to ask for his help. We have to try."

Loli looked unsure but she couldn't think of anything else to do. "If you say so, Ella."

A priestess finally persuaded Horus to let her look in the box. At first Horus resisted, but then he let her see. On looking down at the face before her the priestess let out a small gasp.

Ella still wasn't convinced when the priestess pointed out the distinct likeness of the face to the portrait that she held before her. The priestess didn't just have the very old portraits to go by; she had one of the goddess painted by the great, great, great grandfather of the present Cleopatra—when Isis wished to be seen.

"I tell you that it is she. This is Isis—the one who is all. You are a daughter of Ptolemy. I'd have thought you would have been the last person to lose faith in the goddess," said the priestess.

Ella didn't understand that last remark. The priestess knew full well that there were many non-believers now.

The young woman became even more insistent. "It is she. It is Isis."

With great reverence and care the followers of Isis moved her body into one of the upper chambers. Horus followed them. They chanted and cried as they washed the body of their goddess.

Ella finally told her father what had happened to Sophia and the baby. Ptolemy shook his head and said nothing. He became distracted and started to fumble through some old papers on his desk.

Loli tugged at his sleeve but he ignored her. "And the woman we brought back. She is the goddess. The dead cannot die, unless she is brought back. You do believe me, father?" She began to cry. She was tired, exhausted, and thought that her father wasn't making any effort at all to help.

It was Ella who ventured further. "If it is, father, wouldn't it explain why the dead do not cross over?"

Ptolemy looked up. "It would."

"Will you come to the temple and look?"

Ptolemy sat down in his chair and looked seriously at both his daughters. Loli had been crying and Ella looked exhausted. He gripped the arms of the chair and leant forward. Could it really be Isis? Isis dead? It was an outrageous idea, but he would go with them.

It took some time to get through the streets to the temple. They packed a strong leather bag with all that Ptolemy thought he would need, not least the *Scroll of Dedi,* although Ella thought it pretty useless, as it hadn't worked on the dog, and some other old dusty manuscripts. Ella had no wish to go through the filthy catacombs again, and they all knew that more of the living dead could be hidden away there, so they made their way through the snow-laden streets. It took ages, but they even managed to avoid the colourmen.

The priests didn't seem too surprised to see Ptolemy and hear what he had to say to them. They listened intently to what he wanted. A room was quickly prepared and the covered body of Isis placed upon a table before Ptolemy. He lifted up the white cover and stared intently at the body before him. The head had been placed at the neck, and a white piece of linen placed across there in an attempt to make the body look whole.

Ptolemy looked thoughtful. The gods had taken human form before. Could this be Isis?

A priest touched his arm. "Do you really believe that it could be her?"

To Ptolemy, the goddess, an Isis who had been destroyed, was unthinkable. "If it is her…"

"It is father. It is…" said Loli.

"If it is, don't you think that if I could put this right I would? All my life I have believed in life after death. I have believed in Isis."

As their father continued to look upon the face of the woman Loli pulled Ella a little distance away. "I never told Swin about the baby, Ella."

"Good girl. I know." Ella looked clearly troubled, but needed to get Swin out of her mind for the moment. "Father—the ritual you showed to me?"

Ptolemy laughed. "You saw what happened there. A silly piece of magic that didn't work. I very much doubt that it would work this time, too."

"Why not? Will you try?"

"It won't work, Ella. This is so much more important—different."

Ptolemy looked at Loli and Horus, whom he hardly had given a thought to until now.

"For what I need to do I need to be alone, except for Ella."

The priests acquiesced, escorted Loli and Horus away, and left Ptolemy with Ella.

Ptolemy rummaged through his bag and took out the various scrolls. He looked unusually frustrated. "It's all useless, Ella. For what we have to do, I don't have the knowledge."

The door behind Ptolemy creaked a little, and he turned to see who would dare to come back. Amazed and dumbstruck, Ptolemy stared into the face of Anubis himself. He wore the jackal-head and towered above mere mortal men. For a very long time, Ptolemy had wondered if the gods would return, and now it had happened. Ptolemy lost his balance and staggered back towards the table, with a protective arm holding Ella back.

"I'd have thought that you might at least have waited for me," said Anubis.

Nepythys stood behind him, a hand around her son's waist. The colourmen also entered the room—six of them, all carrying guns. Nepythys looked at them and then pointed to the body of Isis.

"Take the body."

Two of them clumsily picked her up and Ella shouted at them for being so rough. The colourmen just laughed as a third picked up the head, the long black hair, covered in blood, almost trailed on the floor.

"What about them?" said a colourman.

"Just bring Ptolemy and put the scrolls in the bag. The others are nothing to us," said Nepythys.

There was no living human being that would dare to challenge the jackal-headed god. As they left, the priests fell to their knees before him. The colourmen carried Isis, and another pulled Ptolemy along roughly by the arm. The priests knew that they could not do anything. Nepythys felt her strength leave her again. And when Anubis left the temple, he changed back to his mortal form. As he did so he fell to the floor, much weakened by the transformation. Nepythys held him in her arms.

"You should never have killed Isis. This could be the end for us, too."

"No. We will regain our power. Once Isis is restored, so will we be. And then I'll have to think what to do then."

"She'll want revenge."

"I know," said Nepythys. She placed her hand on his cheek and tried, at that moment, not to think of the consequences of what she had done.

Once Anubis and Nepythys had left, the priests ran to see if Ella, Loli and Horus were still alive. Ella reassured them that they were unharmed. Some of the priests fell to their knees again and wept openly. They prayed for the immediate return of their goddess. Ella had nothing to say to them.

Before she left, Ella checked on Sophia and the baby. They looked the same as the last time she had seen them. Sophia was sitting on a bench with the child in her arms, rocking to and fro. She wondered what thoughts drifted through Sophia's mind now, if any. Was she thinking of Swin? Ella put such thoughts out of her head. It was her father's safety that concerned Ella more, now.

Swin spent the rest of the day in the opium den. It was there, amongst the wandering dragons of smoke that he realised he had lied to himself for too long, and that Sophia and the baby had escaped the suffering of becoming the living dead. For many days the opium had eased his grief, but then frightening visions came with the pipe. He saw Sophia holding his child, wandering the city looking for him, calling his name. The visions came, and always in the strangest shades of blue. In the violet darkness, they would come to him with their cobalt blue eyes and cyan skin. The colour of death to him. It's all my fault, Swin thought to himself in one moment of lucidity—I should have looked after them more. When the Chinese woman offered him one more pipe, he dashed it from her hand and left the foul smelling opium den. Ella had been too quick to get rid of him earlier. He now knew where he would find Sophia; not at the Ptolemy house, but in the temple of Isis.

Once inside the temple, Swin leant unsteadily against the archway and looked at the pitiful sight before him. He had to make himself look at the decrepit elderly woman who should have been dead by now, and the diseased child who was curled up in a ball of rags. The man who had his ribs crushed by a wagon, but still he lived. So much pain and suffering, Swin lowered his head, ashamed to stare. He could not bear to see, and the smell was unbearable. As he turned and picked his way through the undead, he felt a cold hand touch his. He drew it away quickly. He looked down, and there was Sophia with the baby clutched to her chest. Swin gasped and cried out. Sophia spoke his name and tried to touch him again. He crouched down low. It was the first time he had seen the baby. A tiny thing with his hair colour, but the grey of her skin caused revulsion within him that he was ashamed of.

"Swin. Help us from this. Do what you can. She suffers, as do I." His wife could hardly talk. Swin tried to be strong.

"Sophia. When you and the baby died, I lost everything. Life has been almost impossible without you."

"We've missed you so. Help us, Swin. Save us from this hell."

The man with the crushed ribs crawled towards him and grabbed hold of his arm. The elderly woman stared at him through milky eyes, and Swin knew that he could stay no longer. Perhaps he thought about the consequences of his next action, perhaps it never crossed his mind. With tears in his eyes, he held his wife and child to him briefly, and then fled the temple, tripping up over the rag child. He heard it cry out. Was it in pain? How could the dead feel? Perhaps the sensations returned from time to time and they remembered what it was to have been human. Something had their souls trapped in their withering bodies like shrivelled leaves, waiting for the wind to crumble them to dust.

Swin rose to leave, and Sophia tried to grab hold of his hand.

"I will come back."

He left quickly, and with a determined stride, returned to the opium den.

When Ella did not find Swin at his house she looked in the first place she knew Swin frequented, and that was, indeed, the opium den. The Chinese woman took her up the stairs and never said a word to her about him; just silently opened a door and frowned. Ella saw Swin, hanging from a beam. She fell to the floor and sobbed, "I'm so sorry Swin…so very sorry. She could see that he was dead by just looking at his face.

The Chinese woman looked nervous and afraid, "I didn't know that he would do this. I couldn't know." The woman explained how he had come to the opium den and sat down with her, chatting about his wife for a while. He had quietly and patiently lit a pipe; he had five in all, so the old woman said. Then he got up, and she thought he had left. It was only when she went into a back room for a spare mattress that she had found Swin hanging from a beam. He must have climbed up on a high window ledge, wound some rope around the beam, and silently slipped to his death without a sound.

Ella had the body cut down and asked the proprietor of the opium den to borrow a cart and two men to help with the body. This she was more than willing to do, to get the body off the premises. She didn't want the authorities informed. It would be bad for business too—very bad. Ella had the body taken to her house. As she walked by the side of the cart, she thought she saw Swin move. He had been covered with a blanket and she knew that, if watching the others was anything to go by, that he would rise from the dead soon.

They all knew what must happen next. Within a few hours of dying, Swin stirred. His arms and legs hadn't stiffened too much at all. There were deep dark circles under his bloodshot eyes, and he looked up at Ella. Ella had him back. That was all that mattered to her at that moment.

Swin couldn't speak at first and indicated that he wanted to write.

Paper and a pen were given to him and even though he was weak he managed to write with a shaking hand.

"I left her, Ella. When she wanted me most, I turned my back on her and the baby, and ran from that place. Take me to the temple. Let me at least be with them now."

Ella couldn't stop crying. She kept on apologising to Swin over and over again.

"It's me who doesn't deserve to live," she said.

Swin wrote something more, "You can't be held responsible for this, Ella. It was my choice. My guilt." He put his head back. The terrible rope burns on his neck were in full view. He held Ella's hand and pressed it gently.

Sophia let out a small cry when she saw him. Swin took his newborn child in his arms, and cried. The blue bruises on the baby's grey skin reminded him of the colour of the irises he had so loved to paint as a child.

"This has to end," said Ella, "to be done with."

Ella looked at the family before her. Sophia stared at Ella. Sophia tried to reach for a memory that escaped her again. She kept on crying and looking up at Ella, then at Swin. She couldn't know, could she? thought Ella. Sophia had never known about what had happened. Sophia tried so hard to remember, but the images in her head kept fading away. Ella looked away and cried again, because she loved Swin and she felt so sorry for Sophia. Ella cried for the suffering that the family had endured, and she was determined that she would do everything she could to put it all right. It all began, and would end, with Isis. Ella rose from the cold stone floor, turned away, and left Swin and his family to their grief.

Sophia gazed upon her husband's face and found the memory she had been searching for. She recalled the street where it happened, the shadowy figure before her, and then the pain hit her with such force that she cried out loud. She had remembered who had taken her life.

When Loli was finally asleep in the large bed, Ella left the room they usually shared and sought the small bedroom off the main corridor where she usually stole away to—to be alone. She kept some opium there, too. Ella then took far too much of it. She drank wine with it, too. She cursed herself, tossed and turned on her bed, crying one moment and then staring blankly into the corner the next. Aulus quietly entered the room. When she saw him she started to cry again.

Her skin looked violet under the eyes…heavy-lidded. "I've always despised you, Aulus, but now, perhaps not so much. I'm far worse than you."

"I doubt it Ella. I've done some terrible things."

"We are probably well suited. I'll never marry you, though. You know that, don't you?

"I know that, Ella."

"We might have been a good match. I've done something terrible."

"What do you mean?"

Ella rolled on her side and started to sob. "It's my fault, you know. Swin didn't kill them. I can't understand why you would accuse him, and use blackmail towards me. You know he didn't do it."

"I know that, too, Ella. I made it all up, and I regret that now."

"But why are you so sure that he didn't?" said Aulus.

"It was me. I killed them." Ella buried her face into the pillow. Aulus put out his hand as if to touch her shoulder. He then drew it away.

"You aren't capable of such an act."

"I am. I am." Ella started to cry again. Aulus could hardly hear her words. Suddenly, she sat up. Her blonde hair hung limp and wet from the tears by the side of her pale face.

"Why was she out that night? She should never have been out that night," said Ella.

Aulus tried to calm her down. She gulped for breath.

"I was coming from Memphis Square. Someone followed me. I was afraid—afraid of the plague, and afraid of who was there. It was very dark. Someone stepped out of the shadows in front of me and grabbed my hand.

My other hand was on the gun in my pocket. I couldn't see the face…I panicked, took the gun from my pocket and shot her. She must have found out that I loved Swin…and was trying to talk to me…"

Ella started crying once more.

"Ella, calm yourself. You didn't mean to kill her. It was an accident."

"I didn't tell Swin. She's dead because of me. He cannot bear the sorrow and now the guilt is eating away at me. How could I have done it…and the baby? It isn't over, even now. Swin never loved me."

"I think that you can never force someone to love you, Ella. I think of all people, I have learnt that."

She had difficulty in sitting up. Aulus helped her. Ella held her stomach tightly and was sick over the bedspread. "I'm sorry, so sorry for everything. I really want to die."

"Sit there, Ella. Don't move. I'll get some towels. Don't lie down."

Aulus found a bowl in the bathroom. He filled it with some water and picked up a towel. As he re-entered the room he saw Ella at the chest of drawers, fumbling through some things. By the light of the kerosene lamp he could see quite plainly what it was when she pulled it out. Instantly, he dropped the bowl which fell to the floor with a loud crash. He grabbed her hand that held the gun.

"That isn't the answer Ella. Think of Loli!"

"But I can't carry on like this…"

"What would it do to Loli if you killed yourself?"

"What would it do to her if she found out what I did?"

"There are reasons why some things never come to light, Ella. All families have the darkest of secrets, carefully guarded. Secrets that they don't want anyone to know about."

"I can't get through this, Aulus. I can't." Tears ran down her face.

"You will get through it—for Loli's sake, if not your own."

Ella was surprised at how gentle Aulus was, but not as surprised as Aulus. He thought about what Sleeward had said to him about his son. He remembered the pain in his voice. Aulus thought about the last time he had really cared about someone. He couldn't think when that was. Aulus cared now. He put the gun in his pocket, and then went for another bowl of water and washed Ella's face with a damp towel.

Aulus stayed with her for hours, holding her and telling her it wasn't her fault. She begged him not to tell her father, and she promised that for the sake of Loli she wouldn't try to kill herself again. When Aulus was almost assured that she wouldn't, he left the Ptolemy house.

Chapter 14

The weather turned suddenly even colder again. It had, in fact, started snowing even more, and the streets around the palace were deserted, as most sat beside fires in their homes or around the odd brazier on a street corner. The cold weather drew the living dead out for some reason. The colourmen did well picking them off, one at a time, as they wandered out of an alley or away from a loved one who had left them only for a short while. One young woman, with dried blood on her clothes, walked barefoot through the street. The colourmen claimed her instantly and bundled her into a carriage. Over the next few days the cold weather, strangely enough, brought even more of them from their hiding places, and more reports of the poor creatures began to appear in the newspapers. Those that had tried to hide their dead had a hard time doing so. Day by day unrest grew, and the population of Manceastre again demanded answers. A few more riots broke out, but were quickly subdued.

The palace laboratory was deep underground, and like the mausoleums, had a network of passageways and secret entrances underneath. The colourmen had been busy, and brought to Clovis and his researchers all the walking dead who had been found in the city. Hidden from Clovis was the mummy that Aulus had been paid to unwrap. He was secreted away in a plain sarcophagus until the colourmen could get it to the buyer. They did not see what was left of his body convulse spasmodically. The old mummies that they had found never did that. Other mummies in the city were turning to dust, but not this one.

The team of scientists were far more concerned with the recently deceased, and why they would not die. The methods they used to try to kill the undead were horrific. All poisons were used, including arsenic, used in massive quantities. Whilst some explored the use of chemicals on bodies, others cleaved skin from bone and took samples to be examined under the microscope. They studied the capillaries to see if blood still ran through them. It did not. Drastic measures were taken to render the dead, and that smell sickened all. It was useless. If limbs were hacked from the body they still twitched, and severed heads still tried to use lips to scream. The dead would not die.

A slave had a leg hacked off, blood poured along the pink marble floor, as he watched, screaming in great agony, until he bled to death. He then awakened to scream once more. Suddenly, something kicked in, and the pain went away and he fell silent. Finally, he slipped into a state of torpor and just stared blankly at his torturers.

Some of the undead could talk, and they tried to explain their predicament, but mostly failed, dissolving into tears as they stared at their grey hands that tried to clutch at the living, to ask questions that remained unanswered. Hearts were cut out as the corpses screamed, and heads were removed from bodies to see if the dead could still move. In all cases, they did. Isis, however, did not move.

Clovis took it all into his twisted mind. He relished the scene, and then in a moment of reflection he stared at a still beating heart and wondered…if there was such a thing as a soul, and if there was, did it really reside in the heart or the head?

Nepythys and Anubis became increasingly more restless; nothing the scientists tried seemed to have the remotest impact on Isis. Hers was the only body that showed no sign of remedial life. They tried reading from the *Scroll of Dedi* that they had taken from Ptolemy, and recited their own incantations. Nothing worked. Each time they put her back in the cryonic chamber, Nepythys would scream and shout at Anubis and the scientists, demanding of them answers they could not give, and asking what they would do next? In a laboratory, where the best scientists from all over the world had been gathered, there could be found no spark of life in Isis.

There were many 'operating theatres' beneath the palace. Steam-driven machinery powered all the tools— the sound of steam escaping when a drill was used was a strange sound. When used on the undead, who had gone beyond pain, there was an underlying hiss now and then, as the drill penetrated skin and bone.

Out of one room came a team of doctors, wearing surgical gowns and masks, their clothes splattered with blood. They had been working on the recently dead. Fixed on the walls everywhere were notices reminding everyone of the importance of wearing masks and washing hands. There were boxes full of clean masks and covered boxes for placing the used ones in, which were equally full. Metal boxes with alcohol-based cleansing fluids hung on the walls, above patches of the spilt substance on the floor beneath. The dowdy corridors weren't all that clean. The only worry was if the doctors or scientists picked up something from the undead.

In another operating theatre, a group of scientists had finished the complicated operation of attaching the head of Isis to her body. The stitches around her neck were ugly and pronounced, but the scientists considered they had done a reasonable job. Isis resembled the Frankenstein creature that Clovis was always ranting on about to them—although all the body parts of Isis were her own. He threw a copy of Mary Shelley's book down on the table every time he met with the 'doctors and scientists.' In his madness he howled at them that restoration was possible. It had to be. It was in the book. He said that in that story all it had taken was a little science.

Nepythys and Anubis now had access to the body of Isis, but what use was a lifeless Isis? What they needed was for her to be restored, so that they could regain their power, the loss of which they attributed to her death. Then, work out how to retain it when they killed her again. They would ensure that there would be no resurrection, this time. Isis had a face the colour of alabaster, and the ugly wounds around the neck looked grotesque. But, her face still looked beautiful.

The priests had washed and braided her hair and her face had been made up with blue eye shadow and black kohl. Nepythys regretted that she had killed Isis, but only because she could not get rid of her permanently. Nepythys thought she saw a shimmering light hover over the body of Isis, but she blinked and there was nothing. There was no love left in Nepythys for anyone except Anubis. There hadn't been for centuries. She thought of Isis as an obstacle, who even in death, stood in-between her and total power, and she needed to think just how she was going to get it.

Clovis hovered over Isis. He didn't believe a word of what the strangers had said to him about her, but she wasn't like the rest; she hadn't come back to life.

"So now you have her body, what are you going to do to help me?"

"We are going to help you get rid of Cleopatra."

"And how are you going to do that?"

"Isis has been Queen of the Underworld since before Alexander the Great, and favoured her chosen ones. I was a young goddess then, and accepted the way of things. But for the last two thousand years, since she honoured Anthony and Cleopatra and their descendants, I have grown restless. The world isn't of my making. I have no influence over it. If the battle of Actium that brought down Octavian had been reversed, I would have had all the power. If you recognise me, I will help you defeat the armies of Cleopatra. If you recognise me, I will make you emperor of the entire world. You will build temples in my name, and erase the name of Isis for all eternity."

"You expect me to believe that this was once Isis?" said Clovis pointing at the body.

"Is it so beyond your comprehension? That there is something more to life than science and machines? Why can't there be both?"

"Science and machines might just be a lot more reliable. They don't turn on you."

"I wouldn't be so sure of that, Clovis."

"She isn't much of a goddess now, is she? So, I get to be emperor?" said Clovis examining the body with eager eyes but being careful not to touch it.

"Why settle for anything less? You can have the entire world. You will be emperor. I can't change the past, but once my power is restored I can ensure that I'm worshipped in the future. Once restored— if she can be restored, Isis will have to be bound forever. I shouldn't have killed her in the first place. I know that now. Think of it Clovis, all that power."

"An alliance between us? A mortal and an immortal?"

Nepythys smiled and said nothing.

Anubis laughed, but Clovis was too wrapped up in the moment, imagining just how much more he could do when emperor, or perhaps now, even a god. Nepythys smiled indulgently, and thought that she would learn how to kill Isis without affecting her own strength, and then, perhaps she would wipe mankind from the planet. Anubis saw the look on her face and laughed even louder.

Over the next few days, once they had convinced themselves that Clovis had no interest in them, Ella and Loli decided to stay in the Ptolemy house for the time being. Aulus stayed with them. Ella was at a loss as to what to do next. She had never been that close to her father, but now that she realised just how much danger he was in, she was afraid for him. When Nepythys had finished with him, what would happen then? Loli hadn't stopped crying all the way home. Horus tried to comfort her with an explanation that Clovis would want to keep him alive. Ella noted his kindness. There didn't seem to be much of a reason for Horus to stay at the temple, although the priests had begged him to. Ella bombarded him with questions, some were answered, but with most he just gave a shake of the head or a shrug.

"We have to get them back," said Loli.

"And how do you propose we do that, Loli? The palace is guarded," said Aulus.

"If we could get in, we could kill Nepythys. Kill Anubis," said Loli. "Perhaps that will bring her back. I don't know. The new Governor General can die for all I care. I just want to get everything back to normal. Perhaps we could enlist the help of the Empress?"

"Enough, Loli. She is probably on her way back to Rome."

"In this weather? I doubt it. We have to go after her to tell her that her beloved Isis is dead and her sister intends to help Clovis become emperor in Cleopatra's place."

"She wouldn't believe us."

"Perhaps not, but if you were in her position and you worshipped Isis, and the undead were just that, wouldn't you try to find out if there was a grain of truth in it?"

Aulus glanced up from his papers. He had obtained a map of the palace from a slave who, when well paid, would steal anything. He had also told them that Clovis had Ptolemy. Loli sat on a low couch, legs under a warm winter skirt, stretched out before her. She hadn't even bothered to remove her cloak.

Ella wondered how on earth they could possibly think that they could succeed in setting Ptolemy free.

Finally, Ella removed Loli's cloak. She poured wine into glasses and gave one to each. She put a little more into one glass and offered it to Loli. Loli took it gratefully. Ella slipped a black pill into her own glass. Aulus noticed.

Aulus pointed to the map. "My contact tells me that Clovis has many underground cellars under his palace where there have been strange things happening, so much so that his slaves are talking about it all the time, and some are running away."

"What strange things? That isn't unusual is it? Apparently everyone, except Cleopatra, seems to know that Clovis is quite mad."

"Do you think they have taken Isis there, Ella?" asked Loli.

"I'm certain of it," said Aulus.

"Can we go to the palace?"

"We just go up to the palace door and ask them if they have a goddess?" Ella asked, shaking her head at Loli.

"I know a few people who would help," said Aulus.

"They would help us get in?" asked Loli.

"I think that the person I'm thinking of would help. She knows of the terrible things that go on there."

Loli's hand shook and she spilled some wine on a blue rug.

"Do you think that they have hurt our father, Ella?"

Ella sat down beside Loli and held her closer. She hardly ever did that, and now she wished that she had done it more.

Aulus suggested a plan. "The first thing a new Governor General is given is a new tomb. A gift from the Empress. He will have a mausoleum and the chief embalmer to work on the plans with the architect. These are almost complete. I could represent the family whilst you go with Licinia to find Ptolemy. He is already at the palace so Clovis might send for him. I'll have to hope Clovis sees me first, before he does that. I'll stall him as long as possible." said Aulus.

"Why would they still want our family to organise that?" asked Ella.

"It is the custom and the traditional gift on the swearing in of a new Governor General, from the Empress. She's already commissioned it. I could go. He'd hardly refuse her gift."

"Will he see you straight away?"

"I don't know."

"You think that he'll see us?" asked Loli.

"Not you, Loli," said Aulus.

"Yes. Loli should come," said Ella. "She got into an awful lot of trouble last time I left her behind."

"He won't see us straight away; it certainly won't be for a day or two. I know that Licinia can get you and Loli in whilst I keep Clovis busy showing the plans to him. Sefu will go over the plans with me, but he will not be going. You go inside with Licinia, who is well known and is rarely stopped. She's one of Clovis' favourites."

"You aren't an architect, Aulus," said Ella.

"I just need to represent the family. As for knowing what I'm talking about...I've scammed often enough Ella. You know that—you know me."

"I thought I did, but I'm not sure now."

Aulus left the house now and then, but always returned before nightfall. He was willing to give a ten year old the attention that the other adults, including her sister, did not want or couldn't, in Ella's case. Ella barely held herself together, but managed somehow. The air was fraught with tension, but Aulus was thoughtful and kind to Loli. Ella and Aulus spent much time in her father's study talking to the chief architect, Sefu, who agreed to step aside and let Aulus go in his place. He was very ill, anyway, but found the energy and time to aid them, if it meant saving his old friend, Ptolemy Child. Aulus also went to see Sleeward a few times, but he sought Ella's company more and more to talk and reassure her that it would all work out.

Ella and Licinia talked about what they would do once inside the palace. Licinia brought over a gown of dark cyan and umber for Ella to wear. The gown was cut low and almost exposed her pale breasts, but Licinia scowled at her when she tried to pull it up.

"You really will need to act as a whore. Have you never seduced a man? Never mind. Don't answer that. It is a stupid question."

Ella blushed. It had been she that had first made an advance to Swin. She had wanted him so much.

Loli picked her favourite clothes. The full deep pink scalloped edged skirt with tiny red roses sewn along the hem that came to just above the knee and a ruffled white blouse. Ella looked at her. She remembered one time when Loli wore the clothes, and that had been when Sophia had been on the embalming table. Why did children of their family have to be taught about the process at such a young age? Why should anyone have to be surrounded by death before they had learned about life? They surely should be more preoccupied with the living and playing. What children were left, during these times of plague, had forgotten how to play or were too overwhelmed by the fear of the sickness that they stayed, or were made to stay, indoors by their parents. Ptolemy had given Ella and Loli quite a lot of freedom, perhaps too much.

Horus said very little and sat for long periods of time, alone.

It was about a week later when they got word from the palace. Clovis would see Aulus. It seemed to all that Clovis was mildly amused by the fact that he had Ptolemy now working for him, as the family struggled on with their duties, and Aulus helping them out. Mind you, Clovis thought that the Child family must have little to do with the dead these days—whilst he did.

The architect had finished drawing up the plans, which had been commissioned long before the old Governor General's death. The tomb, although Clovis hoped it would be a very long time before it was used, was to be far more elaborate than that of Claudius Ptolemaeus Tiberius. Clovis would expect that.

Both Aulus and the girls went to the palace at the same time. Aulus pretended not to know the girls and held back a little. Licinia was her usual charming self, flirting with the guards. Aulus couldn't help but raise a smile, because if they attempted to raise her skirt they would get more than they bargained for. He was also relieved when he saw them waved through the gate. Aulus had little difficulty in getting in after he had shown the tomb plans to the guards.

The girls were taken to Clovis' private apartments and told to wait. Safe in the knowledge that Claudius would be some time pouring over the plans with Aulus. Licinia quickly found one of the secret passageways in that part of the palace that led to the underground chambers. Licinia had spent a long time learning about the layout of the place. She had fully intended to eventually use that knowledge to leave the palace after killing Clovis one day. She should be doing that now, she thought, but no, she would help Ella and Loli get to their father. Licinia ran back to the girls, who were more than thankful to be out of Clovis' bed chamber. Ella knew all about Clovis' preferences, just in case they had to entertain him. She had fully intended to kill Clovis, too, by any means possible if he had placed a hand on Loli. However, Licinia had assured her that he would be wanting to know how much more splendid the new tomb would be than anything that had ever been accomplished before. Even so, Ella was relieved to get Loli out of Clovis' rooms.

"He's a monster, Licinia," said Ella, looking at the strange mechanical things she saw lying on the floor of the chamber. She didn't want to know what they could be used for.

"He certainly is," agreed Licinia.

Clovis had waited for Aulus in the enormous library. It contained so many books, which Aulus doubted that Clovis had touched, let alone read. At first Aulus felt slightly unsure of himself, but he smiled cheerfully at Clovis and explained how they could decorate the interior of the tomb in a more elaborate manner. It would be perhaps, grander than the tomb of the last Governor General.

"Yes. I want it to be that large, but put more gold paint on the walls. There wasn't enough in old Claudius' tomb. I want more gold. I want the figures on the walls to be bigger too. More god-like. Clovis smiled too. He was a happy man. He had Nepythys, who might actually be useful to him once her power was restored, and he always had his alternative plan. He had spies paying people off among all the remaining nobles, and soon he would wipe out Cleopatra and her dwindling army. The plague had been bad in Britanniae, but it had decimated Rome.

"And of course, you'll use the best artist." Clovis didn't want a name; he just wanted a tomb fit for an emperor.

"Of course."

As chief embalmer it had been Ptolemy's role to ensure that the artist, and there was usually just the one for continuity's sake, achieved the desired result; to illuminate the everyday life of the deceased. Clovis seemed interested in the splendour of it all, but not the exact detail.

"We'll use the best. It is important that it be correct. There will be *The Book of the Dead* for him to do, too. "

"I doubt if I will be needing that any time soon, but best to have it anyway."

"Of course."

"Yes. Just do what you have to do to make it the best tomb, ever. Make it twice the size of the last Governor General's one…twice the size."

"But the cost."

"Hang the cost…Cleopatra will pay."

As Aulus discussed the project, Clovis smiled all the time. What a fool, thought Aulus. Power in the hands of a fool and a madman can be a dangerous thing. The quicker this meeting was over the better, and then he would go and find Sleeward.

At first Ella thought it strange that the guards didn't stop them. She realised that they simply thought girls no threat at all. They were able to walk freely about the palace, but that freedom was not for all. She had seen one man searched thoroughly. One guard flirted a little with Licinia—he knew her, so the girl smiled and lingered whilst Ella and Loli moved on a little, and then they waited for her to catch them up.

Licinia soon caught up with them. She knew where the cryonics chambers and the laboratories were. They had good, solid doors, but were unlocked.

"What now?" asked Loli.

"When inside we have to think of a reason to be there," said Ella.

"Why don't we tell the truth?"

"What, Loli? That we have come here to work out how to get our father out?"

"Not that truth."

"I don't see…"

Licinia put a finger to her mouth. "Shhh… someone is coming. Over here."

The girls ducked down a corridor but could just see who had descended the stairs and was standing outside one of the laboratory doors. A man held a box. Before Ella could stop her Loli stepped out and went right up to him.

"I'm here to see a woman," said Loli.

"Here?" The guard looked confused.

"Yes, she is, and she asked me to meet her here."

The man looked at her doubtfully. Loli was not to be deterred.

"She's working here and she wanted me to help," said Loli.

At that point Ella threw her hands up in the air and stepped out into the corridor.

"There you are, Loli. I've been looking all over for you."

"Is this the woman?" He pointed at Ella.

"No, don't be silly." said Loli bluntly.

The guard cleared his throat. "Now look here. What's the name then of this woman who asked you to meet her here?"

Loli hadn't thought that she would be asked. She looked confused for a moment then tried her sweet smile, the one she always used on her father. The man adjusted his belt, frowned at her, and waited patiently for her to reply. Loli was also very much aware of the gun he carried, too. She knew Ella had a gun and she would get one on her fourteenth birthday, thought Loli. But, she didn't know that Ella, for obvious reasons, had left hers at home, knowing that they would all be searched on entrance to the palace.

Licinia stepped out from her hiding place.

"Is this the woman, then?" asked the guard.

"No. Don't be silly. She definitely isn't the woman. Well she isn't a woman exactly..."

"That will do, Loli," said Ella.

Suddenly a colourman appeared in the corridor. Loli recognised him as one of the men who had taken something that belonged to them from the cooling cabinets. She held her breath. He had the smell of death on him.

"Hello." He smiled at Loli to reveal ugly brown uneven teeth.

"Everything all right?"

"This girl is looking for a woman," said the guard.

Both men laughed.

"Well, there are quite a few females in here. Some have been here a while and don't look too good now," said the colourman.

"I'd know her if I saw her," said Loli.

The colourman lifted one eyebrow, "would she be in cryonics...the freezer?"

"Hopefully," muttered Ella.

"You do have the right to be here? I suppose you must have, as no one gets past the perimeter security in this place. Completely locked down it is. Follow me."

He can't be taking us in, can he? thought Ella.

Ella looked inside. It was the smell that hit them first, and although the decaying process had been halted in its tracks, they were still the walking dead. Some of them stopped wandering aimlessly around as the girls entered the room. One of the dead men smiled at Loli. His tongue had turned black around the edges. A terrified Loli hid behind her sister. She had been getting used to the dead in the embalmment parlour, but not this. This was just too awful. The colourman shut the door behind them. Ella kept to the wall of the room with her sister behind her. They were in a room containing some dissection tables. Six of them in all. On each table lay a body in various states of dissection. Some with body parts missing. One of the undead watched, while a doctor, in fact he looked more like a colourman, cut into the dead man's arm. His victim looked pathetically at him. The doctor laughed at him and carried on dissecting the muscles of his arm. Another worked on the man's brain, peering down into the folds, and then he used his scalpel. He must have sawn the top of the skull off to get to it. A few bands of white connected the two hemispheres. His patient seemed oblivious of the work going on above him. Why weren't they screaming in pain, thought Ella? They moved through the rooms, silently.

Sleeward and Aulus stood in the doorway. They had come to find someone, too. They quietly made their way through the building. Behind one of the crates Sleeward saw something move, and he made a grab for it. He held on to the arm tightly. He pulled it into the lamplight. It was a thin woman, who looked fragile and afraid. Sleeward let her go and carried on searching. They hadn't caught up with the girls yet.

In one room, Ella gasped when she looked at the last table. Upon it was the young boy with no eyes that she had seen in the alley outside the opium den. Upon hearing her footsteps on the stone floor, he turned his head towards her. It was a pitiful sight. Two doctors wearing masks looked up, and then one plunged his fist into the chest cavity of the boy. With a scalpel he cut through the various arteries and held up the heart. The boy stared at the ceiling, seemingly oblivious that the terrible act had been performed upon him. One doctor placed the heart in a steel dish and prodded it with another scalpel, before returning to the table.

Loli tapped Ella on the shoulder and pointed underneath the table. Loli didn't take her eyes from the place she was looking at. She had found her own pet dog, Juniper.

"Juniper come here, come here to me," said Loli.

The ragged dog lifted its weary head and growled at her.

"It's me, Loli—come to me."

Again the dog growled and this time it bared its teeth, also, to reveal a grey tongue. It appeared blackened around the edges, too.

"Be careful, Loli. He doesn't recognise you. Leave him."

"Leave him. I can't leave him, he's my dog."

"Loli. Look at him closely. He isn't your dog anymore."

Loli kept her distance and looked carefully at him once more. She sighed. "All right Ella, but can we come back for him later?"

Ella looked about at all the degradation—the terrible things that were being done in the name of science. She suspected that terrible things had been done in the name of religion, too. Ella looked at Loli, who seemed more concerned with her dog than the inhumanity of what was going on around her. Ella pulled her away.

The colourman was way across the room. He beckoned for them to follow and the girls, hesitant at first, followed him.

"So what does...this woman look like?" The guard asked.

"Black hair," said Loli.

"There are plenty here with dark hair."

Sleeward and Aulus entered yet another room. They searched anxiously, too.

"He has to be here." Sleeward whispered to Aulus.

Ella and Loli were sickened by what they saw, but they could not look away. There was a large marble slab in the centre of the room. The kind they had in some of the fish markets, and on the slab was Isis. Her long black hair spread over the black marble and almost to the floor. Her white body had turned slightly grey, and there were large stitches across her throat. Large black tubes were suspended from the ceiling and narrowed as they entered her body by way of syringes. From other exit sites, something was leaving the body, but it didn't look like blood. Whatever they were doing with Isis, it didn't seem to have anything to do with giving her life. There was a terrible smell, like rotten peaches. Ptolemy stood by the body. He was reading from one of the many scrolls that lay in a heap on a nearby table.

Ptolemy looked shocked to see them...then angry.

"You should never have come to this place. Have you seen what is going on here?"

"I've seen bad things in the embalmment chambers, Father."

"Not like this, Loli. Clovis and his science, and now his interest in magic. He expects me to have a part in this. They also want me to find a ritual to raise her after this is finished. No good will come of it. She will be a monster."

"Then don't do it," said Ella.

"I've already been told what will happen to you and Loli if I don't."

"We came for you, Father. Aulus is with Clovis. We came for you." Loli started to cry.

Ptolemy held her close. "Shush Loli. It will be all right. We'll think of a way out of all this."

Ella stared at Isis. "Why doesn't she get up and walk like the other dead people? I don't understand."

There came the crash of metal against metal from another room and raised voices. The scientists rushed out of the room to see what was going on. Ella and Loli quickly joined them.

Sleeward had a doctor upon the floor and sat on his stomach, punching him repeatedly in the face until it was a mass of blood mixed with flesh, and not much more. Aulus stood behind Sleeward. Sleeward kept on shouting, "You bastard! You bastard!" He saw the scalpel next to him on the floor and drove it into the heart of the doctor, twisting and turning the knife, as if he was going to prise it out from in-between the ribs. Pick it out, bit-by-bit.

Ella saw her chance. She found a white coat lying on the floor and put it on. She grabbed Loli once more by the arm and backed into the room where Isis lay attached to the needles and tubes. Isis just stared at her. Ella didn't have much time, so she pulled at the intravenous lines attached to the body. Dark fluid splashed onto the floor. Ella looked at the lifeless body of Isis. What had the doctors done to her? There was more shouting from the room next door. No guards to be seen. They must have put the commotion down to the first stage that some of the undead go through in those first awful hours when they feel pain, before the nervous system seemed to shut itself off from what was happening.

Sleeward appeared in the doorway carrying Luce. Sleeward found his voice with some difficulty, "I shouldn't have left him alone."

The boy seemed to instinctively bury his face in his father's jacket.

"It's okay, son…they won't get you. I'll take you where you will be safe. You hear me? This will all be over soon."

Aulus looked over Sleeward's shoulder. "There isn't just Luce, Sleeward." He nodded towards the others.

"I said that we would help each other but how can we all escape?"

"The longer you talk the greater the risk that we will all be caught."

"You'll have to move fast then. Follow me."

Ptolemy and Aulus carried Isis between them. There was no time to even throw a cover over her body.

"What about Licinia?" asked Loli.

In the commotion, Licinia had disappeared.

"She'll be all right, Loli. She isn't leaving with us," said Ella.

Sleeward led them down the corridor, down other longer corridors, that led deeper into palace underground rooms, until they came to a door that was slightly ajar, leading the way to the catacombs.

Aulus shouted at Ella. "Get the door open, look quick!"

"Where to now?" asked Ella.

"They wouldn't believe that we would take her back to the temple. We should take her there," said Aulus.

"Shouldn't we take her home?" asked Loli.

"That will be the first place Clovis will send his guards."

"I think that the temple is a bad idea," said Ella.

"We'll have to take that chance. We'll work out what to do when we get there."

Once through the door to the catacombs Ella closed the door behind them. She was surprised to find that it could be barred from the catacomb side of the door.

"So, Sleeward. Are you coming with us?" asked Aulus.

"Yes! Can't think of anywhere else at the moment."

Ptolemy looked pale. Loli had never seen her father in such a panic. He caught his breath. "Let's get going. Before they get through that door."

Licinia was caught as she tried to find Clovis. She realised that this was the time to try and kill Clovis. The brave Licinia, was brought before Clovis and taken to the room where he loved to paint. He looked at some of the unfinished paintings and he looked at Licinia. He knew that Isis had been taken but mad as he was he wanted to deal with Licinia first.

Clovis issued some instructions to a slave out of earshot of Licinia. She felt a shiver run over her body as Clovis smiled at her. Two slaves soon returned carrying the most fantastic gown Licinia had ever seen. Clovis signalled that she should accompany the slaves to a small anteroom. Clovis paced the marble floor stopping in front of each painting in turn. Wine was brought in. It was a deep indigo colour and tasted of blackberry and pepper. It seemed to be a long time before Licinia was brought before him.

Licinia looked stunning in an ivory full floor-length gown covered with intricate black latticework. Tight at the waist and it billowed as she walked. The slaves were dismissed.

"Do you think Cleopatra will like that dress, Licinia? I have had two made up—both identical."

"What woman wouldn't—it is a beautiful gown," Licinia looked afraid and puzzled. "Why have two made up that are the same for her?"

"I had to see if it worked."

Licinia took a step towards him.

"No. Stay where you are. I want to watch."

"Watch. Why watch?"

"You'll see."

They were alone. Licinia looked up at the paintings and feared what might happen next …suddenly she let out a scream and started to pull the gown from the front of her body. Clovis called for two guards. They placed their gloved hands on each of her arms and held her still. Clovis smiled as Licinia's skin turned red near where cloth met flesh. As it blistered she screamed. No one would come to her aid. The poison from the dress sank into the pores and she lost consciousness. Her skin corrupted until she breathed no longer.

Clovis smiled again, "It works well." As he turned his back on the body he wondered how the two slave girls were bearing up. He could hear their screams from quite some distance away. Clovis then had Licinia's body taken away and incinerated.

Chapter 15

Once back at the temple the priests opened the door and fell down upon their knees when they realised that Ptolemy had brought her back. He carried Isis into the great library and placed her on a couch. A priest quickly covered Isis' naked body with a sheet. He was astonished that the others had not found something to cover her with before now. Isis seemed to have changed. Her face—no sign of decay. Was something happening to her? Could this woman be Isis? Could she be the goddess who had ruled the underworld and defeated nearly all the other gods? Ptolemy put those thoughts to one side.

"Look, her eyes are open," said Loli.

"I thought that nothing you did would restore her?"

"Perhaps she is just like the other undead after all. Perhaps one of the scrolls really did work, Father?"

Ptolemy didn't answer.

Isis didn't move. Her eyes had opened but there was no hint of recognition that she knew where or who she was. After about an hour she found that she could move her hands, then her arms a little. Whatever Clovis' doctors had done, and what Ptolemy had read, must have sparked some life in her. Something of her was back. Isis looked more human than goddess; in fact she looked less than human. It didn't take them long to realise that what was before them was far from what they expected. Isis said little. She stared into space as Ella and Loli washed her body and put her into a white gown. They helped Isis to stand and she hesitantly took one step, then another, slightly turning her head either to Loli or to Ella searching for a memory from a forgotten world. Isis stumbled.

"Take it easy," said Ella kindly.

Loli didn't say anything. All this was too complicated, too much for her to handle. There was too much going on. The scientists had put grotesque stitches into Isis' neck and the skin looked swollen and sore. How could dead flesh react like that? Loli tried not to look and stared at her hands instead. How could the gods look so human? How could they become so weak? thought Loli. The undead must be allowed to pass over to the underworld, and in restoring Isis, her father was going to try and make that happen.

With the *Scroll of Dedi* in front of him, Ptolemy began the incantation again, hopefully to fully restore Isis. Ella turned the pages as Ptolemy recited. He spoke in an ancient language, and the room seemed to dim and brighten...in turn. Then, to Loli, it was if the room then began to vibrate a little, and figures moved slightly backwards and forwards. She thought she heard a different voice and not that of her father. His words were repeated, over and over again. Was that a response to the ritual? All in the room looked quite surreal. Faces didn't look quite right. Distorted. What was happening? Aulus looked a little shaken and sat down abruptly on a chair. Then Ptolemy stopped speaking and all seemed normal again—if you could call trying to restore a goddess normal.

Everything seemed to return to how it should be, and then it was Isis who began to shake violently. She stopped abruptly and sat up. Her hair seemed to swirl around her in slow motion and settle, and her white hands trembled. She tried to speak but could not find the words.

Isis looked confused, unaware of who or what she was. She tried to speak, but couldn't. Her mind struggled to recognise her surroundings. In the bringing back, had Isis lost a part of her mind? Her eyes rolled and the lashes flickered and then she found the memory she was looking for, and it wasn't noble in nature. Rather, she was a force of nature and as this force grew, elemental...wild within her, her eyes steadied and fixed on Loli. Loli hid behind Ella, terrified of the strange creature. Had Ptolemy brought back something of Isis that had been suppressed and should never have been restored? As she quickly learnt to use her limbs once more she paced up and down like a caged animal. She walked right up to Ptolemy, a few inches from his face, her wild look and hair almost forcing him to back away, but he stood his ground. He tried to smooth her hair away from her face but she slapped his hand away. He thought that she was going to bite him so he kept his arms firmly by his side. At one point she started to cry and fumbled with her gown.

Ella remembered how as a child she had gone with her mother to the asylum and had seen a mad woman there act in the same manner. Had the spell, the bringing back of Isis, plunged her into the same madness? Isis could not speak, and with every attempt she grew more frustrated and violent, until Aulus and Ptolemy grabbed hold of both of her arms. She then did something that the priests would never think a goddess would do.

Isis started screaming. It started with one long high-pitched scream, and then she repeated it over and over again. Loli was sent away. The priests, after they got over their shock, tried to calm her down. She did after a while, and then they took her to the cellars. She started to claw at her own skin, at her arms, and already she had a deep scratch down the side of her face. They didn't see a choice, and cried when chains were brought in. Isis. Her wrists chained together and then the chain wound around a solid metal steam pipe. One priest tested it to see just how solid it was. It was. In her desperation Isis sunk down to the floor and wept. Suddenly, she stopped crying and started screaming again, and just as abruptly stopped.

Loli could hear Isis, and she was quite a distance away. Loli sat on a couch in a room on a higher level of the temple. She imagined that Isis had some terrible memory of being beheaded. Loli's father had to do something. He had to. She ran the temple library and paused outside the library door. She could hear voices.

Ella listened to what her father had to say. "I'll need to try again but I don't think I can do much. If I had access to more books, one book in particular..."

"Again. After that?" said Ella.

"We'll give her some time to quieten down and then we'll try again."

Loli listened outside the door for a few minutes more then went back to the little room, lay down on the bed, and cried. She was confused. Had they brought Isis back or not? Isis was a monster. They had all done this to her. They should have left her with Clovis. After a few minutes the screaming started again and Loli ran back to the library. She burst into the room.

"We can't leave her like that. Kill her. Can't you kill her again?"

"Loli!" said Ella.

"I can't stand this anymore. She isn't a goddess. She's an animal. This isn't how people let alone goddesses should behave. Tell me she'll get better."

"Loli, something has gone wrong. We'll perform the ceremony again," explained her father.

"No—kill her. Nobody should live for thousands of years. It isn't right. She'll be alive long after I am dead."

"She's Isis. Isis—the mother of all," said Ptolemy, solemnly.

Ella held Loli as she sobbed and Ptolemy, for once, looked uncertain of what to do next. Aulus had grown fond of Loli. To Ella's annoyance, Loli ran over to Aulus for comfort, too.

"We can't kill her, Loli. I doubt if we could truly kill her now," said Aulus.

"You have to do something." Aulus held Loli tightly whilst Ella stood open-mouthed at the look of concern on Aulus' face.

It was Ella who descended the stone steps to see Isis. It was Ella who talked to her and tried to get some sense out of her. Isis struggled to speak. For the first hour Isis muttered incoherently and pulled at her chains. She rambled on and answered her own questions with nothing that made sense. Her sentences were full of unusual associations and illogical connections. Ella kept her distance and walked around the room trying to understand anything of what Isis was talking about. Isis strained at the chains so hard that at one point Ella thought that she would free herself. Isis' wrists bled where she had been struggling to get free. Ella wondered how Isis could be so weak. She also felt sorry for her.

Without warning Isis calmed down and seemed to find some sort of balance.

"For all our sakes set me free."

Ella was startled.

"You've all lost so much. The dead are trapped in some half-life. This has to stop," added Isis.

Ella thought of the undead…of Swin, Sophia and the baby. Perhaps Sophia remembered, occasionally, a little of her past life, and when she looked upon the face of her tiny daughter, was reminded of the life that had been taken from her.

"What can be done?" asked Ella.

"Free me." Isis pulled sharply at the chains and it made Ella wince to see the blood on her wrists.

"I can be strong again. I can make sure that the dead pass over to the afterlife."

Ella began to cry. She thought again of Swin and his family, suffering, and of all the dead waiting to finally die.

"Remove the chains. I'm different now. Recovered. Let me go to them as I have always done. I can set them free. I know what haunts you so."

She was the black-eyed goddess. Her eyes, unfathomable before, unreachable…now seemed to soften a little. Ella couldn't take her own eyes off her. She had to do what Isis wanted.

Isis seemed so calm—so quiet at that moment. Ella took the key out of her pocket, picked up the padlock that held the chain together and unlocked it. As she did so Isis held her head to one side and looked at Ella in a curious way. Then a smile spread across her face.

"You remind me of myself when I was a child. You don't say much, but have the look of someone who knows too much already. Someone who keeps secrets and not all of them good."

Ella looked away. She knows, thought Ella.

"Go and find Diodorus. He will bring the other priests with him. The most loyal. I have to get stronger to be able to fight my sister, Nepythys."

"You remember what she did?"

"I have now the memory of my death."

"What will you do?"

"When I'm fully restored I'll decide what to do."

When Ella returned with the priests—six in all, they sat at her feet whilst Isis told them of how she would be worshipped by all once more and that the dead would be received in the afterlife. She would become powerful again. "I am your goddess. Restored to you. Keep faith with me and I will restore the old ways for all."

Diodorus had spent the totality of his life until that point in the service of Isis. He wanted so much to believe. "Isis. We will follow you," said Diodorus and touched the hem of her dress in reverence.

Isis turned to Ella. "Where is your father?"

"Asleep."

"Good. You will come with me. I may have need of you."

Isis did not mention her son, Horus, at all.

Ella didn't resist—she didn't want to. The scroll had partially restored Isis—why was she not the powerful goddess once more? What was missing? She seemed a quieter creature not the monster that had been chained up earlier.

For one brief moment she felt faint, and Isis caught Ella by the waist and looked deep within her eyes—as she did so, some dim memory stirred within her. She saw a terrified young woman, her skin a deep olive colour and her black hair flying wildly about her, who ran for life up the steep steps, making for the temple in Ephesus. They dare not take me from there, she thought. She stumbled once cutting her knee on the sharp stone, blood oozing down the inside of her leg and staining her white gown. Before she reached the door to the temple the soldiers cut her down. Mark Anthony had sent his soldiers for the sister who had plotted against Cleopatra. She was buried in an octagonal-shaped tomb, which looked like the Pharos lighthouse in Alexandria, and forgotten for two thousand years. Mortal sisters. Rivals. Once close, but when it came to ruling Egypt, they would do anything for the throne....even kill each other.

Isis suddenly let go and for Ella the memories did so too.

Ella and Isis found Swin and Sophia with the baby, huddled in the corner, in one of the rooms. There was no one else with them. Sophia cried and the baby just occasionally tried to latch on to Sophia's breast and then its head would roll back.

Ella fell to one knee and looked intently at the baby, at Swin and Sophia. Swin couldn't stand the look of pity in her eyes or was it regret? He suddenly felt so tired, so very, very tired. Sophia looked afraid of Isis, and Ella.

"What can we do for them?" asked Ella.

Isis towered above them, clutching the edges of her dark cloak as if trying to keep herself in control, and hold on to her sanity.

"There is one thing I can do now."

"What is that?"

"I can help them to the afterlife."

"You can?"

Isis closed her eyes and shuddered a little.

"Ella. Leave us alone."

Ella gave her a puzzled look.

"Ella, you need to leave. No mortal or half-mortal has ever witnessed this."

No sooner had Ella left the room than Isis put her arms out to Sophia. She shrank away. Isis moved forward again this time with more determination.

"Come quietly to me Sophia. Let me help you." Isis once more leaned over her.

"Let me look after your child."

Sophia shrank back. Isis composed herself. Sophia looked upon the face of the goddess. She couldn't take her eyes from her. She felt calmer, and gave her child up to her.

"Here, let me hold you, little one. Shush. Soon your suffering will be over."

Isis cradled the baby and held her tightly.

"Have you named her?"

"Her name is Aelia."

Isis began an incantation. Sophia heard the child's name and she turned to Swin looking for some explanation as to what was going on. Swin seemed unresponsive to her, his eyes fixed upon the child, and the so-called goddess who said that she could help them.

"I will aid Aelia to pass over to the underworld where she will dwell on the fields of Aaru forever."

Isis stared at Sophia and as Isis completed the rest of the incantation the baby gave one weak cry of alarm. Sophia could see the tiny hands flailing in the air and then suddenly they dropped. Isis let the baby fall from her arms onto the cold stone floor. Sophia screamed and tried to reach out to the baby, but in her weakness couldn't move far. Swin seemed to be in some sort of trance and did nothing. Isis turned to Swin and stared intently at him, her black eyes—the black death, fixed upon him. He slumped to one side. Before she could scream again Sophia fell into silence, and closed her eyes for the last time.

Sophia's scream brought Ella running. Just before the door opened Isis covered the baby with Sophia's shawl and placed her in her mother's arms. Isis stood before Ella and held her back.

"They are at peace now—they have passed over to the afterlife."

Ella collapsed to the floor and wept. When she could speak she looked up at Isis. "What of the others?"

"Bring them to me. Bring them all."

It was, in fact, Isis who went to them. She stepped defiantly into each dark cellar room, and dismissed Ella, and the priests. Each time she crossed a threshold the dead passed over and were released from their torment and nightmares. There was still a madness about Isis, but the dead did not rise again. Perhaps the worst was over. Then Ella stifled a sob as she remembered how she had loved Swin so very, very much. Guilt sat heavily with her. She had told Aulus everything. Had that been wise? Could Aulus have changed so much, recently?

It was Isis who led the way in the darkness, holding a lantern before her. They came across more of the undead. One was a young man, well, what was left of him. Isis knelt before an old man, half his arm was missing, and he lifted up the bloody stump to her.

"Look away, Ella. This is between him and me. The crossing over of a soul isn't for mortal eyes." She glanced at the priests. "You too."

They all complied. Ella felt sick, dizzy at one point. She wanted opium. That was all she could think of. She hid her face. When she heard the rustle of skirts next to her she looked up and saw Isis standing with raised arms and a look of rapture upon her face.

"They are at peace now. They go before me to the underworld," said

Isis.

Ella looked down at the old man. He had crossed over. His stump bled slightly. The smell of rancid blood hit her nostrils. The young man next to him was truly dead, too and his flesh looked to be quickly decomposing before them.

As they made their way through the foul smelling catacombs they found more of the wretched victims who had been maimed and ripped apart by Clovis, and Isis helped them to cross over, too. She released them from their torment and each time she did, she told Ella and the priests to look away.

When they left the catacombs, they found the walking dead that the families had tried to hide. Isis talked in a soft calm voice to them all. Isis set the undead free. None resisted her. Why would they? Without hindrance, each door was opened to the goddess. The relatives and friends of the undead dropped to their knees before her and thanked her for her many blessings. She got to the undead before the colourmen, now. She found those that should be hers in houses, factories, near the mausoleums, where some supposed they should be. Some she found down by the ship canal, sitting quietly as if waiting for the ferryman to take them away. Most seemed confused. They stared at their hands and wondered what was happening to them. It was finally over for some, but not all. Some of the undead still managed to hide in the warehouses, or crept silently onto ships, not knowing who they were or what they wanted. Some fought back feebly, as if they would rather clutch at the remains of their life than pass over and face the judgement of Thoth. Thoth was dead; killed by Isis, but they did not know that. The priests soon calmed them down with stories of the fields of Aaru, the heavenly paradise to come, the reed field, reminiscent of the earthly Nile Delta. Those who had some recollection wept for those that they would leave behind.

Some she did not get to soon enough. A group of drunken sailors found one young man cowering by the barrels belonging to the vinegar factory and knifed him over and over again, laughing each time he stood up. They tormented and taunted him, bound him with ropes, and then one of the warehouse men broke the group up and released the young man, telling him to go on his way. The warehouseman felt sorry for him. By the confused look on his ashen face he did not know which direction that would be.

It was useless to give the undead food. They only brought it back up again. Whatever curse that kept them from the afterlife left them little hope. One poor woman wandered into a field and started scratching away at the earth, hoping to bury herself, so ashamed was she at the way her grey flesh hung limply from her body.

Isis came across the young man the warehouse man had helped, and released him from his burden. As she progressed towards the ship canal, more were helped on their way to the underworld, and a strange calm fell upon that part of the city of Manceastre. Word of the return of Isis spread quickly. The priests had brought enough gold with them, and they bought passage on one of the smaller but faster steamships. Isis stood on the deck and stared intently down at the ice. It slowly began to thaw.

Isis knew that the only one who could help her to become all-powerful again was Wadjet. Isis would also need *The Book of Thoth*.

"Gather your belongings for a sea voyage. We go to the great library—to Alexandria," said Isis.

Isis placed her hand on Ella's heart and Ella felt a chill run through it, her hands turned blue with the cold, and one tear fell from her eye—as it hit stone it splintered into tiny ice crystals. Isis smiled at Ella and guided her towards the quayside. Isis held her close to her, as they both looked out across the ice-cold water...Ella had a vision of the first Cleopatra. A warrior queen who was used to getting everything she wanted. She manipulated, fought, and set her sights on Rome. She would do anything to have an empire. Mark Anthony lay asleep by her side in his opium dreams, but she was far from sleep. Naked, she left the bed, and walked across the white marble floor—over to a white vase full of Egyptian Blue irises and picked one up. She thought of the mother goddess, Wadjet, and prayed for her guidance and strength. Cleopatra picked up her cloak from the floor where Mark Anthony had thrown it and wrapped it around her shoulders. When she stepped out onto the balcony and looked out upon the city she saw that the heavens were black and there was no star in sight. Only the moon cast its light upon her anxious face. She reminded Ella of Loli. Cleopatra heard a movement behind her and turned slowly, thinking it to be Mark Anthony. He would want her back in bed with him she thought. It wasn't Mark Anthony who pulled her close to her. It was a woman. Cleopatra had been held by her before, and as Cleopatra offered her the flower, the vision faded.

Ella looked at Isis.

Isis smiled.

Chapter 16

It was bad enough that the plague cut the populace down and then the dead could not pass over to the afterlife...there were some who were determined to add another threat to a fear-ridden city.

"Let's go over it again. We don't want to make any mistakes."

"Are you sure this is the right stuff? We don't want a repeat performance of what happened when the other lot tried. Bunch of amateurs. He should have let us get on with it," said Glaucus.

"Himself provided it this time. It should do the job."

"Are you absolutely sure that it is the right stuff?" repeated Glaucus.

"There were bits of our men lying all over the road. We won't have any more accidents, will we now?" Leto looked up at Glaucus.

"Not with me in charge there won't be. We act immediately. This won't be left lying around long enough for any accidents. Do the other ones know what they are doing?" Glaucus looked nervous.

"Been over it three times with them. They know where the others are now. The filthy dead are getting together in other places. Like they are waiting for something."

"Good. We will use the catacombs to get in. Not many go down there now, get in through that way."

The men made their way through the blue-black darkness of the catacombs. Leto began to sweat and held his gun tightly in his right hand, by his side. Glaucus knocked on the small temple door. No answer. Another knock and the door opened slightly. Glaucus put his gun through the gap and shot at point blank range then he pushed the door roughly; he lost his balance and almost caused Leto to drop the explosives.

"Take it easy. Are you bloody mad?"

Leto eased his bulky body through the door held open by a guilty looking Glaucus. Looking guilty not because he had just killed a priest, but because he had nearly blown all of them up. Leto then glared at him and stepped over the body of the priest.

Leto looked down at the body covered in blood. "Didn't do much good for you, your religion, did it?"

Glaucus spat on the body and ran up the steps. At the top two priests appeared summoned by the sound of gunfire. They saw the dead priest at the bottom of the steps, saw the explosives the men were carrying, and held their hands up before them.

"You can't do this. Think of these people," pleaded one priest.

"What people? Corpses? Do you think that we want the undead walking around carrying the plague with them? We've had enough of them."

The priests pushed at the colourmen and tried to force them back. Leto, who was getting nervous carrying the explosives, began to curse under his breath. The priests surged forward again. Two shots rang out. When Glaucus and Leto found the few remaining priests they tied them up in the cellars. The men seemed surprised to find that all the dead who lay in the corners of the basement were the walking dead no longer. They were, in fact, all quite dead now.

"Perhaps it is all over," suggested Leto.

"Perhaps it is," agreed Glaucus, "but let's make quite sure, eh?"

They quickly set the charges and gave themselves plenty of time to get away. This time they didn't bother going through the catacombs and just strode boldly out of the temple doors.

The explosion, and others in different parts of the city, could be heard for miles.

Ptolemy, Aulus, Horus, and Loli had been searching for Isis, and Ella. They got to the temple after the goddess and Ella had already left. The temple was badly damaged and a servant to the priests told them that he had seen Isis, Ella and some priests leave before the explosion.

No one had taken much notice of the small steamship carrying Isis, Ella and the priests which had already left the quayside. The captain on board *The Alexander* looked incredulously at the water. The ice had vanished as quickly as it had appeared. Cleopatra ordered the preparations to depart for Rome. *The Alexander* had a top speed of twenty-three knots per hour, not bad for a heavily armoured steamship. Her captain told Cleopatra that if they dropped Gaius off on the coast of Italy near Rome, depending on the weather, it would take four days, then two more days to Alexandria. She was discussing the plans with Gaius when a legionary appeared in the doorway of her cabin.

"Your highness. Some people wish to come aboard."

"For what reason?" asked Gaius.

"They said…" Here the legionary hesitated.

"Yes?"

"That they know what is happening in the city and they have news."

Cleopatra looked at Gaius.

"Search them for weapons and then bring them in," said Gaius.

On entering the cabin Loli fell to her knees. The others bowed low. Loli began to cry and spoke quickly. "Empress. Isis…has taken my sister. I don't know why. We were told by a warehouse man who loaded supplies on to a ship that they have gone to Alexandria and…"

"Slow down child, let the others speak."

Ptolemy stepped forward. "Would it be so hard to believe that Isis has returned?"

Cleopatra breathed deeply. "Finally," she whispered.

Ptolemy continued. "Isis was killed by Nepythys, but has risen again. But she is not the deity you would expect."

"What do you mean?" said Cleopatra.

"She is different. One moment she is Isis, and the next she is not."

"What are you trying to say man? Say it straight," said Gaius.

"Isis is quite mad."

Gaius laughed. The words just seemed too ridiculous to him but Cleopatra was not laughing. She was thinking that perhaps, it was why Isis had not appeared to her family for generations.

"How do you know all this?"

Ptolemy told Cleopatra of all that had happened in the last few days, of how Isis had not risen like the other undead. Clovis, and then he, had tried to restore Isis and failed. She had been partially brought back and she had started to claim the dead again but she was not the deity that they had all once worshipped. He didn't have the knowledge to help restore her as she once was. He then told of how Isis had taken his eldest daughter with her. A small steamship had left not long ago.

"What would you need to know to restore Isis fully?" asked Cleopatra.

"*The Book of Thoth*. That…is supposed to be in the great library of Alexandria."

"And if you find it do you think that Isis could be restored?"

"Possibly."

Cleopatra looked again at Gaius. "Our plans wouldn't have to change much. These people would come with me to Alexandria. By the time we return you will have raised the army and we might have solved some of our problems. We deal with Clovis and Nepythys with Isis on our side."

Gaius looked doubtful. He knew that the simplicity of that statement and subsequent plan would turn out to be far more complicated, but at least he got to bring back his army.

"We'd never catch them up," said Gaius.

Cleopatra was determined.

"If we leave straight away we can catch them up. *The Alexander*, once under full steam..." said Cleopatra.

"She isn't that fast ..."

"Still, we might. It is also important that you get to Rome as quickly as possible, Gaius, and then I will go on to Alexandria."

Cleopatra turned to Ptolemy. "And if Isis and her priests get to this book first? Can they fully restore her?"

"I'm almost sure that they could, but the book has power beyond that. I don't know what would happen if the intention to use it is not only to restore Isis, but also used for some other reason."

Loli sat cross-legged on the floor. She stared at animal skins that sat on it, too. She desperately wanted Ella back, and wondered if Isis could be as cruel as Nepythys. Loli heard Cleopatra's voice drifting through the air to her. Loli looked up at her father and she heard Ella's name mentioned more than once. She felt dreadfully tired. Wine was brought in and she could hear the drone of voices as plans were made. The cabin felt warm and safe. Loli curled up on the thick, comfortable sheepskin rug, in front of the Empress, and fell asleep.

The shudder of the steamship awoke her. She sat up, unfamiliar with her surroundings. Loli was in the lower bunk of four, two on each side of the wood panelled cabin. It was daylight; she could see it through a small porthole in the cabin wall. Loli had been covered with warm blankets and for a moment she remained, nestled beneath them, until she remembered why she was there. Ella! She wanted Ella!

Ptolemy was still asleep in the lower bunk opposite her. Above him, Horus also slept. She got out of bed, put a foot on it, and peeped over the edge of the higher bunk on her side to see who was there. Aulus? Of course it would be.

Aulus blinked, rubbed his eyes and stared at Loli. Her eyes were all puffy with crying and she looked like she would start again. Aulus looked at her troubled face.

"Come up."

Loli climbed the ladder and sat on the edge of his bunk.

"We'll find her, Loli."

"She's probably dead already. Isis is mad. You heard father. I don't even know why she took Ella."

"She took some of the priests, too," he said as if that would cheer her up.

"But they wanted to go."

"Do you think that we will catch up with them?" Loli brightened up a little.

"We might."

"What would happen then?"

"There are at least a hundred of Cleopatra's soldiers on board, Loli. They might be able to take a few priests."

"And Isis?"

Aulus didn't answer.

They never did catch up with the other steamship. It always seemed to be just ahead of them on the horizon, but all efforts to get to it failed. It always seemed to be exactly the same distance away, day or night. Aulus didn't speak much in the four days that followed, just stayed mostly in his bunk.

Loli made friends with Cleopatra's slaves and was soon adopted by Tjuya Meresamun, who told her of the temples in the east and of the many stories of how the gods came about. Some had said that they came from the stars and seeded mankind. Others recounted how they had known that the gods had played games with people, and that there were times when gods lived a long time amongst humans. When they had appeared to Alexander the Great, they had never revealed their origin, only that their power had a source, and that source was unknown. Loli listened and tried to understand, but all she could think of was Ella, and that perhaps the gods were more cruel than people.

One afternoon she approached Horus and asked him what he remembered of how he came to be a god.

"I have no memory of how I became a god, but I do remember some things. I remember having a temple dedicated to me, Apollonopolis Magna, later known as Edfu. It was near Luxor. Before Isis made me into this boy-god, I recall that I fought Anubis there. His jealousy knew no bounds and as a consequence we nearly killed each other. I know that."

"And since then?"

"I don't remember much. He still wants me dead, though."

Loli shook her head. She still couldn't understand how sisters and cousins could turn against each other.

Chapter 17

When *The Alexander* berthed at Citavecchia, Gaius was in a foul mood. He'd been arguing with Cleopatra about her going off on what he said was a wasted journey. It had ended badly and he couldn't wait to get away from her. Loyal though he was, she had tested him to the limit. They should never have gone to Britanniae in the first place. If she had listened to him, over a year ago, Cleopatra would have had Clovis killed, and they would have all been saved the trouble they had now.

Gaius warmed his hands near one of the braziers. Would he ever get warm again, he thought. His old back injury was playing up, and he turned his back on the fire to warm it and try to ease the pain. A slave gave him a cup of warm wine and some cheese. He ate quickly and gulped the wine down with one eye on the darkening sky. Whilst he drank, a messenger reported to him of the recent events in Rome. Cleopatra appeared briefly on deck, but on seeing Gaius, hurried below.

Citavecchia was about three hours on horseback from Rome. Gaius sent for horses for himself and some of his men and took his leave of Cleopatra. *The Alexander* was part of a fleet of fifty ships and before he left he shouted orders at the captains to get them loaded with coal and made ready for battle. He made sure that orders were issued to take the Chinese mercenaries with them. Most barracks and the training camps for the recruits were close by anyway, so it would not take long to gather an army together. They weren't all as well trained as they would have been by spring, but there was no helping that. Then his thoughts turned to the problem at hand, and he prepared to set out for Rome.

He hadn't liked the idea of *The Alexander* going off without him and he had tried to talk Cleopatra out of following the so-called Isis. They wouldn't be able to catch her anyway, but he was still worried. Cleopatra was determined to search for Isis and go to the Library of Alexandria. Cleopatra wouldn't listen, and although he did want to be by her side, he would have to gather an army quickly, and get back to Britanniae.

Gaius thought about the fact that he hadn't been away long from Rome,

165

but he hadn't wanted to go to Britanniae in the first place. Clovis was a fool, and a mad fool at that, but a mad fool could still be a danger. If any of the royals had been paid off with promises of land and power whilst he had been away, Cleopatra's rule would be undermined further. Fear of the latest plague, and that it had been sent because Isis no longer supported Cleopatra, was spreading, too. He had heard that from men in his own ranks.

The roads were bad from the port to Rome. It had started to rain as soon as they had left and it didn't drain away as quickly as it usually did, so the journey took longer than expected. The landscape was stark and cold, but the summers of the last decade hadn't been much better, since the massive volcano in Krakatoa in the 1880's, had put paid to good crops for a few years. Each grey summer had resulted in a shortage of food, and another opportunity for plague to spread. In previous years it had taken a hold, but not as badly as it had since the eruption. Gaius remembered his youth, where he spent many happy summers at his grandfather's vineyard outside Rome. Each summer spent playing with his cousins, running around the vineyard, until all were dizzy from the heat. Each summer tending the grapes with the slaves, and sitting at his grandfather's knee, whilst he told stories of the early empire of Anthony and Cleopatra. The glorious reign, where society flourished and the empire grew larger, as their children and their children's children built upon their success. A far cry from the ruined empire of the 1890's.

Horses and men were freezing by the time they got to Rome. It was now sleeting and Gaius could hardly feel his fingers. He had to get a slave to remove his leather gloves so he could read the letters, which had been about to be sent to him in Britanniae. Nothing seemed to be wrong in Rome, but there was something Seto, the councillor who had been left in charge, wasn't saying. He suspected that from the tone of the letter.

Gaius needed a bath after his journey. He had his own bathing room in his house, but he had left orders for his staff to lock up the house, or most of it, until his return. So, he sent someone ahead to have it opened up and for Thaddeus, one of his household, to meet him there.

After he had wiped most of the mud off himself, he quickly changed his clothes and made for the public bath-house with Thaddeus. It was late afternoon, and he'd probably run into a few people he'd rather not. But, he needed to be seen as back, in control, and the bath-house was the hub of gossip and intrigue, as it had been for thousands of years. Two thousand years of the empire, which now was more unstable and poorer than when

Anthony and Cleopatra had formed it. Two thousand years of Roman and Egyptian culture, or rather a curious mixture of both. Anthony and Cleopatra could have got rid of the history books relating to the nature of the power and customs of each civilisation, but they had chosen not to do that. They had not been book burners, and Gaius couldn't make his mind up if that had been foolish or admirable. There were some who hoped for the return to a Roman or Egyptian Empire, and had never accepted what they called a mongrel breed of both. Recently, before he'd left for Britanniae, he had heard speeches on street corners calling for a return to pure Roman rule. Although the army had been modelled on the Roman rather than Egyptian one, it had been well paid, and soldiers were given large pensions when they retired. However, there were others who now hungered for the old Roman ways.

Gaius had a hot bath in one of the private side chambers, during which Thaddeus rubbed thyme oil into his skin. He wondered why the baths had been almost empty, unusual for that time of day.

He asked Thaddeus, "Where is everyone?"

"Most are in their homes today. The dead walk and scare those who come across them in the streets." Thaddeus though better of saying any more on that topic, as he could feel Gaius' shoulders stiffen under his touch. Gaius turned over and sat up.

Thaddeus stepped back. Gaius quickly dressed himself without any help from him. He knew when to step back. Three times Gaius had tried to give him his freedom, and three times he had said to Gaius that he had no need of it. So Thaddeus had stayed with him, to run his business affairs in Rome. He had become a friend, at times offering advice to Gaius, as they had poured over maps together long into the night.

"How is the Empress?" asked Thaddeus.

"The same as usual—pig-headed, impulsive, devoted to a goddess who has deserted her. She is on her way to Alexandria."

"Does she plan to marry Clovis?" Thaddeus looked worried.

"No. She'll never marry. She says she will, but she won't. By the time she dies, who knows who will be spared the plague and be in control of this ramshackle empire. Cleopatra has gone off after a madwoman who says she is Isis. She should be here to help keep control of what she has."

"But you'll do that as you have always done?"

"I will."

"Gaius, are you not sorely tempted to seize power yourself?"

"I've thought about it."

Thaddeus looked around. "Where's Oppian?"

"I left him at the port."

"You should have left him here with me before you went to Britanniae. I told you that."

"He's been fine."

"What do you do next?"

Gaius told Thaddeus of everything that had happened in Manceastre, and finally Thaddeus told him of what Seto had done.

In the state house, Seto sat at the huge table. He was alone and didn't get to his feet when Gaius entered the room.

"Gaius?" Seto looked surprised to see him.

"Well? I hear there have been riots? Why did you not mention them in the letters?"

"Yes, Gaius. There has been some trouble, but I handled it."

"What happened?"

Seto looked flustered. "Soldiers tried to arrest some people who had been breaking windows in the west quarter. A sniper shot two of the soldiers. One was shot in the head and the other badly wounded."

"And?"

"The people are panicking. The dead are walking around as if still alive, well ...walking. People are terrified that they carry the plague, others have been fighting with the soldiers to get their loved ones back."

Gaius was reminded that Clovis had the colourmen take the undead away, and that the families in Manceastre had tried to hide them.

"What have you done to stop the riots?"

"I did what anyone would have done."

"And that was?"

"We took the undead away."

"Where?"

"The islands...we took them by boat to the Pontine Islands...as we have always done with outcasts. We take them there by boat every day."

Gaius strode across the marble floor and looked out of the window at the now silent city. Seto got up from the chair and stood by his side.

"Did anyone encourage the populace?"

"Atis spoke out as usual. He said that Isis had abandoned us. Nothing we haven't heard before, but he's gained many more supporters since this terrible curse fell upon us. He's calling for a republic. Every few hundred years this happens. We give them a new ruler from the same family. The people are restless. I've said many times before, Gaius; you cannot tax such a small population and expect them to be fine with that. Reduce the taxes for a while. Double the inheritance tax."

Gaius laughed. "Double the inheritance tax? How can that happen when individuals can't be pronounced legally dead?"

"Debase the currency."

Again, another laugh from Gaius. "It is dipped in silver as it is, man. You are still paying the army in silver I take it?"

"We will be."

"We will be?"

"Gaius, you have found it easy enough to get here from the port, but the taxes come from all over the empire and the weather…"

Gaius groaned. "And our wealth continues to be depleted. For years the rich have been hiding away their money, shipping it overseas, having it 'disappear' in the provinces and then following it there and disappearing themselves. We should have stopped it."

"It isn't just that, Gaius. We've reduced the size of each province. The bureaucrats cost a small fortune; we have an expanding bureaucracy who is bribed by the aristocracy…army costs…"

"But there are less people since this latest plague…"

"Less people needed to farm, now that mechanisation of farming has been introduced. Greedy landowners acquiring more land by any means necessary. More people crowding into the cities. The soldiers haven't been as badly affected as the ordinary people. The soldiers are fitter… and anyone with any sense has moved their business away. Rome produces nothing except a breeding ground for plague. We are still getting the taxes in…what little we can, but we need to provide for what is left of the population with little resources."

"We could pay the soldiers with land."

"Each soldier has more than enough land as it is…there is no one to work the land. They are all in the army!"

"But the women work."

Seto laughed.

Gaius was reminded again of Cleopatra, now more a figurehead than a leader.

"I've put in place a curfew and said we've taken the undead away to stop any chance of plague spreading. That seems to have silenced those who haven't lost anyone, for now. But a small group of dissenters have set up a camp within the Piazza Augustus and I've left them there."

"Who are they made up of?"

"Mostly men, but they have women and children with them. They are the ones who protested that their dead have been taken away. I've told them to go back to their homes, but they refuse. I've threatened to do that by force, but they won't budge. Atis is with them, urging them to make a stand. Many look to him to do something, but what, I don't know."

"And it won't take much to start them off again."

"It won't."

At that point a soldier walked into the room and over to Seto. He seemed uncertain as to whom to address. Seto indicated that it should be Gaius, and seemed relieved that it should be so.

"General. I have this message from my commander."

"Yes. Fighting has broken out in the Piazza Augustus after Atis was shot in the head."

"Who ordered that?"

"Sir..." the messenger seemed reluctant to speak.

"Speak up. Who ordered that?"

Seto walked back to the chair and sat down. "He doesn't have to say. It was me. I told them to take the shot if they had the opportunity."

"Fool. You've just made the situation much worse."

Gaius turned his back on Seto. He had never liked him. He'd hardly been out of Rome all his life. He was a statesman, and not a great one at that...not a soldier."

"We'll go to the square and try to calm them down."

"Me? I never go out on the streets, you know that."

"Well. It is about time you did."

Seto sent a slave for his outdoor cloak and reluctantly followed Gaius out into the city. Gaius was troubled. What ran through his mind was that perhaps Atis had been right, and the empire was indeed in need of a republic. He dismissed the thought instantly.

Both Gaius and Seto rode side by side, but as they approached the Piazza Augustus Seto began to sweat. Gaius remained cool. Gaius removed his helmet and someone shouted his name. Before he had left Rome the people had respected him and looked up to him...perhaps more than to Cleopatra to resolve their problems. Some of the crowd that began to gather threw stones at the horses and Gaius' horse sidestepped.

"Easy." Gaius calmed him down.

The second stone that hit the horse caused it to rear abruptly and Gaius was thrown backwards, falling from the horse. He hit his head against stone and was knocked unconscious.

Seto panicked and gave the order to fire on the crowd. The crowd dispersed screaming and carrying the wounded. The stones became quickly splashed with blood. Seto knew then that he had made one mistake too many. The soldiers advanced on some of the rioters who hadn't managed to find an escape, forcing them into a corner of the square where the cavalry towered above them, and every exit was then blocked.

As Gaius regained consciousness a soldier helped him to his feet. Gaius had a reputation for commanding loyalty without violence. He surveyed the stricken and bloody crowd before him. He wondered how on earth they would keep peace in the city now.

It took a week to calm the people down. Gaius took money from Cleopatra's private treasury to give to the victims as compensation for the wilful and despicable act that had been carried out. He met the families of the victims, one by one, and said that their dead would be cared for on the Pontine Islands. Where he couldn't win their confidence, he paid them off with even more money. He made sure any rivals for power were given enough of what little he had to give to help keep order. He needed Cleopatra back. Enough people loved her still and believed in Isis, but only just. Gaius wondered if she had faired any better in her endeavour than he in his. Before he left, he replaced Seto with someone he thought could control the situation until he returned. On the way back to Citavecchia, he wondered just how long it would take to get the northern territories back in line and replace Clovis.

Chapter 18

The wind howled around the tall steamship funnels, and the waves grew higher and lashed the steel deck. Cleopatra called for her captain to come to her cabin.

"Will this weather get worse?"

"I'm used to storms at this time of year, highness. It's a short voyage. We'll be there within two days. The crew are well trained, but if you have your doubts we can turn back?"

"No. We must press on."

"Will there be anything else, Empress?"

The ship shuddered once more as it fought the waves. Cleopatra looked across at the captain. His face was a picture of composure.

"We are in your safe hands, Captain."

The captain left the cabin. Only when he left Cleopatra did he swear, when he lost his footing, as the ship shuddered once more.

Some of the sailors complained that they shouldn't have left port, and the senior officers calmed the soldiers down when they complained, too. The sailors pointed at the change in the colour of the sky, and a rumour spread quickly that Isis didn't want them to carry on, although they did not actually know the true nature of their voyage.

The Alexander ploughed on, and the captain ordered all crates and barrels to be secured. The sea began to get rougher, and the ship rocked from side to side, unsteady, and unable to pick up speed in the swell.

Ptolemy stayed with Aulus in their cabin, and as Loli wandered around the lower decks she grabbed onto anything she could to steady herself. It was too much of an adventure for Loli to resist. She found the smallest oilskin coat she could, and a small stairwell in the bow of the ship that no one was using. With great difficulty, she opened the steel door to the deck. It was the wind that first took her breath away, as if it was some strange entity that wished to draw her life. The steel door flew from her hands and banged against the wall. The sea spray hit her face, and the waves threatened to come over the side of the ship. The captain kept the ship steadily on course, ploughing the gigantic waves as they crashed over the deck. In the distance, Loli stared opened-mouthed as a great wall of grey water came towards them. Instead of the giant wave crashing high over her head the ship keeled over as the huge wave hit one side of the ship. Loli was thrown back into the stairwell and down the stairs of the lower corridors. Incredibly the ship righted itself, and as it did so Loli felt a strong hand pull her up from the floor.

"Secure the door," someone shouted.

Loli slipped once and then found her feet. She struggled for breath and tried to get her soaking hair out of her eyes.

"Are you completely mad?" A soldier held her roughly by the arm as he stared at the over-sized oilskin she wore.

"I just thought…"

"Thought? It is that kind of thinking that will get you drowned." The soldier pulled his own great coat around him. "Stay below deck if you don't want to end up as fish food."

The soldier looked like he was about to throw up and he stumbled down the corridor, falling against the walls, as the ship swayed from side to side.

Finally, the storm gave up. The very sailors that said Isis was against them said that she had now saved them, and Loli was allowed up on deck. She stared out across the ocean and saw the strangest of sights. The sea was settling into hundreds of tiny whirlpools. How calm—how peaceful it was, now that the storm had vented its fury. It was still bitterly cold though.

An old sailor came up to her and stood beside her. He took off his oilskin, shook the water out of the hood, and looked across the water, too. "The whirlpools. They are a queer sight, aren't they?"

Loli nodded.

"The only whirlpools that I've seen ain't been them sort. I've seen the one in the Straits of Messina between mainland Italy and Sicily, but I've heard of a much bigger one—a maelstrom, they call it, off the Norwegian coast, takes in whole ships, whales and all sorts, sucks them down to the ocean bed and drags them along the bottom. I've heard of a sailor so badly dragged across the sea bottom that he had no face when he came up."

"No face," repeated Loli. She looked visibly paler.

"Don't worry, child, the maelstrom is a long way from here."

"You don't get big whirlpools around here?"

"Never have and never will."

"Then why are the smaller whirlpools coming together to make that?"

Loli pointed at the maelstrom that had suddenly appeared some way off on the port side of the ship.

Loli ran below and started shouting about what she had seen from the deck and another sailor was sent to find out what was going on. He soon returned... his face pale with fear.

"The captain says he is trying to get around it, and The Pharos is in sight."

Cleopatra heaved a sigh of relief. That would mean a safe harbour. Then she looked anxiously at Tjuya Meresamun and remembered the tarot card that she had shown to her and recalled her words. *"This is a difficult one. It can denote the strength of purpose or the coming of danger. The Tower is an important one for you, as it can represent the punishment for being presumptuous or too proud concerning the pursuit of forbidden knowledge. You must act with humility lest it may destroy you."*

At that moment, the same storm that hit the Pharos lighthouse, hit *The Alexander*. The next moment the ship encountered the maelstrom. The steamship heaved to one side as the great bulk of it struggled against the current of the enormous whirlpool. The ship creaked and groaned as it was pulled into frenzied and unfathomable vortices. The water seethed and swirled, the outer ring of the whirlpool rolled to resemble the eternal snake, chasing its own tail. *The Alexander* was dragged along inside the whirlpool that was as big as some small islands, and then with an almighty creak it began the dreadful descent. It heaved along and dropped headlong into the next circle of hell. Then it went around and then down into the next, from one eternal moment to the next, each circle pulling it further away from a safe horizon.

Loli screamed and grabbed hold of the nearest person, which was Aulus. Cleopatra and Tjuya Meresamun went down on their knees to pray to Isis and Wadjet, as the ship was swept in circles by the power of the maelstrom, until the ship tilted too much and they lost their balance. They clung to anything that offered stability. Cleopatra prayed harder.

"Wadjet if you ever had a care for us at all—save us now."

Cleopatra's voice could not be heard over the noise of the maelstrom. Aulus held Loli close to him. Loli could not get to Ptolemy. He had been thrown across the cabin and a table that had not been fixed to the floor pinned him to the wooden panelled wall. The great steam engine of The Alexander hissed and vented steam, enraged by the pounding the ship was getting by a force of nature, which was more powerful than it. All looked to be lost. Cleopatra felt that she would soon lose consciousness through disorientation and fear. Sea water found its way down each corridor, sweeping the crew off their feet. Most drowned quickly. Others, from horrific injuries, and some were blistered by steam. *The Alexander* sank to the ocean bed. Cleopatra, and those who had been chosen by Wadjet, were not on board.

The ship that took Isis, Ella and the priests to Alexandria had a far more uneventful journey. But as they berthed, the rain began to fall heavily, and the wind raged across the city. They didn't waste any time in getting to the great library. The librarians let them in to look at what they wanted. The library was free to all. It was more like twelve libraries in one, with rooms dedicated to many of the main subjects that interested Cleopatra. It was her library, but shared with all. It was one of the largest in the world. On two levels, and held up by beautiful pink pillars of marble engraved with gold, it was indeed impressive. Founded over two thousand years ago, during the reign of Ptolemy II, it was made up of gardens, lecture halls and meeting rooms, and the Peripatos walk, where scholars talked of Socrates, Aristotle, the Neoplatonists and mystical philosophy. The bookcases of the main vaulted library held books on mathematics, astronomy, physics and the natural sciences. Isis knew what she wanted. She walked slowly between them until she came to an alcove in the wall. Above the alcove were written the words...

THE PLACE OF THE CURE OF THE SOUL

Ella looked on as Isis pulled valuable scripts and fabulously bound books from the shelves and threw them across the floor. Ella froze. She didn't seem to know where she was or what she was doing there. A few people who had been reading rose from their chairs and tried to reason with Isis, as if she were just a madwoman who had wandered in. They shook their fists and shouted at her, saying that she was destroying the most precious things on earth. The priests were amazed that she should treat the books with such disrespect, and they begged for her to stop. Isis' black eyes fixed upon her priests and they fell silent. A strange supernatural wind blew through the halls and flung books across the rooms. Papers fluttered everywhere, like little white birds looking for a safe place to land.

Isis smashed the glass cabinet that contained the *Pyramid Texts*, scanned them eagerly, and focused on one page in particular. Her mouth followed the text…

A GOD WHO FEEDS ON HIS FATHERS AND LIVES ON HIS MOTHERS

While Isis became engrossed in that script, one priest, Diodorus, was drawn towards a book bound with gold leather on a shelf just in reach. He pulled it down and opened it. He could hardly believe that such a valuable and important book should be left lying around with the other books. Perhaps to put it amongst the others was the best place to hide it, but he doubted that somehow.

Isis didn't hear Diodorus speak. As she searched, she couldn't hear him over the sound of books crashing to the floor. He had been reading for some time before she felt the effect of the incantation upon her. Before she could get across the great circular room, Isis felt her blood run cold; such was the power of the binding upon her. She reached out to him and suddenly froze. Her arm hung in mid-air. The priests looked around at the piles of books and precious manuscripts that littered the floor. Diodorus put *The Book of Thoth* in his leather bag.

Ella blinked and stared at Diodorus and the ransacked library. "What has happened? Where is Loli?"

Diodorus put a hand on her shoulder. "I'll tell you all of what has happened when we get Isis out of here. The people who have left will bring others back here. We have to leave."

Ella nodded.

The priests tried to think of somewhere they could take Isis, get her away from the people of the city. She had done enough damage, and soon someone would turn up to see what was going on.

"We'll take her to the lighthouse whilst we study the book."

"To what purpose Diodorus?"

"To fully restore Isis."

"Do you really think that possible?"

"I do."

Ella thought that Diodorus seemed so certain, but she could not know that doubt lay heavily on his heart.

They quickly made arrangements to get Isis to Pharos. They didn't think that they had much time before Isis would be free again. The great lighthouse at Pharos was the first place that they could think of to take Isis, which might be strong enough to contain her, and where they might not be disturbed.

As they proceeded along the causeway, Diodorus looked up at the great lighthouse. The building was square at the base, and was as tall as the skyscrapers that they were familiar with in Manceastre. The lighthouse was surrounded by the sea, except for the east and south side, and it had been built as a beacon to lead the way to a safe harbour. The side that faced the sea was inclined, and each level skywards was smaller than the last. The doorway was above ground level, and a ramp supported by sixteen arches led to it. At the top, four marble slabs lay across four more upright marble pillars, so at that point the building opened to the elements and the sky.

Isis lay motionless on a straw pallet in the cart that the priests hauled along, beneath the towering landmark. Pharos was one of the seven wonders of the ancient world. As a boy, Diodorus had learned of them all. The great pyramid of Giza, The Hanging Gardens of Semiramis, The Statue of Zeus at Olympia, The Temple of Artemis at Ephesus, The Tomb of Mausolus, and the last one…how could he forget it…The Colossus of Rhodes, which had stood astride a great harbour. All gone now. All except The Hanging Gardens of Semiramis and The Pharos, which had both been maintained throughout the centuries.

Ella walked beside Diodorus.

"How long can we keep her like that?" She pointed at Isis.

Diodorus shrugged. "Who knows? I took the words randomly from the script. I have no idea how long their power will last."

Whatever had bound Isis, and therefore allowed them to transport her to the lighthouse, might lose its power soon. As if responding to this suggestion, Isis moved her outstretched hand slightly. Diodorus and his brother searched through *The Book of Thoth*. Diodorus had been taught that the book contained powerful spells and could bend nature to its will. Again he read from the book, and looked at Isis to see if the words were having any effect. Nothing. Diodorus put the book back into the leather bag as it began to rain harder.

For the second time since Ptolemy had partially restored Isis, she found herself bound in chains, but this time not in a dark basement embalming room, but bound to the four marble pillars on the very roof of the great lighthouse of Pharos. The storm clouds gathered around her as if the very elements wished to wreak vengeance upon her, or had she called them to her? A lightning bolt flashed across the sky. Isis raised her head and laughed madly as the thunder roared, and torrential rain fell. She yanked and pulled at the chains like some wild animal, instead of the revered deity she once was. For the second time on seeing her in chains, Ella pitied her, but nothing would convince her to set her free, as she had done before.

Isis was tormented. She babbled on about it being the beginning of the end, a day when mankind would be no more. She cursed that the gods had ever created humans, spat and writhed as if the ghosts of the dead gods themselves hurled themselves at her. She cried, whimpered, then rose up and cursed all before her once more. Her black hair flew wildly, as if strands were serpents seeking freedom and revenge. Once she looked straight at Ella, and Ella buried her face in her hands, so terrifying was the hatred upon the face of the goddess. Then Isis called out names Ella had never heard before, and more black clouds began to gather on the horizon and move towards the lighthouse at incredible speed.

Others prayed to older gods. Amidst the chaos, Wadjet answered the call for some caught in the maelstrom. Ptolemy, Aulus, Horus and Loli were taken by her to the small beach at the foot of The Pharos. Not Tjuya Meresamun. Loli looked about her, tried to catch her breath and pulled the wet hair from her face. Her father grabbed her and held her tight. Aulus tried to help Horus to his feet. They heard a scream above the roar of the wind. It came from the top of the great tower before them.

The rain stung Ella's face and the thunder deafened all who tried to speak. It became louder. Isis laughed again and shouted at the clouds, as if demanding that some primordial force act on her behalf. And yet she could not break her own chains. The wind howled around the pillars of the lighthouse and still the storm built in momentum. The sea churned up and brought all manner of creatures and wreckage, even the remains of dead sailors, to the surface that should have remained in the watery grave. Huge waves swept across the far side of the lighthouse, as if they, too, would free her from her bondage. Ella and the priests went down the stone steps and took refuge just below the marble platform where Isis stood. A sad group of travellers, they looked. Their wet clothes clung to them as they shivered. Some priests fell to their knees, then looked about helplessly as they realised that they had no goddess to pray to. Ptolemy again prayed to the old goddess, Wadjet, and begged her to intercede.

Ella again felt herself weaken. "Is there nothing we can do to stop this?"

Diodorus took a deep breath and reached for the leather bag. Suddenly Ella screamed at the sound of thunder, and a bolt of lightning struck part of the lighthouse above. The Pharos shook momentarily and Ella thought that the marble ceiling would fall upon their heads. They all cowered in a tight group close to the wall, furthest away from where some rubble fell into the room, leaving a hole in the wall. They could see the city beyond. Lightning struck buildings and toppled them easily. Diodorus turned away from the dreadful sight. Ella's heart sank. She thought that they only had moments left before the lighthouse would once more be struck and the lighthouse would fall into the harbour. She wept and thought of the sister she would never see again, of Swin and her home, and she found herself praying to any deity that would aid them.

As suddenly as the great storm had started, it stopped. Ella lifted up her head and saw, through the hole in the wall, the terrible destruction that had befallen the city. She picked through the rubble on the floor before her, followed by the others, and found a way up the stone steps to the roof beyond.

The four marble columns were still intact. On that floor lay the chains that had held Isis captive, but Isis had disappeared.

Suddenly Wadjet appeared before them all. The goddess. Half woman. And with the head of the cobra. She stood before them against the setting sun, in a blue, flawless sky. She was twice the size of any mortal and as the snake tongue flickered from side to side, each could hear her voice in their heads.

"It is time to end all this. In the name of all the gods who have been before me we will have the final judgement of all."

Ella looked down at her hand and saw it fade before her. She felt dizzy. The same happened to the exhausted survivors down on the small beach. Ella looked up at Diodorus and saw his face fade away against the blue sky. When Ella recovered she realised she was standing next to her little sister Loli, with Ptolemy, Diodorus, Horus and Aulus looking about them with bewildered eyes. Ella started back. Before them was an angry mob with stones in their hands. She saw someone throw a bottle. It spun in the air before it hit a wall and a flame shot across the ground and up a wooden door.

Ella screamed when a hand grabbed her arm and dragged her down a side street away from the mob. Aulus cried out and ran after her. The others followed. Ptolemy held Loli's hand tightly as they escaped from the crowd and hastily followed whoever had Ella. When Aulus grabbed the shoulder of the man who held her he saw that it was his friend, Sleeward.

"Come on," said Sleeward, "let's get out of here before they come after us. They won't care who they attack, and Clovis'men will be here soon."

Sleeward took them to a safe house. He took them to one place no one bothered with too much anymore. Of course Ella knew it well and thought of poor Swin. It was the opium den in the middle of Langsoon.

Chapter 19

Isis sank slowly, her arms spread wide as if to embrace her final destiny. Down to the submerged palace. Her hair a black mass of petrified snakes. Isis, calm now, looked about her at the ruins of the ancient palace that had lain there for over two thousand years. It had once belonged to the great Cleopatra, who Isis had raised above all others. Nepythys had wanted to destroy that Cleopatra. Isis remembered walking alongside the favoured one, her Cleopatra, the one she loved most. She was proud of her achievements and of the greatest city in the world. Isis recalled how they sat on the marble benches and looked out over a calm sea during a molten sunset. All had been possible then. And now those same feelings flowed through Isis. As the current gently pulled her down, she found herself face-to-face with her likeness. Perhaps it should all end here, she thought. It was the statue the first Cleopatra had dedicated to her. Isis looked at the marble representation and remembered more. She had once been noble, a guardian of a queen and now she recalled her own cruelty, and felt a shiver of remorse. Then that memory was gone and all Isis could see was a proud face, determined and resolute—an eternal Isis.

Wadjet then claimed Isis. Her cobra head now transformed to that of a woman. Wadjet's heart was full of pity as she caressed the face of her daughter. Wadjet then took Isis to Taposiris Magna on Lake Mariut, fifty kilometres west of Alexandra... built by Ptolemy II. Above a large tomb and within the city necropolis he built a smaller replica of the Pharos for his descendants. Isis stirred. She didn't remember anything of her brief time in the ruins of the first Cleopatra's palace. She buried her face against the shoulder of her mother and cried.

"Do you remember that you have a son, Horus?"

Isis shook her head and looked around as if the hieroglyphs and paintings on the walls were strange to her. Wadjet thought long and hard as to how she could best help Isis.

As Wadjet and Isis walked through the myriad tunnels beneath the temple, Wadjet showed her the riches of Egypt and Rome. The tomb had never been broken into, and indeed its location had been kept secret for over two thousand years, since the death of the Empress and Emperor of Rome. Silently, Wadjet and Isis moved through the underground burial chambers until they came before the statue of Alexander. Isis paused.

"You loved him most of all," said Wadjet.

"I don't recall. I don't recall loving anyone—ever."

They walked on to the great chamber. Before them lay two sarcophagi. Wadjet pointed at the inscriptions.

"Anthony and Cleopatra."

Isis looked blankly at the two sarcophagi. By the side and to the back of the coffins were the stone centurions who now guarded them in death. Both held a spear made of gold and a sword.

"Why are you showing me these?"

"To help you feel again. You loved Cleopatra once."

"No longer."

Wadjet passed her hand in front of the sarcophagus. There was a great rumbling sound and slowly, steadily, the great marble lid moved to one side. Suddenly it stopped. The sarcophagus was surrounded by a small platform. Slowly Isis climbed the three steps that led up to it and gazed on the masked face of her Cleopatra who had lain there undisturbed for two thousand years.

"You see before you your great Queen. Why do you desert her descendants now? You who were born before the great Alexander, and you rejoiced in how wonderful this world could become. But even before Nepythys killed you, you swallowed the bitterest pill, and you refused to come to the aid of the present Cleopatra. You became corrupt, and more a sign of death than of life eternal. Now, her people curse your name instead of worship it. They blame you for the plagues that cut their loved ones down before they have had a chance to blossom. You are the canker on the lotus flower. Look upon the death mask of Cleopatra—so like your own. Is she not of you? In this place you built your temple, within the one of Osiris, and you took his cult for yourself. You fought to eliminate his name from history. When Alexander conquered Egypt, you were by his side and he, followed by the Ptolemy dynasty, were favoured by you until now."

Isis. The pale face—the black eyes. Whatever she was thinking, she concealed it well from Wadjet.

"Do you want to be cursed by all until the end of time—until the end of days?"

"I have no memory of all this. Only of what I am now."

"You are more an animal than the divine being you once were."

"Then you should pity me."

"I do and want the first, the only Isis restored."

"I was dead and now I live. Isn't that enough?"

"But perhaps on borrowed time."

"You would kill me?"

"If I had to, I would. If there is no other solution. You are the plague on mankind. You are the darkness that terrorises this once fair world. In times past it was The Phorcydes, the monstrous children of Phorcys and Ceto, who plagued mankind and sought their downfall. The Gorgons—Euryale, Stheno, and Medusa, the most infamous of all, who turned men to stone. The Graeae—Deino, Enyo and Pemphredo. Wasters of cities. Echida, later named the Mother of all Monsters and the She-Viper, and finally Ladon, the serpent-dragon, who fought Heracles and won. All would be proud of you. I am not, Isis. All monsters, but you are the most feared now, of all."

Isis placed her hand on the elaborate funeral mask of Cleopatra. The kohl-black eyes stared back at her. Beneath the mask was the body of the once beautiful Cleopatra, and Isis vowed that Nepythys would not succeed again. Nepythys would die and her dog-son Anubis. Isis would do anything to live and become more powerful. In that moment she knew what she had to do.

Isis turned to her mother and held out her hands. "Perhaps there is still hope."

She remembered the words from the Pyramid Texts.

A GOD WHO FEEDS ON HIS FATHERS AND LIVES ON HIS MOTHERS

At that point Isis knew what she had to do to become more powerful. Only a god can kill a god. Isis moved swiftly. She grabbed a sword that was at the feet of one of the stone centurions and plunged it into the body of her mother. Wadjet stared open-mouthed, at her daughter, as Isis twisted the sword in deeper. Wadjet tried to transform her head into that of a cobra. At one point the transformation was made and her head darted forward, her enormous fangs, missing her daughter's throat by inches. It was useless. Wadjet felt her power drain from her and she sank to her knees. Isis pulled the sword from her mother's stomach and with speed cut the heart out of the body. Isis put the heart to her lips. When she left the tomb she knew what she would have to do. With her new-found strength she would seek revenge.

Nepythys, far away in Britanniae, felt stronger, too. So did Anubis and Horus. Loli looked into the grief filled eyes of Horus and felt a shiver run down her spine, too. When Nepythys had killed the favoured one—Isis, the remaining gods had become weaker, but in the killing of her own mother, and the eating of her heart, Isis had found new strength and so had the remaining gods, Isis would seek Nepythys out. She would finally have her revenge on her sister and Anubis. Nepythys also knew now that the next time she confronted Isis—one would die and the other, rather than become weaker, would become all-powerful.

Cleopatra could feel the warmth of the fire on her face before she opened her eyes. Through the flickering flames she could see a young woman sitting before a large tapestry. The woman hummed to herself, and in her hair strips of gold burned orange from the glow of the flames. She had the longest hair Cleopatra had ever seen—it trailed along the floor around her sandalled feet. With a small pair of scissors the woman cut a strand of hair, entwined some of it, and threaded a needle. She wore a long black dress, her white shoulders exposed, but she did not shiver like Cleopatra did.

The tapestry—immense, encircled the room. The walls looked to be made of blue marble. Rich rugs adorned the floor, mostly violet and green, but the creatures worked into the background were golden and of the sea, it seemed. Huge columns embedded with lapis lazuli held the ceiling up. The lapis lazuli glinted blue green by the light of the huge fire that crackled in the centre of the room. Cleopatra sat on a golden couch the like of she'd never seen in her palace in Rome. Oddly enough, she wasn't afraid. The woman was caught up in her task and didn't seem aware of her at all. She spoke without looking at Cleopatra.

"My name is Neithotep. I am the first Egyptian Queen. Neithotep, originally the goddess Neith, but I chose to be like you. I was human, for a time."

She pointed to the crossed arrows and shield that hung behind her on the wall. They symbolised her role as a goddess of war.

"I wanted peace. My union with Narmer of Upper Egypt brought Upper and Lower Egypt together." Neithotep again pointed to the tapestry and at the symbol of a falcon and one of a catfish for Narmer.

Cleopatra searched for the memory. And then she found it. When a girl, Cleopatra had been inspired by Neithotep. She had been a great queen of Egypt and reigned five thousand years ago.

"Many do not remember me now, but you do. I am now both queen and goddess. Isis has imprisoned and bound me to this place. Even Wadjet could not free me. I know all about you, Cleopatra. Your ancestor, the one who united Egypt and Rome, was of Greek descent. Did you know that?"

"I did."

"You are descended from the Macedonians."

"I know that too."

Neithotep pointed to the figures and hieroglyphs on the tapestry. "These are your ancestors all the way back to Anthony and Cleopatra. Here—the battle of Actium where your empire started and there..." the woman pointed to another part of the tapestry near the end; the part which was unfinished.

Cleopatra recognised herself in the tapestry. Neithotep had cut and used her own hair on the pale canvas. Her skill as a needlewoman was evident in that she depicted faces in great detail. Cleopatra recognised Gaius, too, and felt afraid for him. He stood before a mob in Rome. She knew some of the buildings. Gaius sat astride his horse and the mob hurled stones. Some soldiers had opened fire on the crowd. The undead were there, too. She was reminded of the way Julia had looked. Further along were *The Alexander*, the maelstrom and people struggling in the water.

Cleopatra pointed at the maelstrom and her hand began to shake. "I was there...what has happened to the others?"

"A few survived."

"Are they here?"

"No. At the Pharos. Wadjet has taken them there. I was given the task of looking after you and to keep you away from Isis for a time. See...you are here in the arms of Wadjet."

Cleopatra laughed. "Why would she want to keep me away from Isis? I've waited for her for so long."

"Isis is mad and her sister is not much better. You must stay away from both for the moment."

As her eyes searched the tapestry Cleopatra saw The Pharos and then a blank canvas. Cleopatra looked confused.

"You were a queen and now a goddess?"

"Merely a servant to Wadjet."

"A servant who weaves my destiny."

"No. One who will record your destiny. That is all."

Around the room there were many chests and Cleopatra wondered what they contained.

Neithotep walked across to one of them, her pale sandalled feet making no sound. She lifted the lid of one chest and pulled out another tapestry, which she laid upon the marble floor. Cleopatra knelt down to look at it. She recognised the scene immediately. She saw the Sphinx, and beneath it were many passageways, some looked to be flooded with water, and beneath the level of the water was a great tomb.

"Here lay the body of Osiris."

"What do you mean lay?"

"This is how the tomb looks now, and it is, as you see, beneath the water. But Osiris was never there for long. He was taken away to protect him from further violation from Isis."

"She killed him?"

"Remember, Cleopatra…only a god can kill a god. Yes. Isis killed him, but had his earthly body mummified and placed within the chamber under the Sphinx…"

With a swift intake of breath Neithotep faltered a little and then straightened and screamed. The sound of it echoing around the room made Cleopatra step back to seek a way out of the room.

Neithotep once again pointed at the tapestry. Cleopatra could not understand what she said. She spoke in a language unknown to her. Neithotep placed her pale hands on the tapestry. The scene had appeared without any of her skill. Her only hope that she would ever be free had vanished. Cleopatra looked at the tapestry. She recognised Wadjet but in this depiction Wadjet lay on the ground and Isis stood over her.

Neithotep tried to regain her composure but sank to the floor and stared once more at the tapestry.

Cleopatra gently touched her arm. "Am I now a prisoner here?"

"No, you may go where you want. Wadjet did not bind you here. Only I am bound. Stay here for a time though until the worst of what Isis will do has passed. You will be safe here with me."

"My safety isn't reason enough. How do I rejoin my companions?"

"Will it and it will be so."

As Neithotep was about to say something to Cleopatra, Cleopatra thought of where she wanted to be and Neithotep was left once more to her terrible solitude. The first thoughts that rushed through Cleopatra's head should have been of being reunited with Gaius, whether he was still in Rome or back in Manceastre, but what thought flashed through her mind could only cause her more fear and dread. Before she realised what she had done she delivered herself into the hands of her enemy, Clovis.

Chapter 20

Gaius returned from Rome to Manceastre with as many steamships and legionaries as he could in the short time he had given himself to complete his mission. The weather had, thankfully, been on their side, and now he felt he had enough legionaries to get rid of Clovis once and for all. It didn't take him long to get his soldiers to the city wall. They marched quickly, looked strong and able, too. A little green, some of them, but ready for the fray. What they lacked for in experience they made up for with enthusiasm. All were in traditional armour. Warm clothing to keep out the cold. Woollen trousers and jacket emblazoned with the insignia of his legion. Each wore a thin brass cooulus helmet with cheekpieces. All eager for battle, and honour, and would follow Gaius anywhere. Just like his dog Oppian.

"In the name of Cleopatra open the gate," he shouted at legionaries on the city wall. He saw the garrison commander, Vibius Laenus, momentarily look down at him, and then leave the rampart. The legionaries, when their commander was out of earshot, just stared at Gaius at first but one lanky looking one finally shouted down.

"We take our orders from Clovis, and Vibius Laenus."

"I am Gaius Anthony Sosius, general of the army of the Empress Cleopatra. I order you to open the gates in her name."

More legionaries peered over the ramparts and laughed with their comrades. The gates remain closed.

Gaius sighed deeply and he bellowed at the guards above the gate. "I command you to open the gates or it will go badly for you if you don't."

The lanky one shouted in reply again. "You'll kill us, or even if you don't, our Governor General will."

"I'll pay you double what Clovis is paying you now."

The legionaries mumbled amongst themselves, a few shook their heads. Clovis had tortured some of their comrades after disobedience, and all very well knew how Clovis had used the terrible brass bull on a slave. Word of that had spread quickly. Clovis made sure that his spies and men at the top were very well paid. The legionaries didn't have much to complain about either. Most of them had been born in Britanniae and there had always been a dislike of the legions from the Mediterranean.

For three days Gaius pounded the city walls and called for the occupants of the city to give up or the siege would be made worse for them. Finally the steam driven ballistrae was assembled. It was a contraption that uses levers and springs to deliver spherical stones to the city walls at great speed. However the old Governor General, Claudius, had for reasons of his own that had never been truly understood by his people, been busy reinforcing the city walls over the last few years. The outer walls had been reinforced with metal between stone with a wide walkway along the top. The walls were over sixty feet high and although Gaius had many legionaries the defences held firm. The army within the city used steam too. They used the giant steam driven crossbow, the Scorpio. A great, powerful machine, capable of firing metal bolts to a great distance. Gaius made sure that his tents were pitched well out of range of the hideous machines.

Gaius' legionaries, usually brave, were becoming unnerved. They were unaccustomed to their dead comrades rising and wandering the battlefield, arms outstretched, looking for comfort from their fellow soldiers. All their friends could do was bind their hideous wounds and sit them by the campfire at night, watching them stare at the flames with white filmy eyes. Others seemed to act just as they had done before they had been killed, and demanded that they wanted to fight. Ones who had lost limbs were kept quiet in the tents, and guards placed outside. Morale was low. Soldiers shook their heads at the site of an undead army pleading to fight for their Empress and being incapable of doing so. Few soldiers had the appetite to eat.

Sleeward and Aulus used the catacombs to get out of the city. Sleeward decided that he would join forces with Gaius to help bring Clovis down. Aulus wanted to go with him. The air smelt of oil, fire and death. The hissing sound of steam stopped, occasionally, and he thought that he heard the voice of his son, Luce, calling his name.

"Why did you come here, Aulus? You would have been safe in the city—hidden away with Ella and the others in Langsoon."

"I've seen enough, Sleeward. I want it to end. I won't stand by and just watch. If I can be of help, I will."

Sleeward nodded and patted his friend on the back. "I know," he said.

Grief stricken, but with revenge in his heart, Sleeward asked to see Gaius.

The young legionary eyed them up and down. "You're more like spies. Why on earth would we want you on our side? What could you do for us?"

"We could help you get into the city. Take us to your general. My words are only for him."

An older legionary who had been listening to the exchange beckoned the young soldier over. "Search them well."

The young one did as he was told and turned to the old legionary, now standing next to him. "Nothing. They are unarmed."

Gaius looked up from the camp fire. He often sat with his men rather than keep to himself in his tent. He had been preoccupied with the fact that, or rather consoled by the news, that *The Alexander* hadn't come back from Alexandria. At that moment he thought that he'd rather Cleopatra was not in Britanniae. Clovis was now completely mad and had declared himself emperor in her absence. A stupid idea. He was already under siege in his own city and even if the other nobles tried to liberate him, Gaius was ready for them. Gaius was eager to get rid of Clovis. He had been allowed too much power for far too long.

Sleeward looked a sorry sight. He was unshaven, wore scruffy clothes and his hair was dirty.

"I can get you into the city."

"How?"

"You know about the catacombs?" said Sleeward.

"Indeed I do. They run through Kares-Bu."

"There are more. On the east side of the city the catacombs go right up to the outside wall. Not far from the Coliseum. There is a hidden door. If your siege proved to be successful, probably Clovis would leave the city by this way. Naturally the main passageway leads to the palace, but there are two more entrances from within the city to it."

Sleeward knew every inch of the catacombs in Kares-Bu, and especially the ones near the Coliseum and palace. He'd often scoured them for victims for the Clovis experiments, until his own son became one of them, and Clovis had experimented on him. He told Gaius about this. He told him about Luce.

"The catacombs had been built long before the city walls had been reinforced. One way leads to the Temple of Isis. There's no point in using that one, the temple will be a pile of rubble. We can get out by another one though. I know where it leads. Then we take Clovis' legionaries by surprise."

"You really think that you can find it?"

"I'm sure of it."

Gaius didn't doubt him. He had dealt with enough men to know when a man such as Sleeward was telling the truth.

"If any of the passageways have collapsed you have machines that could be adapted to dig?"

Gaius nodded. "It is possible."

"Then I suggest you act quickly. I wouldn't settle in for a long siege."

"And why not?"

"Not if you want to save your Empress."

"She isn't here. Her ship isn't here."

Sleeward shrugged. "She's here all right. Clovis has her." He then clenched his teeth.

"And I want him."

Gaius got to his feet. He reminded himself that he had just judged Sleeward to be truthful, but what did he really know of him? He could be just another crazy bastard like Clovis, but Sleeward had a way of getting into the city. He had lost his son to Clovis. Gaius knew when a man was fired by revenge. It was written all over Sleeward's face.

"Get some food and then we'll talk."

During the encounter Aulus said nothing. He'd had enough of Clovis, too. What he had seen in the cellars under the palace had sickened him. He cared about what was happening and wanted an end to Clovis. His friend, Sleeward, looked weak from lack of sleep and hunger. A soldier brought them some food and Aulus made sure that Sleeward ate it. Aulus thought about Ella. One soldier rummaged through a wagon and brought them two bed rolls and cloaks to keep out the cold. Aulus thanked him. The soldier looked surprised. Sleeward stretched out on the mat and pulled the cloak over himself. His hand shook as he did so. Aulus noticed. Without a second thought for his own welfare, Aulus added his cloak.

In the first mist of a cold, grey day, Sleeward and Aulus were taken to Gaius' tent. They were given some food and wine and told that Gaius liked all his men to be informal around him. Gaius indicated they should look at a map. A plan of the city, which showed the city walls. Gaius again instinctively looked for possible weak points in the fortifications. He checked himself and looked across the table at Sleeward.

Sleeward pointed at the map. "Here is the location of the door, small—pretty well hidden. Forgotten by many. You could get your men in a few at a time, perhaps—in small groups. Get the gates open. Then you could try and get to her. There won't be as many guards as you think. Most have been deployed to the city walls."

Gaius nodded his head and the men made their plans.

Chapter 21

Clovis had been busy. Nothing was going to spoil it. Not even the enemy at the gates. He had enough soldiers to deal with Gaius and more were on the way. He wanted a special celebration for the spent populace of Manceastre, some of whom he had brought there especially for the occasion. Some of the undead were in that crowd. He had also made relatives and friends bring their walking dead. He needed all of them there. He had to be seen to be in control and that people were there to listen to him.

It was to take place in the coliseum alongside the gladiatorial games. His advisors, of course, thought him mad to have games in the middle of a siege, but Clovis didn't care. There were few gladiators left anyway. Many had died the year before when the plague had swept the city, but the citizens would be entertained by this one 'event'—and he was certain they would never forget it.

Indeed, the gladiators put on a poor show, and Clovis soon gave directions that they should all be taken away and put to death, elsewhere. He was bored with them, and eager for the real reason he had brought so many together.

Musicians played and the barefoot, young dancing girls came into the arena in pale pink and green dresses, trying not to shiver with the cold. They held long garlands of flowers and pretended to pull something along that was being pushed from behind. Then, that something came into view, pushed by the more muscular men, who didn't seem to have much of a problem. Into the winter sunshine came the brazen brass bull. Clovis cheered. The crowd didn't. Clovis didn't seem to notice. He rose to his feet as the bull progressed to the centre of the arena.

"Today we will have a sacrifice for the gods, and you will help me choose who the favoured one should be."

Grey faces remained silent.

"Well then. Let the gods themselves decide."

Into the stadium walked Nepythys and Anubis. The crowd stared, open-mouthed, and some rose from their seats as if about to go. Nepythys was in mortal form, but Anubis was impossibly tall for a mortal and furthermore, he wore the jackal-head.

"Be seated. Be seated," shouted Clovis.

Nepythys and Anubis. Clovis marvelled at their appearance, but what had they really done for him? It seemed to him that he'd done everything for himself. Why couldn't he be one of them? The words that the archaeologist had read out came back to him.

On that day of slaying the Oldest Ones,
The King is a possessor of offerings who knots the cord,
And who himself prepares his meal;
The King is one who eats men and lives on the gods.

Legionaries appeared at every entrance and the people reluctantly sat down again. A cloud fell across the stadium and the crowd became deathly quiet. Laughing, Nepythys and Anubis climbed the stone steps and joined Clovis in his royal box. Some of the crowd then laughed too, thinking that the man was wearing some sort of strange mask, and his height a product of the inbreeding that had become a rarer sight these days. It would explain his extraordinary size.

Clovis put his hand up and the crowd slowly fell into an uneasy silence.

"The gladiators were a great disappointment, but I have this special sacrifice for you. You will enjoy yourselves, believe me."

A diminutive woman was brought in by two priests, loyal to the new gods. Her wrists were bound by flowery garlands and her head held low. She looked up once, when she heard the thunder of the impact of the ballistrae on the city walls. She knew that a siege could take weeks, and she probably only had minutes to live. The woman was Cleopatra. She wore no crown. Clovis had ordered her to be dressed in rags—he wished to humiliate her completely.

"Here is your Empress. She is the one who has lost favour with the gods. She has brought upon your heads, famine and the plague. Isis has refused to appear before her or her family for three generations. Your families will suffer no more. I promise you that. It is time for change. Let the new gods rule."

Clovis smiled at Nepythys and Anubis.

Cleopatra remembered the words of Tjuya Meresamun.

"There is also this one, the card that represents fortitude and strength.

*As you see the card shows the picture of a woman holding the jaws of a
lion, whether she is prying them open, closing them or simply holding them
it is difficult to say."*

Cleopatra didn't have the strength to fight. What could a weakened
woman do? And even with an army, how could she? Against Clovis,
backed by Nepythys? Against a goddess? Impossible. Even if Gaius was
with her now, she doubted if he could do anything. All Cleopatra's guards
were dead and Clovis had somehow managed to keep the loyalty of his
legions. Cleopatra's legions weren't far away, but they would never get
into the city in time. All was lost.

Clovis looked down on Cleopatra and gestured to Nepythys and
Anubis. "I have the blessing of the gods. We will cure our sick, feed our
children and the dead will be allowed to pass over to the afterlife—to rest
in peace. It is their right."

And when all this is over, I will become a god, thought Clovis. He
remembered the words of the texts.

Nepythys held up her arms to the crowd. "Worship me and I will rid
you of plague. I will feed your children and see that they never go hungry
again. We will have a new time of plenty for all. A new millennium will
be with you soon and with it a new beginning. This, I promise you."

Some of the crowd cheered. Clovis thought it encouraging. "It is time
for a new emperor. I will rule, and promise that you will all live well.
There will be a prosperous time for you."

Slaves had been giving out food and wine as the people had entered the
coliseum and they had been pleased, and thanked the gods for Clovis on
this day. One man hadn't been appeased. When he saw Cleopatra, he
shouted something against Clovis. Cleopatra looked up but, he was quickly
removed by a legionary. Most guessed what the man's fate would be and
were already reconciled to the fact that if they spoke out of turn, they
would meet a similar end. For the moment they didn't go hungry, either.
Perhaps the time of hardship was over.

Cleopatra looked nervously at the brass bull. She suddenly felt dizzy,
and she had difficulty remaining on her feet. Slaves piled wood in a pit
that had been dug out of the sandy coliseum ground. The giant bull was
then dragged over the pit. The slaves poured oil over the wood. Cleopatra
saw the small trapdoor then opened beneath the bull. Surely Clovis
wouldn't—in front of all these people? Cleopatra was then certain of her
fate. The garlands that covered her wrists concealed the rope that bit into
her skin. She felt helpless and looked once more at the entrances to the

Coliseum, hoping for Gaius, hoping someone would save her. She tried to pull her wrists apart, but they were bound tightly and she silently moaned in pain. Cleopatra felt so weak, so defenceless and abandoned by her people. Would no one try to help her?

The two priests pushed Cleopatra forward and she almost stumbled. They pushed her again, and then she stopped abruptly. She was determined that she would not fall into the dirt of the arena. They grabbed her by her arms and brought her closer to the bull. She held her head high. If she was to die, she would show her people that she wasn't afraid.

One woman let out an audible gasp and then quickly put her hand over her mouth and looked to see if any legionary had heard her. They hadn't. All eyes were on Cleopatra and the bull. She was dragged even closer to the monstrosity, and that was when her knees gave way and Cleopatra fell into the dust. One priest went back and hauled her to her feet. The other waited silently as Cleopatra was dragged towards the bull. It began to snow, and Cleopatra looked heavenwards with a prayer on her lips to a mad goddess.

"Isis, if ever I needed you, it would be now. Isis. Don't forsake me."

Isis had never appeared to her. To everyone else it seemed, but not to Cleopatra, and now when she was about to die, Isis still refused her. Had she been such a bad empress? thought Cleopatra. Clovis would rule. The cruel and abominable Clovis would rule—blessed by the gods. Is that the way it had to be? Cruelty wins through above all? She looked up at him. Clovis smiling...anticipating her death and his new empire? The priests had changed their allegiance as readily as the people would. Would no one help her now?

The sky grew darker still, and she was pulled again towards the bull. Cleopatra could smell the oil on the wood, and a legionary stood there now too, with a torch in his hand.

Cleopatra, on seeing the flames, finally lost her composure. "Isis!" she screamed, and struggled with the men who tried to push her through the entrance underneath the bull.

"Isis—if ever there was a time when I needed you most!"

Again, there came a gasp from the crowd. There, suddenly, before Cleopatra, stood Isis, dressed in white. Isis, wearing the white and red combined crown of Upper and Lower Egypt. Her arms crossed and holding the crook and flail. The priests let go of Cleopatra, terrified of the sudden appearance of the goddess. They fell to their knees before Isis and begged for forgiveness. It was a futile gesture. The two priests suddenly burst into flame. Flesh burned to the bone, the melting fat feeding the ferocious supernatural flame. They could not even scream. They were so quickly enveloped by the fire.

Isis calmly walked by the two burning priests and over to Cleopatra. Isis touched Cleopatra's hands. The ropes and garlands fell to the ground.

"I always believed in you," said Cleopatra.

"But it wasn't enough." Isis smiled at Cleopatra.

Isis glanced at the crowd. "They didn't believe."

Clovis felt nervous at this point and looked at Nepythys whose constant smile had fallen from her face.

Isis stared up at her sister. "Finally."

There was a low murmur from the crowd as Nepythys boldly walked down the stone steps. She felt strong. That worried her a little. She knew that this meant that Isis was strong, too, as Nepythys received all her power from her.

"So what now? We both want to be queen of what is left. That isn't going to work, is it?" said Nepythys.

"You killed me once. It isn't going to happen a second time."

"You killed them all. All the gods—even the ones I loved. You have had no thought for any but yourself." Nepythys got to the bottom step, held one booted foot out, and then it hit the ground with a thud.

"And if you rule in my place, would it all be any better? I think that you would clear the land of all mortals and start again. Perhaps with the offspring of you and your son?

Nepythys placed a hand on her belly and whispered under her breath. "And would that be such a bad thing?" The crowd strained to hear her.

Cleopatra looked at both of the goddesses and backed slowly away to the perimeter of the arena. Clovis thought about shouting for the guard to have Cleopatra removed, but what was happening before him was far more important. It was clear to him that his fate was now tied up with that of Nepythys, and it hung in the balance.

Isis turned to look at Anubis, who stood as if ready to enter the arena. Suddenly there was a noise and the sound of scuffling coming from high up in the Coliseum. Shouts were heard and then the cry for arms to be put aside. Someone broke through the guards and scoured the scene, looking for his Empress. It was Gaius. Behind him: Aulus, Sleeward, then Ella and Ptolemy. Loli and Horus appeared. Isis smiled at Horus. She now remembered her boy-god, and soon they would be together, forever.

Ella held Loli close. As she did so, something sharp dug into Loli's chest and she remembered that she was still wearing the pendant, the Eye of Horus. As she broke away from Ella, Horus stared at it. He then looked from the two of them, and down at the other two sisters who sought to destroy each other.

Loli sobbed and clung again to Ella. Then she turned to Horus. There was pity in his eyes.

"Why are the gods so cruel?" cried Loli.

"It isn't just the gods though, is it?" Horus pointed at the brass bull.

Isis smiled at Horus. "My son. At last we find each other again."

Horus turned away from his mother.

Isis spoke again to Nepythys. "In killing me, you took your own power away. It was given to you, by me. "

"I think I know that now."

Nepythys turned to the silent crowd and shouted. "You should hate her for what she has done. It is Isis who you should fear for your lives, and indeed she hasn't finished with you upon your death."

"Would you have acted differently? said Isis, "you kept the secret for long enough."

"Too long, sister."

Nepythys turned to face the crowd. "This is your Queen of the Night. Know the truth. She steals their souls, consumes them. Look at your children now. They should rot before your eyes. But no—they live on in this state, neither living nor dead. Look at them and decide who should be your queen, your goddess. Cleopatra is no better. She, too, let this happen to you. I give you no lies, no eternal life. It does not exist."

Clovis held his breath. The horrified crowd shook their fists and shouted abuse at Isis and Nepythys.

Isis turned to the people, arms held out to the undead, who sat silently between their relatives. "You should give them to me willingly. I take their tormented souls and turn them into something quite wonderful."

"You give them nothing but certain death. No afterlife for mankind. Only power for you," said Nepythys.

"And you, sister, are so benevolent to mankind?"

"You gave mankind lies in return for adoration and when they stopped worshipping you—you deserted them."

"And you would do the same."

"It was you who sent the great plagues. You who left them with no hope, and you who decreed that immortality would only be for the gods."

The crowd grew angry. Some rose to their feet screaming and shouting.

Isis put her hand up to silence them.

"The odds are against you, Nepythys. Your power has been given to you by me."

Isis stared into the crowd at the grey faces of those who should be dead—forever. She extended an arm to those she wanted. One by one they fell before her. The people screamed as their loved ones crumbled to heaps of bones and rotting flesh. The horror—to see their family decompose before their eyes. The children they had nursed. The mothers and fathers who had loved them. The lovers they had pledged their hearts to, forever.

It was a barbaric way to die. Nothing had prepared the ones who loved the dead. It was the inhuman act of a god who cared nothing for life. Isis consumed the souls of the dead—getting steadily more powerful until her eyes blazed with the heat of a thousand suns, and terror filled the air.

With every soul Isis took she felt stronger. Nepythys and the remaining gods felt it, too. Some of the undead got unsteadily to their feet, and then collapsed into the arms of their relatives, and friends. One woman screamed as she held the limp corpse of her child in her arms. A man smoothed the hair out of his wife's face and gazed upon the now decomposing flesh of one once so much loved, and still so adored, he would not push her from him. One by one, Isis took them all. The smell of death was overpowering. Some of the living retched, and held their cloaks to the faces. Mothers and fathers sobbed. Husbands and wives wept. All lay their dead upon the ground and covered their bodies with cloaks. They had protected them for so long, they had lost them once, and now they lost them a second time. The cold wind echoed the wailing of the living, until it rose to the very heavens.

Isis said nothing. She knew that if she failed and did not kill Nepythys, Nepythys would kill her. And this time, instead of becoming weaker, Nepythys would become stronger. There would be no Wadjet to see that the remaining gods didn't overreach themselves.

Isis felt the strength from the souls flow into her, and there was much more. This time, with every soul taken, great secrets seemed to be unlocked within her mind. Wadjet was dead, and with her death her daughter, Isis, was much stronger. She could think back to a time when the gods had been born, and she thought that she was the most powerful of all the gods. But there was one great secret she could not fathom. She searched for a way into it, circled it and tried to break in, but it resisted her. Some power resisted her. When she tried to put a name or an image to that power, she failed—and that terrified her. It was the one secret that could bring about her destruction. She knew that she was the mother of all now…wasn't she? There could be no other force stronger than her.

Isis threw her flail to the ground. "Sister, prepare to die."

"I won't give up without a fight."

"Why would we fight?"

"What do you mean?"

Isis looked towards the high wooden door, the entrance to the arena. She found a combatant that would amuse her crazed mind. She laughed and gestured towards the door. It slowly opened inwards to the arena. They heard the sound of it long before they saw it. A hissing, and then the giant head partly emerged. The winter sun struck the head first, and the crowd shrank back. The bronze burn of it—flat to the ground. Then the length of it came into full view. An Egyptian cobra. It slithered through the sand in the arena, rhythmically to the left and then the right. Its gigantic body plunging fear in the hearts of all there. Suddenly it reared up, twice the height of a man. The flat head—depressed with a broad snout. It spread its collar wide and flicked its tongue. Isis held it with her eyes and it, now silent, waited for a command.

Nepythys was quick to use what power she now had to rise to the challenge. Her creature bellowed from outside the arena and came running in, its hooves stirring up the dust. The Minotaur. Half man, half bull, twice the height of an ordinary man, and the awful red eyes. His chest, although covered, was enormous, muscular, and his whole body encased in armour, except for the head. The armour was the same bronze colour as the snake. The bull: black head, hooves and tail. In one hand the Minotaur held an enormous wooden club, in the other a net. Once more the Minotaur bellowed, shaking the foundations of the high stone wall that protected the crowd from the hideous creatures before them. The cobra made a short stabbing thrust as a warning. The distance between them was still enough for a show of strength before trial. Ella held tightly onto Loli and backed slowly up some stone steps. A woman screamed, and with lightning speed the cobra turned its enormous head slightly. The Minotaur charged forward with his club. The pounding of his hooves matched that of Ella's heart, as she clutched Loli even more tightly to her. One swing of the club and he missed the cobra, but it struck at the metal breastplate. Fangs against metal. It reared again. Nepythys seemed to shudder in response.

The Minotaur swung again and this time hit his mark. The giant snake fell to one side and then its head hit the ground with a dull thud.

Isis fell to the ground, momentarily stunned.

The cobra recovered and slithered around the Minotaur hissing periodically at him. Its quick eyes looked at the Minotaur's hooves, broad legs, anywhere where it could get past the armour and strike. Again the club came down. Again the snake was hit. Again Isis felt the blow. Quickly recovering, the cobra rose up again, its huge bronze hood expanding to its full width. The tongue flickered, tasting the air in anticipation of the kill. It struck again. Its fangs hit the wooden club and this time it embedded one of its fangs in the armour. The length of its body writhed horribly as it attempted to release itself. The Minotaur tried to grab its huge tail but couldn't get a grip on it. The cobra thrashed again, and next time it loosened itself and fell back to the sand once more.

Each time the cobra attacked it struck metal. At one point it rose up so high, as if trying to swallow the bull's head. The Minotaur snorted, bellowed and stepped quickly back, then rushed at the cobra again, momentarily pinning the cobra's body to the ground. The cobra freed itself again. Strike after strike came from it as it entwined itself around the neck of the bull. The hands of the Minotaur grasped around the neck of the cobra squeezing harder until the yellow eyes of the giant cobra bulged with the pressure. The Minotaur's arms then weakened. One strike from the cobra must have hit home, as the Minotaur then loosened his grip enough for the cobra to slither from his grasp.

Isis saw her chance. The cobra stared at Isis and moved its head to one side as if comprehending a telepathic message. Isis looked at Nepythys. To the horror of the crowd the giant cobra moved with great speed along the sandy ground and up the stone steps. The crowd screamed and people tried to run away, falling over others as they did so. The cobra sank its fangs into the neck of the goddess, its mouth taking the whole width of her neck as it unhinged its jaws slightly. It pumped venom into her body until it dripped down her like honey. Then the snake convulsed as if in rapture. Anubis fell upon the cobra and tried to pull it off his mother. No matter how hard he tried the snake would not let go, and then suddenly the cobra wrapped the end of its tail around the neck of Anubis and squeezed tightly. Anubis, the jackal-headed god, struggled and failed to get the coil loose from around his neck. Within seconds Anubis found it hard to breathe. All he could do was stare into his mother's eyes, as they met their deaths, together. As they both breathed their last the giant cobra vanished. Anubis fell upon the body of his mother and the sweet sticky venom that oozed from her wounds became a honey trap to him.

The Minotaur vanished at the same time as Nepythys took her last breath.

Isis—triumphant. A beaming smile upon her beautiful face. Horus looked on, ashamed of his mother. He didn't want her. He wasn't like her. Isis had her revenge. The crowd remained silent. The dead at their feet.

Cleopatra stepped forward. "Lies for all these years. No eternity, and now this. You are the cruellest of all the gods."

"Lies. Cruelty. Yes. Only the strongest survives. You should learn that. You've been too soft with your people, allowed them to turn their backs on me, and now I'll turn my back on you—on all your people. I'll begin again and your part in this is over."

"You saved me just to kill me yourself?" said Cleopatra.

"I haven't quite decided that yet," replied Isis.

Ptolemy and Diodorus looked anxiously at each other and spoke in low tones. Even so, those nearest to them backed away, afraid that the voices would draw the attention of Isis to that part of the Coliseum.

"Give me the book, Diodorus."

Diodorus kept a firm hold of the leather bag. "You know of the curse, Ptolemy. If you do this you will surely lose one of your daughters."

"And if I don't, this madness will go on and there is no telling what will happen next."

Ptolemy closed his eyes as if taking one brief moment to satisfy himself that it was the right thing to do. He reached for the bag.

Diodorus pulled away. "I already have a cursed life. I've read from the book before. It's too late for me and I have no children to lose."

Ptolemy stared into the eyes of Diodorus, took a deep breath and nodded.

Such is the power of words that they don't have to be shouted to the heavens. Diodorus whispered them, barely audible to himself, but powerful nonetheless.

The enormous wooden doors creaked open once more and the crowd again uttered prayers, not to Isis or Nepythys but to any god who would listen. Utter silence. Rotten bandages flapped in the cold wind as the mummy entered the arena. It was obviously centuries old. Part of the chest cavity had been cut away, and it was from here that most of the bandages hung. Only the recently dead, who had not already had their souls stolen by Isis, had risen before. This one was different. However, each foot of this mummy did not crumble, as it touched the earth. The brown bandages flapped as if trying to wind themselves around the body again and deep black holes had been gouged in the face, where eyes should be. It could not see and yet it did. It dragged its feet and limped along, intent on its purpose.

Isis knew who it was. "Osiris," she muttered.

Through a ragged mouth it began to speak. "You recognise me then. You who brought an end to my life and finished off most of the remaining gods."

Isis said nothing. The sky darkened and the thunder rolled. She shrank back in fear.

"You killed me and now you have killed your own mother, Wadjet. You are a goddess no longer. You feed upon the souls of the very ones you should nurture, and for what?"

The sky grew even darker. It began to snow again—sending a shiver down the backbone of the city. The wind whipped it up into mini white tornados, spiralling around the Coliseum.

"You have come to the end of your allotted time. Gods should die and be reborn again. It should be so." Osiris turned his head towards the place where Horus stood. "Only Horus will be allowed to live this time; he will grow and become a man," he said.

Isis held her breath as the mummy's head turned back to her. Silence. Broken by loud thunder. It stopped snowing.

Osiris stepped closer to Isis.

"The final judgement is not on mankind, but on the gods. In the circle of life and death, we, too, eventually return to a primordial beginning. It is almost the end of days for us. An eternal darkness will bind us to one another. Thoth fixes life spans to mortals and gods alike. Decay awaits us all in the end. I speak for the Demogorgon, the Terror God, and the God of all the Earth, who judges all false gods. Her word is final—and you have failed in her eyes. Cursed are the gods who have committed crimes against each other."

"Only a god can kill a god," whispered Isis. But she knew now that when she had consumed the heart of Wadjet, her mother, she had gone too far.

Isis stood her ground. Her black eyes, that had once held fire, dimmed. Her wild hair suddenly hung limp to her shoulders. Osiris took the final steps towards Isis and crushed his body into hers.

Isis tried to hold her hand out towards Ella and Loli. Tried to speak. "Daughter…" The word trailed off into the wind that echoed around the arena.

Both Osiris and Isis crumbled into dust.

The people did not cry for the loss of their gods, but they lamented for their dead. Their myriad cries reached out to the night sky, out into the darkness, with no hope for an afterlife. They knew now that to be mortal was all that they would ever have. It had all been a lie.

Cleopatra put her small hand up to calm the crowd. She spoke with a new found authority, and her strong voice echoed around the Coliseum.

"I will help you become strong again. We will live without gods. Know that there is no afterlife. Just life here on earth. We will have to learn to live with that. Mourn your dead. The cruel tyranny of Isis has gone forever. The hearts of the dead will sink into the earth and that is all there will be from now on. Earth, air, fire and water. Be satisfied with that. There will be nothing more. Soldiers of Clovis. Throw down your swords, and you will be spared."

There came the sound of metal on stone.

Cleopatra reached out for the hand of Gaius. "Will you rule with me as emperor like the first Cleopatra and Mark Anthony? Can we salvage anything from an empire ravaged by plague and loss of faith?"

Gaius nodded and stood by her side. He took her hand. "It can be so."

"Then let us show the people how we will move forward. Let us begin again."

The people of Manceastre, weakened and terrified, and some crying for the undead they had just finally lost, could only muster a murmur of approval.

We will start again, thought Cleopatra.

Sleeward looked intently at the brass bull, a smile spreading upon his face, which he then turned on Clovis. Clovis looked around for his guards and saw that none would now come to help him. No soldier lifted a hand as, at sword point, Sleeward escorted Clovis out of the arena. It would be a slow painful death for Clovis. Sleeward would make him suffer because of all the suffering Clovis had caused. When all was quiet Sleeward would return, and put Clovis in the brass bull, and build a fire underneath. The thought of that finally eased Sleeward's pain a little.

Ella moved closer to Aulus. He put his arm around her and drew her to him. She didn't resist. Her tears flowed freely now, and he held her even tighter.

Loli looked up at Ella. "She called out, daughter. What did she mean?"

Ella didn't say anything. She didn't know what to say.

Loli then turned to Ptolemy. "She looked at me and Ella. Why didn't you tell us?"

"No, Loli. I swear to you that your mother never looked like her. She isn't your mother."

"But you saw the look on her face and what she said."

"She wasn't your mother, Loli."

"I don't believe you. She must have changed how she looked for you. I have a brother now. He has never been nasty to me. He just kept the great secret about the underworld."

Loli turned away from her father and reached for her brother's hand. She looked down at the pendant, the Eye of Horus, ripped it from her neck and threw it down the stone steps.

"Why did you do that?" asked Horus.

"It is better that we do. The people are angry enough already."

Osiris had said that Horus would grow up to be a man. He never mentioned that he wouldn't remain a god. Horus felt the power within him. He would use it wisely, and perhaps, stop someone else from becoming as powerful as Isis had become.

Loli could not look again into Ella's eyes in case she knew. Loli had not been able to stop herself from taking part in the feast of souls.

The End

Author Biography

Allyson Bird lives on the edge of the South Yorkshire moors in England, with her husband and daughter. Occasionally she is drawn to strange places and people, and occasionally they are drawn to her. Her favourite playground, both as an adult and child, is the village graveyard. Once she wondered what would happen if she took one of the green stones from a grave. She has been looking over her shoulder ever since but has never given it back.

Her debut collection, *Bull Running for Girls*, won best collection, in the British Fantasy Society awards, 2009.

Dark Regions Press published her second collection of stories, *Wine and Rank Poison*, in October of 2010.

She is co-editor, with Joel Lane, of the anthology, *Never Again*, from Gray Friar Press. *Never Again* is an attempt to voice the collective revulsion of writers in the weird fiction genre against political attitudes that stifle compassion and deny our collective human inheritance. The imagination is crucial to an understanding both of human diversity and of common ground. Weird fiction is often stigmatised as a reactionary and ignorant genre—we know better. The anthology was published by Gray Friar Press in September 2010.

Isis Unbound is her debut novel.